An Unlikely Match

THE AMISH INN NOVELS

AN UNLIKELY MATCH

BETH WISEMAN

THORNDIKE PRESS
A part of Gale, a Cengage Company

GALE
A Cengage Company

LIBRARY OF CONGRESS CIP DATA ON FILE.
CATALOGUING IN PUBLICATION FOR THIS BOOK
IS AVAILABLE FROM THE LIBRARY OF CONGRESS.

ISBN-13: 978-1-4328-8909-8 (hardcover alk. paper)

Published in 2021 by arrangement with The Zondervan Corporation LLC, a subsidiary of HarperCollins Christian Publishing, Inc.

Printed in Mexico
Print Number: 01   Print Year: 2021

To all those who have
lost a loved one to Covid-19.

GLOSSARY

ab im kopp: crazy, off in the head
ach: oh
boppli: baby
bruder: brother
daadi haus: a small house built onto or near the main house for grandparents to live in
daed: dad
danki: thank you
dochder: daughter
Englisch: those who are not Amish; the English language
fraa: wife
Gott: God
grossmammi: grandmother
gut: good
haus: house
kaffi: coffee
kapp: prayer covering worn by Amish women
kinner: children
lieb: love

maedel: girl
mamm: mom
mei: my
mudder: mother
nee: no
Nichts zu danken: You're welcome.
Ordnung: the written and unwritten rules of the Amish; the understood behavior by which the Amish are expected to live, passed down from generation to generation. Most Amish know the rules by heart.
rumschpringe: "running around"; the period of time when Amish youth experience life in the *Englisch* world before making the decision to be baptized and commit to Amish life.
sohn: son
Wie bischt: Hello, how are you?
ya: yes

ONE

Esther stared out the window in disbelief as her heart pounded like a bass drum.

"Lizzie, what have you done?"

Two large buses pulled into the driveway, followed by two sleek black cars — limousines, she thought they were called. Esther raised the blinds higher. "You said our guests were *Englisch* executives from a large produce company who planned to have meetings here."

Lizzie scowled. "*Ach,* well, that's what I thought they said." She blew a strand of gray hair away from her face, then tucked it beneath her prayer covering. "That's what the message on the answering machine said, and when I called the man back, he said they were coming all the way from Los Angeles, California. He asked if we had room for them to park their vehicles, and I told him we have eighty acres. I figured they'd go back and tell their fancy friends what a wonderful gem they'd found hidden here in southern Indiana."

Esther took a deep breath and clenched her hands at her waist. "Those *Englisch* folks aren't from a produce company, Lizzie." She turned to her younger sister. "Do you see what is written across the sides of those buses?" She waved toward the window and sighed. "Or motor homes. Whatever they are."

Lizzie scrunched up her face and squeezed her eyes closed, then she lifted her chin and looked at Esther. "I must have made a mistake."

Esther shook her head. "There is a big difference between *produce* and *production.*" She pointed out the window, tapping the glass this time. "Clarkson *Movie* Productions, Lizzie. You didn't give them permission to film a movie here, did you?"

"Of course not! I would have remembered something like that." Lizzie huffed. "I don't know what you're so upset about. They are still paying customers."

Esther raised a hand to cover her forehead. "They made reservations for twelve to stay in the main *haus.* Are we expected to feed all the other people in those buses and cars too? There are bound to be more than twelve, and we only have enough groceries

10

for those staying in the guest rooms."

Lizzie turned away, her chin still raised. "I don't know."

Esther began to count as people started getting out of the vehicles. Six stepped out of the first bus — four men and two women dressed in fancy clothes. They huddled in a circle, eyeing the property from behind dark sunglasses. It was a bright sunny day in the middle of April without a cloud in the sky. Five more people emerged from the second bus as still others began pouring out of the black cars.

Esther glanced at Naomi and Amos, who were standing on the porch of the *daadi haus,* surely wondering what all the commotion was about. They'd known the inn was expecting a dozen guests, not this crowd. Naomi was like a daughter to Esther and Lizzie. She'd lived and worked at the inn before she and Amos married the previous spring and rented the small house. Gus Owens leased the third house on the property, a small cottage. Esther had seen him leave in his rusty black truck earlier that morning. She was grateful he wasn't here now. Gus had a disposition that warranted filtering, to say the least. He was a grumpy old man who spoke his mind no matter how rude or obnoxious his comments were.

"Look." Esther pointed out the window again. "That man seems to be the one in charge. He's gathered everyone around him, and he's doing all the talking."

Lizzie was quiet but kept her eyes on the group. Esther stayed by her sister's side wringing her hands. Should they go outside and greet their new guests or wait until someone approached the house?

Finally, the man who had been talking pushed his sunglasses up on his head and started toward the front door. He looked middle-aged with dark hair graying at his temples. His slacks were tan, and he wore the same color loafers with a short-sleeved white collared shirt that wasn't tucked in.

Esther instructed Lizzie to let her do the talking, then the sisters met the man on the porch.

"Welcome to The Peony Inn." Esther nodded and shook his hand when he extended it. The others stayed where they were, talking among themselves while the bus engines roared.

"Are you who I spoke to on the phone? Lizzie?" He directed the question to Esther, but Lizzie cleared her throat.

"*Nee,* that was me." She tried to smile, but it was brief.

"We have rooms ready for twelve," Esther

12

said as she looked over the man's shoulder. One young man stood off to the side of the group.

"Yeah, that's fine. I appreciate you letting us park our RVs here. We were having trouble finding a place to accommodate all of us and the motor homes in one place."

Esther swallowed hard. "How many should we plan to cook for? We are a bed-and-breakfast, but we usually cook three meals a day for those who rent a room." She hoped he understood without her having to say she didn't have enough food on hand to feed his entire crew.

The man glanced at his phone when it beeped, then looked back at Esther. "Uh, don't worry about meals. We'll have food catered in or have someone pick it up for everyone."

Esther's worries reversed as she thought about all the food she had stocked up, much of it produce that would go bad if not eaten. "The cost of the rooms includes the meals. Perhaps some of your group would like to eat at least part of the time."

"We'll see how it works out. We don't have a set schedule." His phone beeped again, gaining his attention for a few seconds before he looked back at her. "Uh, I think there will only be six people staying in the house. We've got room in the motor homes for everyone else."

Esther thought about all the work she and Lizzie had done to accommodate twelve people, but she nodded.

"I'll go get the six staying in the house." He nodded over his shoulder. "Are those other houses rented?"

"*Ya,* one is leased long-term to a gentleman, and the other *haus* is occupied by a young couple." Esther didn't think she'd ever referred to Gus as a gentleman before. She hoped he would stay tucked away for the next month, but all this activity was more than likely going to upset him. And when Gus was disgruntled, there was no telling what he might say or do.

The man flinched. "We'll have to run the generators for the motor homes most of the time while they're parked here. They're rather loud. I didn't know there would be other residents close by." He paused. "By the way, I'm Brandon Clarkson, the producer. I'll be staying inside, along with my son and four others. I'll go get everyone staying in the house and introduce you. We have a few who aren't thrilled about sleeping in a house without air conditioning." His voice held a tinge of irritation.

Esther pushed through her worry. About

the food overage, the loud generators, and the likelihood that Gus would throw a fit.

"I'll be right back with the others." Mr. Clarkson did an about-face and rejoined his crew.

Esther glanced at Lizzie, proud that her sister had pressed her lips together and stayed quiet. "You can speak now."

Lizzie stretched her arms stiffly at her sides. "Don't yell at me. I didn't know it would be like this."

"I don't ever yell at you." Esther grinned. "I might scold you when you act like a child, but I don't yell." They watched as Mr. Clarkson spoke to the group. "Gus is going to be very unhappy."

Lizzie cackled. "Well, now, there's a silver lining after all." Esther's sister avoided Gus whenever she could. Most people did, but Lizzie and Gus fought like five-year-olds, even though they were both in their seventies. In his own disconnected way, Gus was like family. The black sheep, for sure, with a nasty temper and a foul mouth to match. But he'd been good to Esther during a health scare not long ago. Besides, Lizzie and Esther's mother had made them promise before she died to let Gus live in the cottage for the rest of his life, for reasons she would not share with them.

15

Mr. Clarkson walked back up the porch steps with five others in tow. He introduced Esther and Lizzie, then each person individually. "This is Quinn. She's our art director." He nodded at the tall slender woman with white hair as short as a man's. Then he pointed at the two men on either side of her as he spoke their names. "That's Hal, our director, and Giovanni, our cinematographer."

Esther had no idea what any of those titles meant. One of the remaining unidentified men moseyed up to Mr. Clarkson. "And I'm Jesse, the production designer."

The younger man who had been off to the side of the group earlier was still lagging behind. Mr. Clarkson gestured over his shoulder without turning around. "And that's my son, Jayce."

The lad nodded when he reached the steps but didn't say anything. Most of the people Mr. Clarkson had introduced appeared to be in their late thirties and early forties. Jayce was younger — maybe early twenties. His sour expression was a mystery, but when Mr. Clarkson locked eyes with the boy, he just shook his head and frowned at his son.

He turned back to Esther and Lizzie. "We'll get our things, and then if you'd be kind enough to show us to our rooms, I know we all have work to do." He snapped his fingers. "Oh, I know you don't have Wi-Fi, but can we get cell service inside the house?"

Several guests had asked Esther about this before, so she was familiar with the lingo. "I'm told only one to two bars," she said apologetically.

Mr. Clarkson glanced around at the others. "Everyone just hotspot. It seems a little faster if you only have one or two bars. Do the best you can."

"We have lunch planned for twelve if anyone is hungry." Esther smiled as her stomach churned with worry.

Quinn stepped forward. "We ate on the road, but how nice of you to offer." The woman was dressed in a sleek black pantsuit that was belted with a white sash. A long white necklace and matching earrings completed the outfit. With her short white hair, she reminded Esther of a zebra. Her fingernails were pearly white and long, and the spiked white heels made her appear at least five inches taller than she was. Esther couldn't imagine walking in such footwear.

They all echoed her response, then headed back to the vehicles to get their luggage. All but one.

"I'll eat." The youngest of the group, Jayce, stuffed his hands in the pockets of his jeans. He wore a yellow T-shirt, and the edge of a tattoo showed beneath one of the short sleeves. His dark hair was wild and untamed, landing just above his shoulders. He was handsome and tall with an athletic build, the type Esther thought would be confident, like most English men with such stunning looks. Instead, an air of isolation clung to him, most evident in his dark eyes. This boy had a story. Esther was sure of it. But for now, she was glad at least one person was willing to eat.

Jayce stowed his suitcase in the small room upstairs. It was a far cry from the luxury hotels his father's crew usually stayed in. But Montgomery, Indiana, didn't have such accommodations, and this Amish house was big and had room for the motor homes on the property.

He sat on the bed and gave it a little bounce. Seemed comfortable enough. He pressed down on one of two feather pillows. There was a small desk and chair against one wall, along with a small dresser, and a rocking chair took up one corner of the room. His father probably chose the largest room for himself.

The only reason Brandon Clarkson was staying in the house was because he and Veronica had recently broken up, and she refused to stay under the same roof as him, motor home or otherwise. After dating for two years, Veronica had finally come to her senses and ditched the old man. Out of all the actors and actresses Jayce had been around over the years, Veronica was the nicest. She wasn't just talented — she was also kind to everyone she met. Jayce understood how a woman could succumb to his father's charm, but it never lasted. He eventually showed his true colors.

Jayce was pretty sure staying inside the inn with no air conditioning was not his father's first choice.

He lay back on the bed and flung his arms wide. He liked the quaintness of the room, the smell of freshly cut hay wafting through the window screen on the tail of a cool breeze. But this was going to be the longest month of his life. He'd only agreed to work for his father because he offered Jayce a ridiculous amount of money to basically be a roadie. At the end of the month, he'd have enough money to get his own place and walk away from Brandon Clarkson once and for all.

That was what his father wanted after all,

and it was definitely what Jayce wanted. He didn't have any idea where he would go, but it would be far away from the hub in Los Angeles. His father thrived on the hustle and bustle. Jayce longed for a life that wasn't so busy. The price of freedom was enduring each other's presence for a month.

Jayce's father represented everything he didn't want to be. His dad was greedy, unscrupulous, and had a way of convincing everyone in his life that he was a god to be worshipped. People actually worked hard to earn a place in Brandon Clarkson's world, a world Jayce had been trying to escape since his mother ran off with another man seven years ago. That had been a hard pill to swallow at fifteen, especially since his mother insisted Jayce stay with his father. His dad had been difficult before the split, but his disposition grew progressively worse after he became a single parent. Jayce didn't think dear old Dad missed his mom as much as he let on. It was the blow to the man's ego that bothered his dad most.

Now Jayce was twenty-two and had given up the party life the Los Angeles elites had to offer. It had been over a year since he'd walked away from that lifestyle. He credited God for guiding him onto a different path — God and a girl named Susan. Unlike

Jayce, Susan had been raised going to church. She introduced him to God, and once the acquaintance was made, Jayce knew his relationship with the Lord was going to be lifelong, even after things didn't work out with Susan.

His father didn't credit God for anything, and it was a source of contention between them. Sadly, if Jayce hadn't run with the wild crowd for so long, he would've already had enough money to move out of his father's condo.

He'd done a short stint in college, then tried his hand as an entrepreneur, a venture that might have thrived if not for his father's interference. These days, his jobs came in the form of bartender or waiter.

He and his father lived together as roommates, tolerating each other. It made Jayce sick to watch the man use people, mostly women. But Brandon Clarkson had made a fortune by taking advantage of plenty of men too. The sad part was that he was a brilliant man. He didn't need to flaunt his wealth or treat people poorly. His talent alone could have made him into the better man Jayce occasionally caught a glimpse of.

Jayce thought his father's movies were successful because they included multidimensional characters, all created with the positive attributes Brandon Clarkson kept hidden from the world. But Jayce had given up on any real relationship with his father a long time ago. And his mother was flitting around the country with a man half her age. Jayce couldn't remember the last time he'd heard from her.

Forcing the gloomy thoughts from his mind, he got up and walked to the window. Eyeing the motor homes and limos from upstairs, he knew half of the occupants were whining about the accommodations. Jayce found this small room in an old farmhouse to be a welcome change. And whatever was cooking downstairs awakened his senses and reminded him how long it had been since he'd had a home-cooked meal.

The Amish seemed like strange people. They didn't use electricity, drove around in buggies pulled by horses, and dressed like pioneers. Jayce had Googled the area during the long drive. He was skeptical until he saw his first horse and buggy, and he noticed that the people were dressed like the photos he'd seen online. He found their traditional way of living appealing, in a strange sort of way. Except for one thing. According to what he'd read, they were super religious. Jayce considered himself a man with a strong faith, but organized religion had left a bad taste in his mouth.

From the aromas wafting up the stairs, the Amish were apparently good cooks, and Jayce was hungry. When they stopped to eat earlier, the meal was cut short as soon as his father finished eating and rushed everyone else to hurry up.

Jayce made his way downstairs, hoping the food was as good as it smelled.

A quaint but roomy dining area revealed enough prepared dishes to feed an army. An old grandfather clock chimed just as he walked into the room, and then he was drawn to several paintings on the walls, colorful landscapes with modest wood frames. Some were signed by N. Lantz and others by A. Lantz.

He refocused on the food and couldn't believe Quinn and the others were going to pass this up. Surely they could smell the food too. Hungry or not, anyone should have been lured by the heavenly aromas.

"Wow. That's a lot of food." He eyed the offerings as the two older women who had greeted them walked into the room. "Sit anywhere?"

"*Ya,* of course." The woman who had introduced herself as Esther, and who had done most of the talking, stood off to the side with her hands folded in front of her.

She was a tall, stocky woman. The other lady — Lizzie — was tiny and hadn't said much. Now she stood beside her sister watching him.

Jayce took a seat in the middle of the twelve place settings and eyed the offerings. "Wow," he said again. "This looks awesome." He reached for a large bowl of mashed potatoes nearby. After scooping a generous helping onto his plate, he stood and made his way around the table gathering roast, peas, corn, bread, and broccoli salad. His glass was already filled with tea.

When he sat back down, he said a silent prayer of thanks, unsure what proper protocol was with these people. Then he took a couple of large bites and thanked God again. The food was amazing. The two women were still standing at attention side by side. "Aren't you going to eat?"

They exchanged looks. The petite one — Lizzie — clenched her teeth before moving to a chair across from Jayce. "Well, I'm eating." She looked over her shoulder at her sister. "And you should too. There's going to be a lot of food wasted if more people don't eat." Visibly bothered by the lack of attendance, she frowned even more as she sat. While Esther remained standing, Lizzie lowered her head, presumably to pray. Jayce stopped chewing, which seemed silly but somehow respectful. He started eating again when Lizzie raised her head and began to fill her plate.

When she finished, Esther made herself a plate and joined them. She sat beside her sister, also lowering her head right away. Despite a mouthful of roast, Jayce stopped chewing again and resumed after her prayer.

Jayce had helped himself to seconds before the women finished a third of their meal. "I can eat enough for at least three people." He hoped to quench their disappointment that no one else had joined them for the meal.

Esther cleared her throat. "So, what type of movie is your father making?"

Jayce held up a finger as he finished chewing another large chunk of roast, possibly the best meat he'd ever had. "It's about six people who get stranded on an island, then they find a cave to take shelter in when a storm comes, leaving them trapped inside. One of them is a murderer, but no one knows who."

"There are a lot of caves around here." Esther delicately forked a piece of meat. Her tiny sister ate like she hadn't had a meal in days. She'd piled her plate with almost as much food as Jayce. *No way that little old lady can eat all that food.*

"Tomorrow we're loading up to go to Bluespring Caverns to film. The people running it said they would close it for half a day and offer patrons a free pass for the following day." He helped himself to another slice of bread and slathered butter on it. "This is the greatest meal I've ever had," he said. *The food will definitely be the best part of this gig.*

"*Danki.* I mean, thank you." Esther blushed a little. Lizzie was too busy eating to acknowledge the compliment. "Will your group be spending the night in the cave?"

"Do what?" Jayce covered his mouth with his hand so he didn't spew food everywhere. "I don't see that happening."

"Oh. I just wondered." Esther raised an eyebrow, seemingly amused. "Bluespring hosts a lot of Boy Scout troops, church groups, and students, so they have a section of the cavern set up with electricity, beds, and other accommodations."

Jayce tried to picture anyone from the film spending the night inside a cave. "Nah, I seriously doubt it, but it sounds cool." He pointed to the roast. "May I?"

"Eat all you want," Lizzie said before she rolled her eyes. "Doesn't appear anyone else is going to." She grunted. "Nothing like *gut*

26

food going to waste."

Jayce smiled apologetically. "I'll do my best not to let that happen. I —"

A large heavyset man with a gray ponytail stomped into the room. By the look on his face, he wasn't here to eat. He crinkled his nose. His big jowls jiggled as he shook his head and folded his arms across his chest, resting them on his oversized belly.

"What in the . . . ?" He rattled off words that obviously upset the sisters. The smaller one stood and picked up her plate, firing the man a look filled with anger as she squinted and snarled at him.

"I am forced to eat two meals per year with you. Thanksgiving and Christmas. That's all you'll get from me, you grumpy old excuse of a man." Carrying her plate, she stormed out of the room.

Jayce stifled his amusement. The woman had been mostly quiet up to this point. *What a spitfire.*

"Gus, I have told you repeatedly that you can't use such language in this *haus.*" Esther turned to Jayce, her face red. "*Mei* apologies."

"No problem." Jayce refocused on his plate and began cutting off another bite of roast. He'd noticed the women's accents. Some of their words sounded different, kind of like German.

"Gus, why don't you sit down and eat?" Esther waved toward a chair across the table. "Most of the guests had already eaten before their arrival, so we have plenty."

The man — Gus — turned to Jayce, nostrils flaring. "Who are you? Are those your motor homes causing all that racket outside? Not to mention there are people everywhere — in and out, doors slamming, and someone playing loud music." He faced Esther before Jayce could answer. "This ain't gonna work, Esther."

"Just eat, Gus." She lowered her head, shaking it. "It's only for a month."

Gus let out enough expletives to offend even Jayce, face flaming as his jowls bounced. "And this is surely something Lizzie did!" he added at the end of his rant.

"Dude, whatever your problem is, that's no way to speak to a lady." He reached for his fourth slice of bread but kept his eyes on the man. He was an old guy, but he was big.

"Sonny, you zip it." He pointed at Jayce before he turned back to Esther. "You'd better at least make sure those idiots turn off those generators at night or I won't get a lick of sleep."

Jayce stood. "Sir, I don't know who you

are, but —"

"Kid" — the old guy's finger moved in Jayce's direction again — "I'm pretty sure I told you to zip it."

Jayce took a deep breath, wiped his mouth with his napkin, then set it next to his plate. He glanced at Esther. The poor woman's face was still red, and her lip quivered slightly. He turned and walked to the man, who outweighed him by at least a hundred pounds. He'd held his own in plenty of fights with bigger guys. Surely this old man wouldn't throw any punches.

"You need to leave." Jayce spoke as calmly as he could, but his comment was met with thunderous laughter.

"Shut your mouth, you little runt."

Jayce tensed as he felt a muscle in his jaw quiver. It wasn't cool to mistreat old ladies. He looked over his shoulder just as Lizzie came running barefoot back into the room, carting her plate. She slapped it down on the table and pulled out a chair beside her sister.

"I could hear from the kitchen, and I don't want to miss this." She put her elbows on the table, then propped her chin on her hands with eagerness in her eyes. "Go on, young man. Don't stop."

The old man clenched his fists at his sides

as he turned his attention away from Jayce. "Lizzie, you're like a worm that gets under a person's skin and crawls around until a fellow goes crazy."

"Sir, I have to ask you to leave. I'll escort you out if I need to." Jayce motioned in the direction of the door. "These lovely ladies invited you to join them for a fine meal, which you really should have taken them up on. But instead, you're talking like a fool and being rude." He stepped closer to the man, who was now shaking with rage. "So you're going to leave. You just need to decide how. On your own or with my escort?" Jayce raised an eyebrow.

Hands still fisted at his sides, Gus glared at Esther. "We will speak about this tomorrow. As a renter, I have rights."

He stomped out of the room grumbling, each step heavier than the one before.

"Don't let the door hit you on the backside on the way out!" Lizzie yelled, her eyes lit up with victory.

"It's not funny, Lizzie." Esther blinked back tears as she turned to Jayce. "*Mei* apologies again."

Lizzie stood, walked around the table to where Jayce was standing, and put a gentle hand on his arm. "It's not our way to be physical, *sohn*."

"I didn't know that, and I meant no disrespect." Jayce paused. "I was hoping it wouldn't come to that, but I couldn't stand watching him speak to either of you that way."

"As I said, it's not our way." Lizzie displayed a perfect set of pearly whites that couldn't possibly be her own teeth. "But I would have paid *gut* money to see you knock the meanness out of Grumpy Gus Owens." She guided him to his chair. "You sit. I'll be right back."

Esther's eyebrows drew together in an agonized expression. "I'm so sorry."

Jayce stared into the woman's kind eyes. "You've apologized three times, and you shouldn't. That guy is the one who should be apologizing."

Lizzie rushed back into the room balancing four pies on her arms with the precision of a seasoned waitress. She set each one within Jayce's reach.

"Pecan, rhubarb, apple, and key lime." She batted her eyes at him. "You should have some of each."

Jayce couldn't help but smile. He'd somehow stumbled into food heaven.

He was reaching for a slice of apple pie when his father burst into the room.

"I was in the shower, but I could hear all

31

the ruckus even with the water running." His eyes blazed in the familiar way Jayce had seen before. When he was younger, the expression was usually followed by a good smack across the face. These days, his old man knew better. "We haven't even been here a day, and you're already stirring up trouble!"

"*Nee*, it wasn't his fault at all, Mr. Clarkson," Esther said, echoed by Lizzie.

But the damage was done, and Jayce felt his face seething red with embarrassment. He pushed back his chair, scraping it against the wood floor. After thanking the women for a wonderful meal, he left the room. He stormed out the front door, past the motor homes and the small house with a couple sitting on the front porch, then he turned onto the road and kept walking.

Two

Evelyn tried repeatedly to pick up Millie's hoof so she could see what the horse had stepped on, but each time the poor girl whinnied and pulled away from her. Drops of blood spotted the pavement on the back road that led from her house to the Bargain Center where she worked.

"You've got to let me have a look, Millie." She scratched behind the mare's ears, hoping to calm her.

Evelyn had brought her mother's emergency cell phone, but the battery was dead. Her mother had asked her to charge it when she got to work, which wasn't going to happen anytime soon at this rate. Both of her brothers left for work over an hour ago. Her father was busy in the fields. Her mother said she had no plans today, so it was unlikely anyone would be coming to her aid.

Unless someone happened by, she might be stranded for a while. She bent at the waist and tried again to look at Millie's foot, but the horse neighed with even more agitation. When Evelyn stood, she caught movement out of the corner of her eye. Someone had just rounded the corner and was heading toward her. The only people who lived on that road were Esther and Lizzie, along with their renters. *This man must be a guest at the inn.*

Evelyn raised a hand to her forehead, blocking the sun's glare as she waited for him to get closer. He was tall and apparently not Amish since he wasn't wearing a hat. That was all she could see until he came into full view a minute or so later.

"Hey, you okay?" He raised a bushy eyebrow that hovered above eyes as dark brown as a moonless night, obscure and intense.

Evelyn felt a shiver run the length of her spine, despite the warm weather. She opened her mouth to say something, but a warning bell sounded in her mind.

"Are you staying at The Peony Inn?" Her voice wavered, but if he was a guest of Lizzie and Esther's, maybe she could shed this unexpected fear. He was a tall English man, muscular with unruly long dark hair. Evelyn was small, weighing in at about a hundred and twenty pounds and only five foot two.

The man nodded, then reached into his pocket and pulled out a phone. "Do you need to call someone?" He glanced at Millie, whose leg was still bent at the knee.

"Um . . ." Evelyn began to tremble, but the man smiled, and everything changed, softened. Even his eye color seemed less intense.

"*Ya,* I might need to borrow your phone, but *mei* horse . . . She, uh, has something in her hoof." She nodded at Millie but quickly looked back at the man as she tried to figure out why she was so unnerved by his presence. She didn't know him. He was a stranger. *It's normal to be cautious around a man I don't know.*

"Want me to have a look?" He stuck his phone in his back pocket, then tucked his dark hair behind his ears — hair much too long for a man. Before she could answer, he made his way to the horse and began rubbing her neck. "What's her name?"

"Millie." Evelyn didn't move as she tried to calm her erratic pulse. *What is wrong with me?*

"Hey, Millie. Did you step on something?" He moved his hand to Millie's nose, and Evelyn was about to tell him the mare didn't like her face touched, but Millie leaned into him and nudged him with an acceptance

Evelyn hadn't seen before. She believed animals had a sense about people. If Millie trusted him, then Evelyn would try to do the same.

"I was on *mei* way to work, but Millie stopped abruptly and has been holding her leg like that for about fifteen minutes, refusing to budge." Evelyn eyed the blood that had pooled below Millie's hoof. "Not that I blame her. But every time I try to see what's wrong, she pulls away from me."

"Hey, girl. Are you going to let me have a look?" He alternated between stroking Millie's nose and scratching behind her ears. Then he ran his hands down her sides, talking softly near her ear. "Please don't kick me in the face."

Evelyn squeezed her eyes shut when he leaned over, sure that he was indeed going to get kicked in the face. But when she opened one eye, he was standing with a sliver of glass in the palm of his hand.

"It's not very big, but it was keeping her from putting pressure on it." He offered the glass to Evelyn, and she slipped it in her apron pocket. She'd put it in the trash at work. "Do you have anything to wrap around her foot, like to stop the bleeding?"

Evelyn thought for a few seconds. "I-I don't have anything in the buggy." She

36

wished her pulse would slow down.

"What about that thing on your head?" He pointed to her prayer covering.

"Nee!" She gasped as she raised a hand to the top of her head. "I mean, no. I can't take this off." *Not even for Millie, and especially not in front of a man I don't know.*

"Okay, sorry. I didn't know. This is an old T-shirt I'm not terribly attached to." He lifted the yellow shirt, revealing what she'd heard her brothers refer to as a six-pack.

"No, no, no!" She turned away and quickly untied her black apron. "Here, use this." She pushed the apron toward him.

"Really? It'll get blood on it." He eyed the garment, frowning.

"It's fine. I have plenty more at home." There was probably an extra at work she could use for the day.

He shrugged and folded the apron into a small square with the ties hanging out, then tenderly lifted Millie's hoof, placed the square cloth on it, and gingerly wrapped the thick strings around her hoof and leg to hold it in place. When he was done, he stood.

"How far do you have to go?" He lifted a hand to his forehead, blocking the sun.

"Not far. A few miles up the road to the Bargain Center." She paused and leaned

37

over to run her hand down Millie's side. "I'll call a vet when I get there." She gave the animal another long stroke down her flank. "We recently had a farrier out to shoe all the horses, so I'm surprised this happened."

"The glass was stuck at an angle inside the shoe, but it won't hurt to have it checked out. You don't want it to get infected." He took his phone from his pocket again. "Do you need to call anyone now?"

Evelyn studied the man for a few moments. He was handsome. In an English sort of way. She tried to picture him without all the long dark hair he seemed to be hiding behind. Yet there was no hiding the intensity in his dark eyes.

"*Nee*. I'll use the phone at work to call the vet." She took a deep breath and forced a smile, anxious to get on her way, but also curious. "How do you know so much about horses?"

He shrugged. "I don't know a lot. As a kid, I was sent off to summer camp pretty often, and they had horses. I remembered that there's a certain way to touch an ailing horse to keep the animal calm." His left eyebrow rose a fraction. "Fifty-fifty shot. I could have gotten kicked in the face just as easily."

Evelyn flinched. "Well, I'm glad you didn't, and *danki* — I mean, thank you for your help."

A smile filled his face. The lopsided grin was cute, in an adolescent sort of way. She could tell by his features that he was close to her age, maybe a year or two older.

"I like your accent," he said. "I've never been around your kind of people before."

A tourist. Montgomery was becoming more and more of a destination to get a glimpse of Amish life. Some folks were glad because it brought income to the community. Others, particularly the elders, weren't so fond of the visitors.

"I'm Jayce, by the way." He extended his hand. Evelyn paused, but her hand found its way into his firm handshake.

"Evelyn." Her cheeks felt warm as she pulled back her hand.

He scratched his forehead. "You said you're on your way to the Bargain Center. Is that like a Walmart?"

"We have Walmarts, but they are too far to go by buggy. I guess you could say the Bargain Center is like a mini Walmart." She paused, searching for a way to explain. "A *very* mini Walmart, but it has most everything a person could need. Groceries, a deli, household items, gifts. But no clothes, if that's what you're looking for."

He looped his thumbs in the back pockets of his jeans. "Could I ride with you? I forgot a few things at home that I'd like to pick up."

Evelyn was caught off guard and unable to do more than nod. What would her coworkers think when they saw her pull into the parking lot with this handsome English man?

"If it's a problem, no big deal." He shrugged.

"*Nee,* it's not a problem." It was the least Evelyn could do. She climbed into the buggy and waited for him to sit beside her, then she slowly tapped the reins. "I'll take it slow and easy."

"I'm in no hurry." He pulled out his phone and focused on it for a few minutes.

Evelyn kept a close eye on Millie, relieved the horse wasn't limping. Finally, she turned to her passenger. "So, what brings you to Montgomery?" No wedding ring, so he didn't have a wife who'd brought him along on a tourist trip.

He lifted his eyes to hers, but she quickly looked back at the road.

"My dad owns a production company. He's wrapping up a movie, shooting a final scene or two here." The man — Jayce —

40

spoke in a low voice, but there was an air of contempt that made Evelyn wonder about his relationship with his father.

"You're making movie scenes at the inn?" Evelyn couldn't believe Lizzie and Esther would allow such a thing. Or that the bishop would consent.

"No. We're just staying there. Some of us are staying inside the house, and we have a couple motor homes too." He raised his eyes from his phone and shook his head. "We'll be here about a month, and I'm dreading every moment."

Evelyn wasn't sure what to say, but when he refocused on his phone again and didn't offer an explanation, she cleared her throat. "This part of Indiana is very lovely. Hopefully you'll have time to do some exploring when you aren't working."

"Yeah, it's pretty here. The location isn't the problem. My father is." Sighing, he still had his head down as he punched buttons on his phone. Evelyn had been right when she noticed the contempt regarding his father.

"He's always wanted me to be involved in his business, but I don't want anything to do with it. I'm only here because he offered me a lot of money to do the heavy lifting. I just have to survive this month of being

41

around him, then I can move out on my own. Maybe even leave LA altogether."

Evelyn was surprised he was sharing so much, and there was no mistaking the bitterness in his voice. "LA?"

"Los Angeles." His eyes were still on his phone.

"*Ach,* in California." She'd heard of Los Angeles but suspected it was a busy place she'd never visit.

After more typing on his phone, he looked over at her. "Sorry. I'm listening. I'm just sending a text for someone to pick me up later. I'm letting him know I'll text again when I'm ready." He set the phone on his lap. "You've probably seen some of my dad's movies."

"I-I've never been to see a movie in a theater." Evelyn had been in her running-around period for three years now, since she was sixteen, so technically she could break a few rules and venture out, but the opportunity had never presented itself.

Jayce's jaw dropped. "You're kidding, right?"

Evelyn shook her head. "*Nee.* I mean, I could go. I'm not baptized yet." She raised a shoulder and dropped it slowly as she kept Millie at a slow pace. "I just never have."

Jayce closed his mouth and rubbed his

forehead. "Sorry, but that's so weird for me. Is it a rule or something?"

"I guess it is. But when we turn sixteen, we enter into a *rumschpringe*. It's a time for exploration, when we can go out into the *Englisch* world and experience life before we choose baptism into the Amish faith."

The left side of his mouth curled up. "No offense, but you look older than sixteen."

"None taken. I'm nineteen."

He scratched his chin. "So for the past three years you've been allowed to go to the movies, yet you've never been?"

"*Ya,* that's right." She paused. Most folks knew at least a little about the way Amish people lived. This man didn't seem to have a clue. "It's a time when our parents turn a blind eye and allow us privileges we won't have after we're baptized."

He stared at her wordlessly for a few long, awkward moments. "I have no idea how God, baptism, and the movies fit together, but you're saying you *can* go see a movie?"

"*Ya.*" Evelyn had dated a few men in her small community, but none had asked her to go to a movie. And it hadn't seemed all that important.

"Are you allowed to date?" He raised an eyebrow, grinning. "What do you do? Dinner and a movie are kind of a thing where I come from."

Evelyn felt herself blush. "*Ya,* we can date." She kept her eyes on the road. "We go out for meals at restaurants, and sometimes we go on a picnic. And there are other things to do."

"Like what?" He twisted slightly in the seat. She'd captured his full attention but wished she hadn't. His eyes pierced the short distance between them, and an unwelcome tension settled into a knot in her stomach.

"There's the zoo, the corn maze in the fall, or we can always go horseback riding." She glanced his way, but quickly faced forward again when his leg brushed against hers. "Uh . . . in the winter, we go on sleigh rides. And there are singings held for the young people. We find lots of things to do."

He was looking ahead but gave her a sidelong glance as if contemplating something, and the longer he was silent, the larger the knot in her stomach grew.

"Well, then." He tipped his head to one side. "We have to go to a movie."

Evelyn's eyes widened. "What?" Was this English stranger asking her out?

He crinkled his nose and frowned. "Wow. What was I thinking? Someone as gorgeous as you must have a boyfriend." A swath of his wavy dark hair fell across his forehead. After he pushed it aside, he said, "You need to make him take you to a movie."

"*Nee,* I don't have a boyfriend." Evelyn's chest tightened, and she wished she'd kept quiet. Now she'd opened a door she wasn't ready to walk through. She was, however, basking in the compliment.

Jayce stared at the beautiful Amish woman far too long, and she refocused on the road. He continued to take in her features. Dark hair tucked beneath that thing on her head, which he assumed had some kind of religious meaning. Green eyes set against a dark olive complexion, like a really good tan from being outside a lot. He'd already noticed her slender figure when her apron was tied around her waist. All other physical details were hidden beneath the dark-green dress she wore.

The few times she'd smiled, her face lit up. The woman was a knockout.

"Sorry." He gave his head a quick shake. "I know I'm staring. I just don't see how someone as pretty as you isn't spoken for." He laughed. "Or hasn't been to a movie. I grew up in a theater. I love movies, which is ironic because I hate my father's business, and I'm not fond of enclosed spaces. I do okay as long as I know I can leave. It's the feeling trapped that bothers me."

"I'm not sure I understand." She glanced his way briefly.

"For example, elevators are a problem. Even going up one floor makes my heart race." He shrugged. "Yeah, weird, I know. I'd flip out if I ever got stuck in an elevator. Luckily, that's never happened."

"I don't think it's weird." She spoke with confidence, like she really didn't think his claustrophobia was odd. She seemed like a sweet girl. Maybe that was why he was over-sharing.

"Theaters, restaurants — even small ones — don't bother me because I can get up and walk out. Tomorrow I'll be in a cave while they shoot my dad's latest movie. Caves are big, spacious, and I can leave anytime I want. If I feel like I'm going to suffocate, I'll walk outside for a break."

She slowed the horse, turned to face him, and with sympathy in her eyes said, "You have to go by boat into the cave. There's no way in or out except by boat."

Jayce felt like a hand was closing around his throat. "You're kidding."

"*Nee*. Each boat holds twelve or thirteen people, I think. To return to the dock, everyone in the boat would have to go back too."

Jayce groaned. "I had reservations about this trip, but I've been in other caves. And they all had easy exits." He leaned his head back and momentarily squeezed his eyes closed. No wonder his father offered him a ridiculous amount of money for this project. In addition to wanting Jayce to move out of his apartment, his father would have an opportunity to humiliate him in front of the crew.

"I'm sure dear old Dad has picked a place that will make me feel like I'm dying." He half snickered, half growled. "Wow. I sound like a wimp. I don't even know why I'm telling you this." He was quiet for a few seconds. "Hey, your people are religious, right? Maybe you can pray for me? You can bet I'll be praying, but I suspect you have a more direct line to the Big Guy."

She laughed and her green eyes twinkled against her olive complexion, which rendered her even more beautiful. *Wow.* "*Gott* hears all of our prayers equally, but I do think when we pray for others He hears those prayers before the ones we say for ourselves."

"Great. I'm going to need an abundance of prayers. As many as you can spare, beginning immediately." He winked at her and was unsure if she saw the gesture at first, but then she began to blush.

"In return for all those prayers, I'm going to take you to a movie." He kept his eyes on hers as they widened. He waited for her to say no.

Instead, she pointed right. "We turn there, and the Bargain Center is on the left a little farther down."

"What night do you want to go to a movie? Unfortunately, I'll be trapped in caves most days. There's bound to be a theater not too far away, right?"

"Um . . ." She looked at him again. "I think the theater in Washington is the closest. It's only eleven miles away, so the horse can make the trip."

He couldn't stop the grin that covered his face. *She didn't say no!* "No, I should pick you up. Isn't that proper protocol, even here? I've got access to cars and drivers. Or we can call a cab or Uber."

She giggled, and her eyes twinkled again as her cheeks dimpled. "I'm afraid we don't have cabs or whatever that other thing is."

"Then car it is. What night and what time?" He rubbed his hands together. "This is going to be great — watching someone experience their first movie."

She pulled into the parking lot of the mini Walmart and right up to a hitching post.

"Well, that's convenient," he said as he stepped out of the buggy and waited for her to tether the horse next to two other horses and buggies. "I guess a few Amish people must come here."

She grinned. "You might say that." She leaned down and unwrapped the blood-stained apron square from around the horse's foot, then straightened. "No more bleeding. But I'll ask the vet to take a look, just to be sure."

Jayce nodded, knowing he was running out of time. "How about tomorrow night at six o'clock? I'll pick you up and we'll eat and go see a movie."

She was quiet. It was out of character for Jayce to be this pushy about asking a woman out. But he didn't know much about the Amish rules and worried he might not see her again. He held his breath and waited.

"I-I guess eating out and seeing a movie would be okay."

She said yes!

"Where should I pick you up?" He heard the eagerness in his voice and wondered if she did too. This would give him something to look forward to.

She started walking toward the entrance as she rattled off an address, then picked up her pace and strode into the store. Jayce repeated the street and number in his mind over and over as he pulled out his phone and followed her inside. He punched in the address and looked up.

Wow. His jaw dropped when he took a few steps inside.

THREE

Evelyn tried to walk ahead of Jayce so it didn't look like they were together, but he stayed close behind her.

"Am I the only person in here who isn't Amish?" His eyes grew wide as he spoke in a whisper. "And there aren't any men."

Evelyn tried to ignore the people peering at them from every direction as she bee-lined toward the back of the store. There was a line of Amish women waiting to check out and several more in the aisle as Evelyn led the way.

"The *kinner* — children — are in school but will be out soon. The store usually fills up this time of day. The women will get their groceries then meet the children at the school, where most of them left their buggies. It's close enough to walk. The men are at work." She pointed to a door that read Employees Only. "I have to go get an apron. Hopefully you can find everything you

51

need." She nodded left. "The deli is that way. To the right, you'll find household items and food."

"Uh, yeah. Okay." He took a few steps to the right before she closed the door. She found an apron, then scurried to the cash register.

"Sorry I'm late. Millie got a piece of glass stuck in her foot." Evelyn switched places with Katie. When she looked at her friend, Katie's expression mirrored those of the women in line, along with the ones who had stopped in their tracks, all of them ogling Jayce like he was from another planet.

"Who is that?" Katie asked as she kept her eyes on Jayce. It was impossible not to notice his athletic physique, and surely they'd all seen those mesmerizing eyes when he walked in the store.

"He's staying at the inn. Esther and Lizzie's place. He found me on the road and helped with Millie." She nudged Katie to step aside and reached for the first item to ring up.

"*Ach,* I love *mei* husband, but that is possibly the most handsome man I've ever seen." Katie shook her head. "I mean, for an *Englisch* man."

Evelyn couldn't deny how nice-looking Jayce was, but she regretted accepting his invitation to supper and a movie. She didn't even know him, and he wasn't Amish. He was age appropriate and handsome, but they had nothing in common. He came from a life she knew nothing about. Clearly he didn't know anything about Evelyn's world either.

She would go to the movie with him, then not see him again. He would be working a lot anyway. She had to admit she was looking forward to seeing a movie.

As Jayce rounded a corner and disappeared from sight, everyone got back to business, either shopping or waiting patiently in line. Katie walked toward the deli, where she was scheduled to work today.

Widow Byler gave Evelyn a curious look as she rang up the handful of items, but she didn't ask about Jayce, nor did any of the other women Evelyn checked out. Everyone began rushing to get in line since the school bell would toll soon.

Jayce breezed past the women, raised a hand, and said, "I couldn't find what I needed, but I'll pick you up at six tomorrow."

Evelyn lowered her head. He couldn't have said it any louder if he'd tried. Now every woman in the store knew she was going out with the handsome English man

53

tomorrow evening.

She slowly lifted her eyes. Most of the ladies were eyeing her with speculation. Widow Byler crinkled her nose from where she stood near the exit. Evelyn didn't say anything and continued ringing up the groceries. The entire town would be talking about Jayce and Evelyn by the end of the day. Montgomery wasn't immune to gossip, and Widow Byler was the queen bee when it came to spreading news.

Maybe she should cancel the date. Except most people wouldn't know if she canceled, so the damage was already done. Maybe she should tell the few ladies still in line that she was going to show him around because he was a guest at the inn. But that would be a lie. No matter which direction her mind traveled, a fib met her at every turn.

She pressed her lips together and stayed quiet. Everyone looked up when a long black limousine pulled into the parking lot. Even Evelyn's mouth fell open. *Is that the way Jayce always travels*? She hoped he didn't show up at her house in that fancy car tomorrow night.

She hadn't factored in what her parents and brothers would think about her going out with an English man, particularly her father. But she would tell them the truth.

He helped her with Millie, and she didn't feel like she could turn down his kind offer of supper. Would omitting mention of the movie make it a partial version of the truth? Both of her brothers had taken girls to the movies.

No matter how she spun it, her description of the evening felt like a lie. What she couldn't tell her family, or anyone else, was how wildly attracted she was to Jayce. And it wasn't just his looks. It was the compassion he showed Millie and the way the horse had nudged him and allowed Jayce to help.

A date with an English man who would be gone in a month shouldn't feel like a threat at all. How much could she possibly feel for him in such a short time? She was probably just getting ahead of herself. They were going out tomorrow night, and that would be the end of it.

Jayce slid into the front seat of the limo. Unlike his father and the others, he preferred to sit up front with their hired driver, Billy.

"What are you doing way over here? You walk all this way?" Billy was about his father's age, but a whole lot nicer.

"I got mad at the old man and took off on foot to clear my head. Then I helped an

55

Amish damsel in distress." He paused, smiling. "A beautiful Amish damsel in distress."

"What was wrong with her?" Billy's eyebrows drew inward in a concerned expression.

"Actually, *she* was okay. It was her horse. The mare had a piece of glass in one of her hooves, stuck right in the side of the shoe. I was able to get it out. Then I remembered I forgot my socks and a couple other things, so she let me ride here with her. She works inside." He nodded to the store as Billy pulled out of the parking lot. "But they didn't have socks or the other things. I'll hit Walmart in the next day or so."

"What were you and your father fighting about this time?" Billy frowned as he turned onto the main highway.

"He was out of line this time. I know sometimes it's my fault, but not this time." Jayce pulled his visor down to block the sun. "There was this older man. He came in the dining room when I was eating." He glanced at Billy. "By the way, you should have eaten when we got there. Best meal I've ever had." He waved a dismissive hand and looked out the window.

"Anyway, this man — they called him Gus — he started basically screaming at those sweet ladies who own the inn. He was really obnoxious and rude. I felt like I had to say something, so I politely asked him not to talk to them that way. Then he tried to get all up in my face. Can you believe that?" He turned back to Billy. "He's probably in his seventies. Anyway, he finally left, and then Dad came barging into the room ranting that he heard *me* from upstairs. He demanded to know what I'd done — said I was stirring up trouble the first day." Jayce shook his head as he told Billy how the women tried to defend him, but his father wasn't hearing it.

"I got up and walked out."

Billy didn't say anything. He'd worked for Jayce's father for a long time, so he knew the man well. But Billy was fair and if asked for an opinion, he'd give an honest answer.

"He was the one out of line, right?" Jayce finally asked.

Billy thought for a few more seconds before he answered. "Yes, I suppose he was. Although, after what happened recently, I can see why he would jump to conclusions."

Jayce leaned back into the headrest and sighed. "That wasn't my fault either."

"But it happened." Billy paused. "You're a good guy, Jayce, but you need to learn to control your temper."

He respected Billy but still felt the need

to defend his actions. "Never once have I lost my cool when it wasn't warranted."

"You might believe that to be true, but a real man will walk away from a physical encounter if he can."

Jayce shook his head. "That's being a coward. And if I hadn't stood up for those women, I would have felt guilty. I didn't think I'd have to hit the man, but he had no business talking to them like he was."

They were quiet for the last short stretch back to the inn until Jayce said, "I asked that Amish girl to dinner and a movie tomorrow night. Can you believe she's never seen a movie?"

Billy slowed the car almost to a stop when they turned onto the road that led to the inn. "Do you know anything about the Amish?"

Jayce shrugged. "They all dress alike and ride in buggies. But man, this woman is gorgeous."

Billy pulled off the road and put the car in park. Jayce could see the inn in the distance and hear the hum of the generators if he listened closely. Gus was probably going nuts about the noise.

"I lived in Pennsylvania for a while when I was around your age, in Lancaster County." Billy paused and waited for Jayce to look at him. "So I know a lot about the Amish. And for starters, they generally don't mix with outsiders. Granted, I don't know if the rules are different here, but I think some things are universal. They are very religious, for one thing."

"I believe in God." Jayce sat taller, feeling a little offended.

"I'm not calling your relationship with God into question. I'm just telling you that the Amish believe in a literal interpretation of the Bible, and one of the things they believe very strongly is that you turn the other cheek. They are *very* passive. They won't engage in a fight, even if provoked. Also, this girl you're going out with isn't like anyone you've dated back home."

Jayce shrugged again. "Her choice of clothing isn't the best, but her beauty makes up for it." Jayce pushed his visor back up and nodded toward the house. "Why are we stopped to have this conversation?"

"Because it's important for you to understand that this girl is . . . pure." He lifted an eyebrow. "You following me? And she'll stay that way until she gets married. So don't pressure her to do anything, not even so much as a kiss."

"I have my faults, but I have never pressured a woman into anything." Jayce fought a surge of anger, feeling insulted again.

"I believe that. I'm just letting you know these people are very chaste." He scratched his chin. "I'm surprised she agreed to go out with you. As I said, they usually don't date outsiders."

"I'll treat her with the utmost respect." Jayce was considerate to women. Billy would be surprised to know he wasn't the romantic conqueror most people probably assumed.

Billy smiled. "I believe that too. I just thought you should have a little background." He put the car in gear and headed toward the inn.

It hadn't been all that long since Jayce had eaten, but his stomach was already growling. He wondered what the sisters had on the menu for tonight.

Esther finished glazing the ham and put it in the oven to keep warm, along with a pot of twice-baked potatoes and pinto beans. The salad was made and in the refrigerator. Two loaves of freshly baked bread sat on the counter. She'd prepared enough for ten people — the six guests, she and Lizzie, and extra in case anyone changed their mind about dining with them. The young man, Jayce, could put away a lot of food. She loved watching people enjoy a meal. It was her reward for the effort and a reminder of the many ways the Lord provided for them.

She was pleased when Quinn and three gentlemen entered the dining room. Hal, Giovanni, and Jesse, if she remembered their names correctly. She suggested everyone be seated while she and Lizzie finished setting the table. Naomi had walked over earlier in the day to help, but Esther assured her that she and Lizzie could finish up.

They needed to hire a new girl who could manage most of the cooking and cleaning. Naomi still helped when she could, but now that she was married and pregnant with twins, her time was mostly devoted to running her own household, as it should be.

Esther was still getting used to the sound of the generators running on the motor homes. She was surprised Gus hadn't returned to complain some more. As she placed the ham in the middle of the table, Mr. Clarkson entered the room. Everyone seemed to sit a little taller. He greeted Lizzie and Esther, then the group fell into a conversation about their plans for tomorrow. If she'd heard correctly, they were going to Bluespring Caverns for part of the day.

Jayce came into the room, smiling, until

he saw his father. His expression fell and he took the seat farthest away from Mr. Clarkson. Esther's heart hurt for the poor boy. He'd boldly taken on Gus, which no one ever did except Lizzie. Jayce had actually gotten Gus to leave. Lizzie only fired up an already smoldering situation when she confronted their renter. No good ever came from encounters between the two.

"I believe that's everything," Esther said as she placed a loaf of warm bread on the table. She and Lizzie had already decided they would eat in the kitchen. Occasionally they joined their guests for a meal, but only by request. This group barely noticed when they left the room — only Quinn threw a quick thank-you after them.

"See, it's not so bad," Lizzie said as she bowed her head. After they prayed silently, she began to cut her ham. They'd each made a plate to leave in the kitchen before setting out the meal for their guests. "They're nice enough."

"There's just so many of them." Esther glanced out the window. "And I must admit, the generators are rather loud. I'm surprised Gus hasn't come back over."

Lizzie chuckled. "He's probably afraid of that boy."

Esther wasn't sure Gus was afraid of

anything, but he had clearly backed down when Jayce confronted him.

"And that boy is right." Lizzie gave a taut nod of her head. "We shouldn't let him talk to us that way."

Esther frowned. "You are as forthright as Gus when it comes to the two of you arguing, minus the terrible language."

"He starts it," Lizzie said, rolling her lip under.

Esther sighed. It wasn't true. Lizzie sometimes instigated the run-ins with Gus. But she was too tired to argue.

They both looked up when they heard footsteps.

"Got room for one more?" Jayce stood in the kitchen holding his plate.

"Ya, ya." Esther nodded to the two empty chairs at the kitchen table, wondering if he left the others because of his father.

Lizzie instantly resembled a lovestruck teenager as she batted her eyes at Jayce, asking if she could get him anything. Esther couldn't help but look away and roll her eyes. If Lizzie knew how silly she looked, perhaps she'd act her age. But anyone who stood up to Grumpy Gus Owens was a hero in Lizzie's book.

"Nah, I don't need anything," he said as he slipped into the chair across from Esther, with Lizzie sitting between them. "I just didn't want to listen to the plans for tomorrow anymore. I'm terrified enough."

Esther and Lizzie exchanged glances, then waited for him to explain.

"I don't like enclosed spaces," he finally said. "I didn't realize until Evelyn told me that this particular cave is only accessible by boat." He sighed. "Meaning I can't run out if I need to."

"Evelyn?" Esther asked, ignoring his concerns about the cave. They only had one Evelyn in their community, but the name was also common to the English. "Is that someone in your group?"

"No." Jayce took a sip of tea before he continued. "When I left earlier, I needed some air and to get away from my dad. So I took off walking. A woman's horse had stepped on a piece of glass, so I helped her. Her name was Evelyn." He grinned. "The woman, that is. The horse was Millie." Pausing, he focused on Esther. "I'm really sorry about my behavior today. I just couldn't stand to see that man speak to you that way. I'm sorry if I overstepped."

Lizzie was beaming, flashing her pearly white dentures. She was clearly smitten with this young lad. It was almost embarrassing.

"I've waited a long time for someone" —

she glared briefly at Esther — "someone besides *me* to stand up to that grumpy old man."

Esther was more curious about Jayce's encounter with Evelyn. If Lizzie was giddy over the handsome English man young enough to be her grandson, what must Evelyn have thought about him?

"It was nice of you to help Evelyn with her horse." Esther tried to sound casual but kept her eyes on Jayce to catch any reaction.

He finished chewing a bite of ham. "It wasn't a big deal. I'm usually pretty good with animals." He set his fork down. Esther was sure he wasn't done eating, but his expression started to mirror Lizzie's, dreamy and dazed. "She's beautiful."

"The horse or Evelyn?" Esther asked playfully. She hoped he said the horse, even though she knew he was talking about Evelyn Schrock. Every single man in their community had courted — or attempted to court — her. She'd even gotten a little serious with one or two. But she always broke it off in the end, saying no matter how wonderful the man was, he just wasn't the one.

The young woman was probably drawn in by Jayce's charming personality and natural good looks. Esther and Lizzie had both lived beautiful love stories, despite their inability to have children. They loved seeing young people find each other and start a life together and had even been known to play matchmaker, but Jayce wasn't a consideration for Evelyn. They were too many worlds apart.

Jayce picked up his fork, stabbed at a piece of ham, and grinned back at her. "Evelyn, of course. We're going to dinner and to see a movie tomorrow night." He took a bite and swallowed. "Can you believe she's never seen a movie before?"

Lizzie was quieter than she'd been in decades as she watched the handsome young man talk. Alarms were ringing in Esther's head.

"We don't go to movie theaters, but young people are often allowed to during their *rumschpringe.* It's a time when —"

"Yeah, she told me. She gets to do her own thing before she gets baptized." He excused himself to go into the dining room for seconds, returning with more food than he'd started with.

How much time had the boy spent with Evelyn? What would her parents think about her going out with an English man? Jayce had nearly perfect features, long hair, and ink peeking from beneath his short-sleeved shirt. That was more than enough to send Jonas Schrock into a tizzy. Looks shouldn't matter, but first impressions stayed with a person, wanted or not.

"Will you be taking her to Washington to see a movie?" Esther knew where the theater was, even though she'd never been inside. "That would be the nearest town to see a movie, and you can get there by buggy."

Jayce finished chewing, then swallowed. Esther remained in awe at the amount of food the lad could eat. "I want to do things the right way and pick her up. Billy can take us. He's one of our drivers. Or I can probably take one of the cars and pick her up."

Esther glanced at Lizzie, whose gaze had shifted from dreamy to concerned. For once they were on the same page. If Jayce showed up in a limousine, Jonas might forbid Evelyn to go in such luxury. Even though Evelyn was nineteen and not yet baptized, she still lived under her parents' roof and must abide by their rules. Given the circumstances, it might be best that Evelyn and Jayce not get too chummy.

"Nee, nee, nee." Lizzie pushed back her chair, folded her arms across her chest, and grunted. "You can't pick up Evelyn in that fancy black car. Her *daed* wouldn't let her out of the *haus.*" Lizzie waved a hand in

the air. "Take one of our buggies."

Esther's eyes widened. "Lizzie, he doesn't know how to drive a horse and buggy." She glanced at Jayce, who had stopped chewing, his eyes ping-ponging back and forth between them.

"If he can drive a car, he can drive a horse and buggy. We'll give him Poppy. That old horse isn't going to kick up and cause him any trouble."

"Lizzie, you don't know that. Poppy is old, but she can be unpredictable." Esther glanced at Jayce. The boy finally swallowed the food in his mouth.

"Uh . . ." He scratched his head. "Would her parents really not let her go if I show up in a limo? Because those are the only cars we brought."

Esther was tempted to implore Jayce to cancel the date. This had disaster written all over it. "I've known Jonas and Mae, Evelyn's parents, for a long time. They are fine people, but . . ." Esther sighed. "Lizzie is right. Jonas might not let the girl out of the *haus.*"

Jayce stared at his plate, then picked up a slice of bread and grinned. "Then the horse and buggy it is. I don't want to take any chances that her parents won't let her go."

Esther tried to smile. They didn't even

know this young man. But when she looked at Lizzie, her sister winked. Esther would have a talk with her in private later and explain the obvious — this was not a situation to be encouraged.

FOUR

Jayce carried as much scuba equipment as
he could under one arm and pulled a wagon
behind him with the rest as he descended
four hundred feet into the cavern. With the
sun still at his back, his chest tightened as
he neared the underground river. He slowed
behind the others when they reached the
platform, reminding himself that daylight
and the ramp leading out of the cave were
just around the corner.

To the right four boats were docked.
Jayce's heart raced at the thought of getting
in one of the narrow aluminum vessels and
going into the cave with no means of escape.
The boats reminded him of his grandfather's fishing boat, except these had been
outfitted to hold tourists with two rows of
seating running down the middle. On the
few occasions Jayce had visited his grandfather, they'd fished on the pond on his
property. Jayce's father grew up on a farm

in west Texas. More than once, he'd told Jayce how he couldn't get out of the Podunk town fast enough. Jayce loved the rural area, the slowness of the town, and the quiet. It was the polar opposite of everything in Los Angeles. No sirens, honking horns, schedules, or traffic. He wished he could have spent more time with his grandparents when they were alive.

He followed Veronica, who was wearing a wetsuit. Cameramen were already loading equipment into one of the boats and insisted they would carry the more expensive gear themselves. There was a flurry of activity as several other actors and crew members hustled to board the boats.

How far into the cave would they be going? His stomach began to twist and churn.

"Jayce, hold up."

He slowed at his father's voice coming from behind him. He turned and waited as the others kept going.

"Listen . . ." His father took a moment to catch his breath. Jayce had seen the man go up and down the long ramp to the river level twice.

"What?" Jayce asked, frowning.

His father put a hand on Jayce's shoulder. "I know how you feel about places without an easy exit, so after everything is loaded, you can hang back. We're only filming one scene, and the setup will probably take longer than the actual filming."

Wow. He'd dodged a bullet. Jayce was about to take him up on the offer when the corner of his father's mouth went up on one side, mockingly. His silent expression spoke volumes to Jayce as he remembered the time the man had forced him into an elevator that took them to the top of a forty-six-floor building. He couldn't have been more than eight or nine, but he could recall the event like it happened yesterday. By the time they reached the forty-sixth floor the first time, Jayce was crying and could barely breathe. His dad pushed the Down button, and they made the trip three more times while he screamed at Jayce to suck it up. The dissatisfaction in Brandon Clarkson's eyes, telling him to toughen up and be a man, had never left his memory.

"No, I'll go," Jayce said as he stared him down, wishing immediately that he'd accepted the get-out-of-jail-free card. Just once he'd like to prove the man wrong. Maybe he would treat Jayce with a little more respect if he saw this through.

His father's smirk expanded as he eased his arm to his side. "Well, okay then."

Jayce tightened his grip on the wagon and

forced himself to meet up with the others at the water's edge. After two more trips for the rest of the gear, it took another thirty minutes or so to get people and equipment stowed in a way that was acceptable to the guides who would be driving the boats. Despite the cool temperature in the cave entrance, sweat gathered on Jayce's forehead and trailed down both sides of his face.

The boats wobbled as everyone balanced themselves and the equipment in the middle. The cameramen clung to their mini-cams and other paraphernalia as if they were children who might fall overboard. Jayce wondered how deep the water was farther into the cave. Standing on solid ground and handing the last of the snorkels and masks and another air tank to Hal, he worried he might toss his breakfast. When he felt eyes on him, he looked to his left. Veronica's expression was filled with sympathy, unlike his father's. Her eyes said, *You don't have to do this.*

Over the years Brandon Clarkson had made his feelings known, often calling Jayce a coward — or something far worse — in front of people. He longed to shut the old man up and show him that he had conquered his fear, but when he stepped one foot into the boat, his head started to spin.

"I think I'll take you up on that offer, Dad, to stay behind." He hoisted himself back to the dock. He could feel his face turning red and wished that just this once his father wouldn't make him look like a fool.

Dear old Dad's eyes shone with satisfaction. "Yeah, I didn't figure you'd actually get in the boat and go."

Jayce trembled, wanting more than anything to get in that boat. But he didn't. He couldn't. As the cavern employees fired up the trolling motors, the boats eased away.

The last thing Jayce saw was his father's smirk.

Esther stared at the pile of breakfast dishes in the sink, then thought about all the laundry that was building up. After their guests left this morning, she'd gone upstairs to tidy the rooms. She'd never seen so many towels used in such a short time. It looked like each person had used two or three. Of course, there wasn't a towel limit per guest, but they were all on the floor — some in the bathrooms, others in the bedrooms — meaning she would need to replace them with fresh towels.

As the kitchen sink filled with warm water, she added soap, then heard Lizzie clomping down the stairs. When she turned around, she saw that Lizzie had beat her to the task. She was carrying an armful of towels.

"These city people are slobs," Lizzie said as she dropped the towels near the basement entrance. She dramatically placed a hand on her forehead. "Don't even go up there, Esther. It's a mess. There are clothes all over the floor. And one of them eats a lot of chocolate bars. The wrappers are just thrown on the floor." She put her hands on her hips, shaking her head.

"*Ya,* I know. I was up there earlier." She turned off the water and faced her sister. "But we've had guests before who weren't very tidy."

"*Ya,* true. But *all* of these guests are messy. Didn't their *mudders* teach them the basics? Hang your towel on the rack. Don't throw trash on the floor of your bedroom. And someone must have gotten up in the middle of the night because they left a half-eaten piece of apple pie on a plate on the bed." Lizzie wrinkled her nose and shook her head again.

"We're too old to do all of this ourselves." Esther turned back to the sink and started scrubbing the dishes.

"I've been asking around trying to find someone." Lizzie sat at the kitchen table. "But no takers."

"We'll find someone." When Esther finished nearly twenty minutes later, she dried her hands and joined Lizzie at the table. "I want to talk to you about something."

Lizzie sighed. "I've been on *mei* best behavior. What have I done?"

Esther grinned. "You haven't done anything. I just don't think we should encourage anything between Evelyn and Jayce. The girl is probably infatuated with him because he's so handsome and charming. But he isn't only an *Englisch* fellow. He's an *Englisch* fellow who lives a life far different from even the average non-Amish person. He rides in limousines, probably lives in a fancy house in Los Angeles, and grew up in a way we can't even imagine."

She held up a finger when Lizzie opened her mouth to say something. "Just let me finish. I know there have been instances, although rare, when someone converts to our way of life. But that would never happen in this situation. It's only one date, hopefully the last one. I don't want to see someone so worldly break Evelyn's heart."

Lizzie sat taller and raised her chin. "These things are in *Gott*'s hands, not ours."

"And how many times have we taken things into our own hands by playing matchmaker? I'm just saying that we can only

76

cause harm if we encourage a romantic relationship between Jayce and Evelyn." Esther paused and shook her head. "This is silly. That boy hasn't even been here twenty-four hours." She propped her elbows on the table and folded her hands together. "I guess that's *mei* point. In less than a day, he already has a date."

Lizzie eased back into her chair. "*Ach,* what I wouldn't give to be fifty years younger. I loved *mei* Reuben, but I reckon young Jayce would have turned *mei* head, too, at that age."

Esther got up and walked to the window. "Some of them must have stayed behind since the generators are still running. They couldn't all have fit in the two cars they took." She tapped a finger to her chin. "Which brings me to another point. Why hasn't Gus been over here complaining?"

Lizzie shuffled over to the window. "Because that young man put old Gus in his place."

"I don't think Gus scares that easily, especially not by someone like Jayce. He was red in the face he was so mad yesterday. Then, nothing. Seems odd to me." Esther glanced at Lizzie. "Have you even seen him outside the cottage? I hope he isn't ill and nothing has happened to him."

Lizzie hung her head, shaking it, before she looked up at Esther. "You're a *gut* woman, Esther, to care about that man when he's given us nothing but grief. I'll be haunted until the day I die about why *Mamm* made us promise he could live here for the rest of his life."

"I'm sure she had her reasons." Esther was as confused as Lizzie about her mother's dying wish.

"But what were they?"

Esther twisted her mouth back and forth as she thought about it for the umpteenth time. "You know I have no idea. We may never know." Recalling the time he'd helped her, she said, "Gus does have some *gut* qualities. He was helpful when I had *mei* medical issues. There is compassion deep within his soul. He just doesn't show it much."

"I'll say it again." Lizzie groaned. "You're a *gut* woman, Esther. Every time I see that man, I want to give him a swift kick in the shin."

Lizzie actually had kicked Gus in the shin a few times over the years. "Well, let's just all try to get along." Esther stared at the cottage from the kitchen window as Lizzie retreated to take the towels down to the basement.

When Gus Owens got fired up about something, he was relentless until he got his way. They'd hired someone a few years ago to mow the grass around the main house, the cottage, and the *daadi haus*. The fellow they employed could only be there early in the mornings, and Gus had thrown a tantrum, saying he couldn't sleep in with all the noise. The man only came once a week, but Esther eventually had to let him go and hire someone else who could tend to the yard in the afternoons. They'd made plenty of concessions over the years to tame his temper.

Esther tried to be kind. She often took Gus leftovers and slices of pie. He was often ungrateful, complained about the choice of pie, and never invited Esther inside, which was a blessing. She'd been in the cottage before, and it was an unpleasant experience. Gus had been there for her when it counted, though. He'd shown a tiny smidgen of himself that most folks never saw — little kindnesses that were bottled up and rarely revealed. Maybe later she'd go check on him.

She plodded back to the kitchen, wiped down the counters, and returned her thoughts to Evelyn and Jayce. Lizzie was right. That boy was a looker. He had a kind face and eyes that seemed to hold a secret.

He was everything a young woman might be attracted to. But that woman needed to be English. Esther prayed tonight would be a onetime thing.

Evelyn paced her bedroom Friday afternoon. She needed to tell her parents she had a date this evening. It would be better for them to know in advance that her date was an English man. A nervous excitement swirled in the pit of her stomach, but she broke out in a cold sweat every time she thought about Jayce pulling up to her house in a fancy car. If her parents saw that and hadn't been warned, it could go very badly.

She sat on her bed and wrapped her arms across her stomach. She'd never been out with an English man. Maybe he didn't consider this a date. Perhaps he just wanted to go to the movies and needed someone to go with. What if his intentions were dishonorable? Would he try to hold her hand or slide his arm over her shoulder? She'd heard stories from her friends about movie dates. If Amish men showed such public affection, would an English man? The thought of Jayce touching her in any way caused her stomach to tense even more. She wasn't sure she wanted to push away any advances he might make. It wasn't just his athletic build that drew her to him. His alluring brown eyes shone with intensity, like he had a lot on his mind and was just waiting to share his thoughts with someone. She wanted to know him better.

After another fifteen minutes of pondering the situation, she heard her mother shuffling around downstairs in the kitchen. It would be easiest to break the news to her.

Evelyn went downstairs and moseyed her way into the kitchen. "*Mudder* — why are you sitting on the floor? What are you doing?" She had pulled pots and pans from the bottom cabinet and stacked them all around her.

"I can't find *mei* double boiler. I've stored it in this cabinet for decades." Her mother looked like she might cry, which was odd, but not completely out of character. Evelyn had read about menopause, and her mother seemed to be in the throes of it lately.

Evelyn wasn't sure if she should say where the double boiler was. Her mother continued pulling pots from the cabinet, and Evelyn cleared her throat.

"*Daed* has your double boiler in the barn." Her mother stopped moving and glared up at Evelyn.

"Why does your father have *mei* double

boiler in the barn?" The words were clipped. She pressed her lips together and lifted herself off the floor. She brushed the dust from her black apron and blew a strand of loose hair out of her face before tucking it beneath her prayer covering.

"He's melting wax with a propane camp stove." Evelyn flinched, knowing her mother was about to blow up. Mae Schrock only allowed Evelyn to touch her kitchen pots and utensils, and even that had been hard for her. Her mother loved to cook, and the kitchen and everything in it were her territory. Evelyn didn't think there was a pot or gadget her mother didn't own, unless it wasn't available in a battery-operated or propane version.

Her mother's face was red, fists balled at her sides. "Why is your father melting wax?"

Evelyn cleared her throat again and shrugged. "He said he was going to make candles."

Her mother threw her hands in the air. "*Ach*! What in the world for?"

Evelyn shifted her weight as she crinkled her nose. "I think to sell."

"To sell?" She groaned, throwing her head back. "What is wrong with that man? Last month he tried to make wine. We don't even drink wine!" Her mother took a deep breath. "And the month before that, he was whittling and carving little animals out of wood."

When she covered her face with her hands and started to cry, Evelyn walked over to her mother and wrapped her arms around her.

"He's ruining *mei* double boiler," she said through her tears. Evelyn thought she'd gotten used to these random meltdowns. The books she'd read said this phase should pass. *But when?*

Now was not the best time to tell her that an English man was coming to pick her up this evening, but the window of opportunity would be closing soon. Her brothers would return from work, their father would come into the house, or her mother would take off to the barn to reclaim her double boiler.

Her mother eased out of the embrace and took a deep breath.

And just like that she was back to herself.

"*Mamm,* I need to tell you something." Evelyn chewed her bottom lip. "Please be open-minded."

Her mother locked eyes with her. "Evelyn, I'm not having the best day." She raised an eyebrow. "Please don't make it any worse."

"I just wanted to let you know that I have a date tonight." She paused, twirling the

83

string on her prayer covering. "And it's with an *Englisch* man, someone staying at Esther and Lizzie's inn." She held her breath and waited for her mother to explode and explain all the reasons this was a bad idea — reasons Evelyn already knew.

"What time is he coming?" She folded her arms across her chest, an action that seemed defiant, but her voice was level and calm.

"Six o'clock. And . . . I'm worried what *Daed* will think." She hugged herself and waited.

"You should be." She opened the door that led to the front porch, then looked over her shoulder at Evelyn. "I will try to handle your father, but no promises. You do know that dating an *Englisch* man is a bad idea, *ya?*"

"*Ya,* I do. But I don't think it's really a date." She was pretty sure it was, but putting some doubt in her mother's mind might not be a bad idea, until she knew where things were going — if anywhere. Evelyn wasn't even sure why she agreed to go. *Not true.* She'd agreed because Jayce was irresistibly handsome. She could still feel the way her insides swirled when he told her she was beautiful while staring at her with those enchanting eyes.

"I'll let your *daed* know." She growled.

"Right after I get *mei* double boiler back!" And with that, she stormed off to the barn.

Evelyn stood speechless. Her news had been trumped by her mother's need to reclaim her double boiler. Perhaps this wouldn't go as badly as she'd feared. Her father would be in the doghouse by this evening.

Esther sipped tea in her rocking chair on the front porch, watching Lizzie teach Jayce how to drive the horse and buggy. Poppy was a gentle animal, but Esther worried if this quick lesson would be enough for Jayce to get himself and Evelyn to their destination and back home safely. Normally they would take the topless spring buggy this time of year, but Lizzie had insisted Jayce take her enclosed buggy, even though she wouldn't give a reason and there wasn't any rain in the forecast. Esther had argued that the young people were going to be hot, but Lizzie ignored her and did what she wanted. Sometimes it just wasn't worth the energy to argue with her.

Mr. Clarkson and the others had returned about an hour ago. Esther and Lizzie prepared extra supper, but only the six guests staying in the house came for the meal. Jayce ate, too, even though he was taking

Evelyn out shortly. Esther offered a few suggestions about places to eat, but Jayce said he'd let Evelyn choose. He was a nice young man.

The sound of a door closing caused Esther to look up. *Oh dear.* Gus was moving across the yard with giant strides, and seconds later Brandon Clarkson came out of one of the motor homes. Esther stood, her heart thumping. Gus was rushing directly toward Mr. Clarkson, and the encounter could not be good.

Lizzie didn't seem to notice as she continued to instruct Jayce. Esther stepped down the porch steps one foot at a time, prepared to intervene.

Gus lifted a hand in the air before he reached Mr. Clarkson. "Hello, Brandon!" he bellowed.

"Good to see you, Gus." When the producer reached Gus, he extended his hand.

Esther tipped her head to the side, bemused.

"How'd the shoot go today?" Gus was holding a container Esther had taken him leftovers in a few days ago. She usually had to go collect the items herself. Unable to recall a single time he'd returned a dish, she took a few more steps into the yard. She wasn't going to miss any part of the scene unfolding before her.

"It went very well." Mr. Clarkson stood in front of Gus, both men smiling. "We've done a lot of traveling, and today we wore everyone out. We're going to take the weekend off, but I'll see you Monday?"

"Yes, sir. Looking forward to it." Gus tucked the container under his arm, then looped his thumbs beneath his suspenders. He could almost pass as an Amish man with his black slacks, blue shirt, and suspenders. But the long gray ponytail cleared up any confusion.

Mr. Clarkson went back inside the motor home, and Gus stomped across the yard toward Esther, pausing to frown at Lizzie, who promptly told him to shut up before he even said anything.

"Do you see how that sister of yours treats me?" Gus handed Esther the empty container. "I didn't say a word to her, and she treats me with such disrespect."

Esther glowered. "Gus, it goes both ways with you and Lizzie. *Danki* for returning *mei* container."

"Yeah, yeah. Whatever." He propped his arms across his belly, which appeared to be growing. Esther couldn't say anything about that. At least her dress covered her own rounded middle.

"What is that crazy woman doing, anyway?" Gus asked with his signature scowl etched across his face.

"She's trying to teach that young man — Jayce — how to drive the buggy."

"Why?" He turned to Esther, his jowls hanging low as his frown deepened. "I don't like that kid."

Esther grinned. "I think the feeling is probably mutual. Lizzie is teaching him about the buggy because he is taking Evelyn Schrock to supper."

Gus shook his head. "I don't see that going well. But I reckon I'll have to do my best to get along with the twerp since he's Brandon's son."

"Um . . ." Esther scratched her cheek. Gus didn't get along with anyone. "What does Jayce being Brandon's *sohn* have to do with anything?"

Gus chuckled, and Esther wondered if she was dreaming. Gus was not the kind of man who found humor in many things. "Well, I guess you haven't heard." He coughed, then rubbed his hands together before resting them back on his belly. "As I explained to you yesterday, I found those generators to be bothersome."

Esther waited, not used to this formal tone Gus was using.

"As for Brandon . . ." He paused to clear his throat, then smiled. "Yeah, we're on a first-name basis. Anyway, when I was telling him my concerns about the generators, he gasped. I was midsentence when he told me I had a certain look he needed for a background person in his movie." Gus stood proud, chest puffed out, causing the buttons on his shirt to look like they might pop any minute. "Anyway, I gotta go. As an actor, I need my beauty sleep."

Esther covered her mouth with her hand as Gus turned and strutted toward the cottage. *What a smart man, that Brandon Clarkson.* He stepped right onto Gus's playing field — and it appeared to be a win for both men. Esther only hoped they could tolerate Gus now that he saw himself as a movie star. Then again, any change in his behavior had to be an improvement. *I hope.*

FIVE

Jayce pushed his sunglasses up on his head. Poppy seemed to trust him with the reins, and she hadn't given him any trouble so far. It wasn't as hot inside the buggy as he'd thought it might be. There was good cross-ventilation, and the sun had been hidden behind the clouds most of the afternoon. He had noticed a strong scent inside the buggy, even with the fresh air blowing in the windows. *Vanilla.* It was a little overwhelming. He hoped it didn't bother Evelyn too much. Maybe Lizzie had spilled a milkshake or something recently.

He found the address Evelyn had given him without any problems.

At Lizzie's insistence he'd worn a long-sleeved shirt so as not to reveal his tattoo. He was proud of the great job the artist had done, and he was proud of the message the tattoo represented, but Lizzie said it would be best. She'd even come at him with a pair of scissors, but that was where Jayce drew the line. He wasn't going to let an Amish woman cut his hair. Apparently, there was only one style for men here, and Jayce wasn't returning to L.A. looking like he'd had a bowl put on his head for a haircut.

Lizzie was a funny old lady. She'd sat him down and lectured him as if this were his first date. He was twenty-two. He'd been dating since he was fifteen. Although, that first year after his parents split up, he wouldn't call what he did dating. He'd partied. But it eventually got old. Things changed for him all around when he entered into a relationship with God. Now he was picking up an Amish woman for dinner. He'd certainly traveled the distance from one end of the spectrum to the other.

At the end of the driveway, he tethered the horse to the fence post, the way Lizzie showed him, then he strolled across the yard and up the porch steps. He was usually pretty good with parents, but Lizzie said Evelyn's parents would be a hard sell, especially her father. He tapped lightly on the screen door, and a few seconds later, Evelyn answered, pushing the screen open so Jayce could enter.

"You came in a horse and buggy?" Her eyes widened in surprise as she peered past him at Poppy and their ride for the evening.

He chuckled. "Yeah, surprise. Lizzie taught me, and I thought you might be more comfortable riding in that instead of one of the limos." Although he was 100 percent sure she would have loved the limo. "Actually, Lizzie thought your parents might prefer this mode of transportation."

She nodded. "*Danki* . . . I mean, thank you."

"Sure."

As he entered Evelyn's living room, he instantly thought of his grandparents. After they'd passed, within a year of each other, Jayce's father had sold the place right away. This farmhouse brought up memories of visits with his grandparents. It smelled like something was baking, for starters, and the wonderful aroma filled his senses when he took a long, lingering breath. Atop the fireplace was a mahogany clock that could have been an exact replica of his grandmother's. He wondered if this one chimed on the hour and half hour in the same way.

With the windows open, a cool breeze floated in through the screens. Even the tan, slightly worn couch looked familiar. There was nothing ornate in the room. No pictures, and the walls were white. But somehow there wasn't anything sterile about the environment either, which was how he often described his father's current home.

After his mother left them, his father sold the house Jayce had grown up in and purchased the most expensive thing on the market at the time that didn't require yard work. Granted, his mother's decorating hadn't exactly exuded warmth, but his father's luxury condo reminded Jayce of some futuristic palace — and not in a good way. Evelyn's home offered a warmth that was missing from any home Jayce had ever known. Only the time he'd spent with his grandparents had given him a similar cozy feeling.

He was still taking in his surroundings when two men about his age came walking barefoot into the living room, eyeing him up and down. Evelyn introduced them as her brothers — Lucas and David. Neither extended a hand, so Jayce didn't either. He wasn't sure what proper protocol was with these people.

When Evelyn's parents stepped into the room, the brothers went upstairs.

Evelyn's father, whom she introduced as Jonas, looked older than Jayce would have expected. He had a full head of gray hair, a long beard the same color, and eyebrows that almost met in the middle of his forehead. His eyes were hooded like a hawk's, and he was frowning as Evelyn introduced him.

Her mother, Mae, was the opposite and appeared too young to have children in their twenties. Even though her hair was salt-and-pepper colored — visible only in a small area outside those things they wore on their heads — she had high cheekbones, bright-green eyes, and a face void of wrinkles. She was pretty in a natural sort of way. Like Evelyn, she wasn't wearing any makeup, and as she smiled, Jayce's stomach settled a little.

"Evelyn's curfew is ten o'clock." Jonas spoke sternly as he raised his eyebrows, seeming to wait for Jayce to counter.

"Yes, sir." Jayce forced a smile. He'd never dated a girl with a curfew. How would they eat, get to a movie in the buggy, and return by ten?

"What are your plans?" Mae folded her hands in front of her, still smiling.

"Uh . . . we're going to supper," Evelyn said before Jayce had a chance to respond. "I'll be home by ten."

Jayce followed her lead when she moved toward the door, stopping to pull a black cape from the rack nearby. He offered a quick, "Nice to meet you," then rushed to keep up with Evelyn.

"Do you want me to drive the buggy?" she asked as they walked across the yard.

Jayce considered the idea since she was surely better at it than he was. He didn't want to do anything to put her in danger, but he hadn't had a single problem with Poppy, and his manhood seemed at stake. He didn't want a girl driving him around.

"I'd like to drive, if that's okay with you." He opened the passenger door.

"*Ya,* fine with me."

Before she stepped into the buggy, Jayce said, "Wait, I better warn you. There's a really strong scent of vanilla in here. *Really* strong." He didn't remember smelling the vanilla when Lizzie was teaching him how to drive and handle the horse.

"It's okay. I love vanilla." She stepped into the buggy, and Jayce waited until her cape was all the way inside before he closed the door.

He untethered the horse, climbed into the seat beside his date, then backed up Poppy as if he'd been doing it his entire life. Within a minute, he had them turned in the right direction and the horse settled into a steady trot.

When he finally looked at Evelyn, she was holding her nose.

"See? It's bad, isn't it? I'm really sorry. I

didn't notice it until I got on the road."

She released her nose, blinked a few times, and said, "It is a bit strong." Then she laughed. "I wonder why it smells like that?"

"I don't know." Jayce shook his head, holding his breath for a few seconds, until he laughed too.

"I can handle it," she said with a taut nod of her head.

"Then I can too." He wanted to tell her again that she looked beautiful. He also wanted to ask her if all those clothes were really necessary. Not that he wanted to see her figure, which he kind of did, but it seemed like overkill.

"I'm wondering how we're going to have time to go eat, get to the movie, and get you back home in time." He grinned as he turned to her. "And I'm guessing I'll be in big trouble if we're not on time."

She shook her head. "Not at all. You won't be in any trouble. Just me. I'll be the one in trouble."

Jayce grimaced. "Yikes. I don't want that to happen." He gave Poppy a gentle flick of the reins until the horse picked up a little speed.

"Don't they have food at the movie theater?" she asked.

"Uh . . . yeah. But they'll only have hot

dogs, pickles, popcorn, candy, stuff like that."

"I love hot dogs, if that food is okay for you." Evelyn smiled and Jayce rejoiced on the inside. He loved theater food. His dates had never been interested in that type of dining, but Jayce still got popcorn every time.

"Yep, hot dogs are fine with me." He looked her way again. "Are you sure?"

"*Ya, ya.* I'm excited to be going to the movies." She folded her hands over the small black purse in her lap. Jayce wondered what was in it. She didn't need money. He would be paying for their food and tickets. She wouldn't have any makeup in the bag. Or a brush. Every Amish woman he'd seen had her hair tucked beneath one of those head coverings. He wanted to ask her but refrained.

"I like the way you talk. You have kind of an accent." Jayce smiled at her. "It's cool. Different. It sounds a lot like German."

She blushed. Soon it would be dark and he wouldn't be able to catch her reactions with as much clarity. "Pennsylvania *Deitsch* is our first language. We don't start learning *Englisch* until we are five. I think that's why we sound a little different to outsiders."

Jayce nodded. He was at a loss for further

conversation. It seemed to him that the Amish were the outsiders, disconnected from the rest of the world. There were a lot of things he wanted to ask about her way of life. Why no electricity? Why no cars? Why the clothes? It must all tie in with their religious way of life, but it seemed so foreign to him. And unnecessary. He stayed quiet.

"How did it go in the cave today?" She cringed as she asked. Jayce grimaced as well.

"My dad gave me an out, told me I didn't have to go on the boat ride inside the cave." He winced as he recalled the smug look on his father's face. "I wanted to go, to prove to him I could, but at the last minute, I just couldn't get in the boat." He looked at her and felt his own face turning red. "It's embarrassing. Especially for a guy."

"I don't think you should be embarrassed. Everyone has something they're afraid of." He wanted to ask what she was afraid of, but he supposed that was up to her to reveal. He had voluntarily told her about his claustrophobia. He hated being dubbed anything with *phobia* on the end of the word.

As the sun began its final descent, it came from behind the clouds and was full force in front of them. Jayce dropped his sunglasses down on his nose. Evelyn opened her purse, and he got to see one thing she carried in the bag. She reached inside and pulled out her own shades. He smiled.

Then blurted, "So what are you afraid of?"

"Birds." She spoke barely above a whisper. "Actually, anything that flies. Birds, butterflies, bees, hornets, and even our chickens. Collecting eggs is usually a daughter's job, but when I was little, I used to beg *mei bruders* to get the eggs. They wouldn't at first, but I'd come back to the *haus* crying every morning, so eventually Lucas took over the task."

Jayce thought for a few seconds. "I understand about bees or insects that bite, but butterflies?" He rubbed his chin.

"*Ya*. I know. It's silly." She shook her head, but then lowered her sunglasses on her nose and looked above the rims. "But animals with wings stalk me. Seriously." She dramatically pushed the shades back up on her nose. It was cute.

He laughed. "I'm sorry. I don't mean to laugh, but butterflies are so dainty." He lifted a shoulder and dropped it slowly. "Just processing it."

"They say you should face your fears." Evelyn sighed loudly. "*Mei daed* took me to the zoo in Bloomington when I was young, specifically to see the birds. He said if I faced *mei* fear, I could conquer it." She giggled, a delightful sound. Kind of child-like and sweet. "I shot out of the bird place screaming and crying, and I got lost. *Mei daed* was frantic. By the time he found me, we were both too shaken up for him to push the issue. He's never brought up my fear of birds again."

"Wow. You're lucky he let it go like that. My old man never lets up about me being afraid of confined spaces. I mean, it's already a blow to a man's ego, but my dad likes to drive the point home every chance he gets, especially in front of people."

He shook his head as he recalled the elevator incident. He considered telling her since she shared her story, but then thought better of it. He'd already made his father out to be a monster, but there had been some good times between them. He just couldn't remember those as clearly as the bad times. Anyway, he didn't need to spill his entire life story to this woman he might never see again.

He slowed the horse when they neared the movie theater. "Wow. I feel like I just jumped back in time. What a cool theater." He studied the marquee, which resembled half a hexagon. "I've only seen theaters like this on TV."

"I think it was built in the late twenties. It was restored not too long ago."

He maneuvered Poppy farther down the street where he saw a single hitching post. "No one will try to steal the horse and buggy?"

She shook her head. "I've never heard of that happening."

"You probably don't even lock your doors at night." He turned quickly to face her. "Not that I'm planning to sneak into your house or anything."

She giggled again. "You wouldn't get far. The entry board creaks, and I'm pretty sure Lucas sleeps with one eye open. If you wanted to sneak in, just throw a rock at *mei* window, and I'll lower a ladder I keep under *mei* bed." She laughed. He was really enjoying that sound.

"The three doors that enter my dad's place all have three locks each."

"Is it because you're worried about burglars?" Her eyebrows narrowed into a frown.

"Yeah, I guess so." He paused. "Or some woman my dad recently made mad. They've been known to come calling after a breakup, and it's not always a pretty scene."

Jayce hopped out and walked around to her side of the buggy and opened the door. "Wow. I'm glad to be out of that buggy. That vanilla was brutal." He took a deep breath of fresh air. "Any idea what movie you want to see?" He hadn't even checked online to see what was playing. After she'd stepped out of the buggy, Jayce pulled his phone from his pocket and looked up the theater they were at.

"Uh-oh. There are only two movies playing. But here are the times and the movies." He held the phone out so she could see. "There are trailers that show a clip of the movie, and there's a description." He handed the phone to her. She scanned the two listings and gave the phone back. He could read the distress on her face, the way she was chewing her bottom lip and blinking nervously.

"What's wrong?"

"I-I don't want to see anything that, um" — she gnawed on her lip even more — "has bad things in it."

Jayce wasn't sure what to say. "Okay. What do you consider bad things? One movie is rated PG-13, and the other one is a cartoon."

"What does that mean, PG-13?" Her eyes widened.

"Uh, well, let's see." Jayce scratched his head. "I guess it means not to bring a kid under thirteen years old. Maybe it has some language or something else inappropriate. Nothing bad or anything, at least not for an adult."

She lowered her head, holding her little black purse with both hands in front of her.

"I'm going to leave the decision up to you." He lowered his arm, wishing he'd looked online at other theaters. But going to a movie farther away would have presented its own set of problems. He would have had to pick her up in one of the limos.

She lifted her head and her eyes met his. "Do you like cartoons?"

"Are you kidding?" He laughed. "I love cartoons, but I'd never suggest that to anyone. They'd think I was nuts for choosing a kid movie over an action-packed thriller." He held up a hand. "Don't get me wrong. I like a lot of different kinds of movies, but I do have a confession to make."

Her jaw dropped slightly. "What?"

"I watched *Frozen*. And the cartoon playing is *Frozen II.*" He scratched his chin. "Wow. Between my claustrophobia and fascination with cartoons, I can feel my manliness taking a nosedive."

She bounced up on her toes. "Do you want to see that one?"

He raised an eyebrow. "Seriously?"

She squeezed her eyes closed. "Sorry."

Laughing, he motioned for her to walk beside him. "Sorry? Are you kidding me? Don't be sorry. I'm heading into a theater to watch a cartoon and eat hot dogs, pickles, and popcorn. I couldn't be happier."

"Are you just saying that?" Her voice held a challenge, but she grinned.

"Nope." He caught her eye and winked. "I'm wondering where you've been all my life."

Evelyn couldn't look at Jayce as she clutched her purse on her lap. She was excited to see a movie finally but worried she wouldn't be able to focus on it.

"I'm wondering where you've been all my life." What did that mean? Surely it was just a playful comment.

When she'd opened her purse to get money for her ticket, Jayce quickly shook his head and said he had it. He also insisted on paying for the food and drinks. Any doubt in Evelyn's mind about this being a date was gone.

It took both of them to carry everything Jayce had ordered. Two hot dogs, two nacho trays, two bags of popcorn, two candy bars, and two sodas. As they entered the theater, Evelyn's stomach swirled with excitement. It wasn't as dark as she'd feared. She wouldn't have to worry about making sure Jayce kept his hands to himself.

"Here's your soda," he said after he placed the drinks in the cup holders on either side of him.

Evelyn lifted the cardboard box in her lap. There were candy bars, nachos, hot dogs, and popcorn. She'd only asked for popcorn, but Jayce ordered her a hot dog anyway. "This is a lot of food," she whispered. The theater was about half full. Jayce had chosen seats right in the middle after asking if she had a preference.

"I hope it's enough," he said right before starting in on his hot dog.

Evelyn picked at her popcorn, despite the temptation to fill her mouth with handfuls of the buttery snack. The soda was good too. Her mother rarely bought soft drinks. Iced tea was the drink of choice at her house.

"I'm in heaven." Jayce took another bite of his hot dog. It was gone in a flash and he was on to the second one after asking her if she was going to eat it. Men his age ate a lot. Her mother often pointed out how much food she had to cook to accommodate her sons' appetites.

Jayce finished the second hot dog, then wiped his mouth with a napkin and twisted to face her. "Are you excited?"

"*Ya,* I am." Evelyn couldn't wait for the screen to light up. She never would have believed her first movie would be an animated film with an English man, but she couldn't have been happier. No worries about language, too much skin showing, or an inappropriate story line.

Then the lights started to dim and she jumped, dumping her popcorn partly in her lap and some on the floor. "Oh no."

"Don't worry, we've got plenty, and I can always go get more." He reached toward her like he was going to help brush the popcorn from her lap, but he stopped and pulled back his hand, thankfully.

"Why is it so dark now?" She heard the tremble in her voice as she shook the popcorn from her lap and onto the floor.

"The movie is about to start. There will probably be some previews first." Jayce continued eating, but his eyes were on the screen.

Evelyn couldn't believe how big the screen was, nor how colorful and bright. She jumped again when Jayce's arm brushed against hers. When she looked his way, she saw that he'd only accidentally elbowed her as he dug his hand into his bag of popcorn. Now he was staring at her.

"Evelyn," he whispered as he leaned close to her ear.

"Ya?"

"Quit being so jumpy and just enjoy the movie. I promise I'm not going to make a move. I won't even try to hold your hand."

She forced a smile, glad he couldn't see the flush she felt filling her cheeks. Instead of trying to deny the reason for her jumpiness, she nodded. An unexpected disappointment assaulted her from out of nowhere, and she didn't think she would have minded his fingers intertwined with hers.

Once the movie started, following several previews, she became lost in the story. Jayce laughed out loud several times, as did Evelyn. It didn't take her long to finally relax into the situation. And the movie was over much too soon.

"Danki — I mean, thank you — so much for taking me," she said as they walked out to the buggy. The moon was high and bright, and she felt light on her feet.

Jayce gave her a stern look. "If you tell anyone we went to see a cartoon movie for kids . . ." He threw his head back, laughing, his long hair falling forward across his face when he finished. "Wasn't it great though?"

"I loved it." Evelyn slid into her seat, and Jayce closed the door and made his way around the buggy.

On the way back to Evelyn's house, they kept talking about the movie and laughing — and occasionally holding their noses. She couldn't imagine what Lizzie must have spilled in the buggy to leave such a strong aroma.

Evelyn didn't start getting nervous until Jayce stopped the buggy in front of her house and turned to face her. He stared at her for a long time, those captivating eyes locked onto hers. If he tried to kiss her, she would let him.

He still held the reins in one hand as he twisted to face her more fully, his knee brushing against hers.

"I know you have a life, and you probably already have plans, but I'm going to risk it. Are you busy tomorrow?"

She noticed a brown leather bracelet around his wrist. It added an allure he didn't need. Jayce already oozed with charm, and his over-the-top good looks and easy manner were like a magnet drawing her in.

"No problem if you're busy." He shook his head. "My dad surprised us and gave everyone the weekend off, which leaves me nothing to do but hang out with him and the crew, which will be terrible. I mean,

Quinn is okay. Hal is okay. Veronica is cool too. She's the biggest star in the movie, but she doesn't act like it. Still . . . if you don't have any plans and feel like showing me around, I'd happily buy you another meal tomorrow."

Evelyn tried to think about any plans she might have for the weekend. Reading a new book she'd bought at a secondhand shop was at the top of the list. Mending her brothers' socks and maybe trying a new recipe for roast. None of it was as important as getting to know Jayce better.

"*Ya,* sure. That sounds *gut.*"

"Fantastic." He rushed to get out of the buggy, looped the reins loosely around the fence post, then escorted Evelyn all the way to the front door. She coughed, struggling to find her voice, but happy to be away from the strong vanilla scent.

After clearing her throat, she thanked him again, but she couldn't seem to get her eyes to look away from his mouth. *Stop staring. Stop staring.*

Jayce cocked his head to the side and smiled. "What? Do I have something in my teeth?" Still grinning, he shrugged. "Because if I do, just tell me."

Evelyn opened her mouth to speak, but somehow her mouth took on a life of its own as she leaned forward and pressed her lips to his, then hurriedly stepped back and momentarily froze.

Their eyes locked. Jayce's looked like they might pop from their sockets.

"Um, *ya,* well . . . Thanks again." She hurried to open the screen and nearly slammed the door behind her.

As she leaned her back against it, she lifted her shaking hands to her chest, her heart pounding like a jackhammer. She'd never done anything like that in her life.

She'd never be able to face him again.

SIX

After Jayce put Poppy in the barn, he continued analyzing the evening as he walked back to the inn. With all the information he'd received from Lizzie, Esther, and Billy, Jayce hadn't even planned to hug Evelyn. He'd wanted to kiss her all night, but more than that he didn't want to do anything to offend her or make her uncomfortable. He reached up and touched his mouth, shaking his head as he neared the house. They didn't even know each other.

Lights were on in the motor homes, and the generators were buzzing. Maybe the old guy, Gus, had gotten used to the noise. Or maybe he'd paid the sisters another visit and they managed to calm him down. He opened the front door and closed it quietly behind him, then tiptoed to the stairway, hoping he didn't run into his father. When he reached the stairs, he felt eyes on him. Turning slowly, he was relieved to see Lizzie and Esther sitting at the kitchen table and went to join them.

"Apple and pecan." Lizzie nodded to the pies as she spoke. She already had a plate and fork set out for him. "We want details."

Esther glared at her sister. "Lizzie, must you always be so brazen?" She turned to Jayce. "We just wondered if you enjoyed the movie and where you went for supper."

He was still focused on figuring out why Evelyn kissed him. But he wasn't one to kiss and tell. He pulled out a chair and sat, then gave the women a brief rundown of the evening.

"That sounds like a nice time." Esther sipped her coffee. Jayce would be up all night if he drank coffee this late.

"Yeah, she's a nice girl." He eyed the pies, trying to decide between the two. Finally, he sliced into the apple pie.

"You didn't kiss her or do anything inappropriate, did you?" Lizzie drummed her fingers against the table. He looked up and paused. She looked different. It took him a few seconds to realize it was because she wasn't wearing her dentures. They had also both replaced their white head coverings with scarves.

Smiling, he said, "No. I didn't kiss her or do anything inappropriate." *But she sure laid one on me.* He lifted the piece of pie onto his plate, pulled it toward him, and took a bite.

Lizzie yawned. "You seem like a nice young man, but I have a special talent for spotting a liar, so I had to ask. You're not lying."

Esther scowled at her sister.

"No, I'm not lying." Jayce recalled the feel of Evelyn's lips on his. It had happened and ended before he even knew. He suspected it was a bold move for her. She'd immediately hightailed it inside without looking back.

"However . . ." Jayce kept them in suspense as he ate another bite of pie. "She's going to show me around tomorrow."

"Really?" Esther took another sip of coffee. "That's nice."

Something about her tone seemed to ask for a response, but he was busy with the pie and not sure how to respond anyway.

"She's Amish, you know?" Esther ran a finger around the rim of her coffee cup while keeping an eye on him.

He raised both hands to cover his mouth and gasped. "You're kidding."

Esther grinned. "Silly thing to say, I suppose."

Lizzie yawned again. "Did you have any trouble with Poppy?"

113

Jayce shook his head. "Nope. I picked up Evelyn and delivered her home safely without a hitch."

"Well, we just wanted to make sure you were a gentleman. I'm sure things are a lot different here than where you come from." Lizzie rubbed her eyes.

"You could say that." Jayce laughed, again recalling the kiss. He stood after finishing his pie and thanked the women. Temptation flowed through his veins like a rushing river, prodding him to tell the sisters that Evelyn had kissed him. Instead, he thought he'd better mention the vanilla. "Lizzie, did you spill something in your buggy?"

"*Nee.* Why?" She slouched in her chair and chewed a fingernail.

Jayce waved in front of his nose. "The smell of vanilla was so strong I worried we might throw up. I don't mean to sound disrespectful at all. I appreciate you letting me borrow the buggy, and it was fun driving it. But . . ." He shook his head. "I've never smelled that much vanilla in my life. Even with the windows open, it was pretty overbearing."

Lizzie shrugged. "I've never noticed that."

Jayce found that impossible to believe, but maybe Lizzie had a medical condition that

114

prevented her from smelling. He decided to let it go, excused himself, and went to bed.

Esther waited until Jayce was out of earshot before she turned to Lizzie. Her sister looked like a rag doll slumped in her chair as she avoided looking at Esther, still nibbling on her fingernail. "Vanilla?" She raised an eyebrow.

"What about it?" Lizzie continued to avoid Esther's inquiring eyes.

"Why would your buggy smell like vanilla?" Esther leaned forward. "And enough to make those young people feel sick."

Lizzie moaned as she straightened in the chair, then sighed. "Vanilla is an apple-desiac. It draws people together and makes them feel romantic."

Esther gasped as she brought a hand to her chest.

"Why do you look so shocked? It was just a little nudge to help them feel comfortable on their first date." Lizzie stiffened as she placed her palms on the table. "I read that in one of my romance books."

Esther held her forehead in her hands before she looked at her sister. "First of all, you need to stop reading those books. Secondly, the word you misspoke has a different meaning from what you think." She shook her head. "How did you get enough of the scent to stay in the buggy and overwhelm the *kinner?*"

Lizzie pressed her lips together, then let out a dramatic sigh. "I left some vanilla candles out in the sunlight behind the barn until they melted a little. Then I smeared the wax on the back seat and floorboards." She paused, raised her chin. "I couldn't smell it all that much so I mixed some vanilla extract and water together, put it in a spray bottle, then sprayed everything in the buggy."

Esther wasn't sure when her mouth fell open, but she forced it closed and thought for a few seconds. "I thought we were in agreement that we should not encourage anything between Evelyn and Jayce." She shook her head. *"Vanilla?"* she asked again.

"I like that boy." Lizzie pushed her lip into a pout, exaggerated by the fact she didn't have her dentures in.

"You don't *know* that boy." Esther stared at her.

"*Ach,* well, I like him anyway." She lifted her chin. "He might not be lying, but he's not telling us something." Lizzie pressed her lips together, moving them from side to side, the way she often did when she didn't have her dentures in.

Esther's sister had smoothly changed the subject, but Esther had to agree with her. "I had the same feeling." It hadn't been anything Esther could put her finger on, but Jayce had seemed to be evading the entire truth. "Maybe he just needs a friend. We can't assume that every time a young man meets a young woman, they will become romantically involved."

Lizzie huffed. "We always assume that. It's what we do."

"Not in this case." Esther picked up one of the pies, walked to the counter, and began covering it. Lizzie followed with the other pie. "It's not just that one of them is Amish and the other isn't." She glanced at her sister. "Jayce grew up with lots of money, in a place where movie stars live, and he enjoys a life far more luxurious than even the average *Englischer*."

"That lifestyle must have a downside." Lizzie ran her hands under the water, then reached for a kitchen towel. "It's obvious he doesn't have a *gut* relationship with his *daed*."

"Downside or not, this time we are staying out of any matchmaking possibilities." Esther had noticed a twinkle in Jayce's eyes when he talked about Evelyn. That wasn't surprising. Evelyn was beautiful, inside and

117

out. She was also smart enough not to let anything romantic evolve over the next month.

"Well, there are still a bunch of sheets and towels that need to be run through the wringer." Lizzie stretched an arm behind her. "But *mei* back has given out."

Esther tightened the strap on her white robe. "We're going to end up in an early grave if we don't find some help."

"I'll keep asking around." Lizzie shrugged. "I just can't find anyone."

They headed toward their bedrooms on the main floor, both yawning. "Sweet dreams, Lizzie."

"You too, Esther."

Evelyn couldn't remember the last time she'd been up this late. It was nearing midnight. Rolling on her side, she pounded her pillow and closed her eyes.

After a few minutes she rolled onto her back and threw an arm across her forehead. How could she possibly spend the day with Jayce tomorrow after what she'd done? She kissed a man she didn't know on a first date. And it wasn't even a good kiss. She just smashed her mouth into his and retreated without a word.

She'd never allowed any man to kiss her

on a first date. Usually she waited several dates before she even considered the idea. *So why did I do that?*

No amount of analyzing would change the outcome.

Forcing her eyes closed, she tried to will herself to sleep. But she continued wondering what Jayce must think of her, how forward she was.

Saturday morning, Esther and Lizzie served breakfast in the dining room before retreating to the kitchen to enjoy some downtime. Mr. Clarkson, Quinn, and the other men were all downstairs by nine o'clock, the time they'd requested breakfast be served. Everyone was in attendance except Jayce.

Esther and Lizzie could hear the conversation in the other room.

"Where's Jayce?" Quinn asked as forks clinked against plates.

"Who knows," Mr. Clarkson replied in an aggravated voice. "He'll probably sleep all day. That's what he does at home. He's lazy."

"Maybe you confuse lazy with depressed." Quinn spoke firmly. "He hasn't been happy in a long time, Brandon."

"He's ungrateful and spoiled. Jayce has been given everything he ever wanted," Mr.

Clarkson said. "And since I'm grossly overpaying him to be a roadie, he'll have enough money at the end of this month to get his own place."

"Everything he's ever wanted?" Quinn was on the edge of raising her voice. "I think all he's ever wanted is love. Things weren't easy for him during your divorce."

"That was a long time ago. He's an irresponsible adult now. And . . ."

Esther cringed when Mr. Clarkson rattled off a sentence filled with words that needn't be spoken aloud. Lizzie had stopped eating and was also attuned to the conversation in the other room.

A chair scraped across the floor, followed by heels clicking against the wood. Quinn must have left the room. A few minutes later, Mr. Clarkson spoke up again.

"I don't know why Quinn is always defending him. She doesn't have kids. She doesn't know what it's like, especially related to Jayce. I spent almost twenty thousand dollars getting him out of jail and on legal fees. She overlooks things like that."

Esther and Lizzie locked eyes.

"I wonder what he did," Lizzie whispered.

One of the men cleared his throat. "Let's just let it go. It's our day off."

Esther wasn't sure which of the men had

spoken up, but the room had gone silent.

"I thought someone named Veronica was Brandon Clarkson's ex," Lizzie said, her voice still low.

"*Ya,* but I think that woman is his ex-girlfriend. He must have had a wife he divorced when Jayce was younger." Esther was still wondering what had landed Jayce in jail, especially since Evelyn would be spending the day with him. They really didn't know him at all.

"It doesn't sound like that woman, Quinn, cares for that Clarkson fellow too much either." Lizzie took a sip of coffee, her head still turned toward the dining room.

"It isn't our business," Esther whispered.

"But Evelyn is our business. We've known her family since before she was born." Lizzie shook her head. "Although I'm having a hard time picturing Jayce in jail. He seems like such a nice youngster."

"We've known that *youngster,* who is a grown man, for only a few days." Esther stopped buttering her biscuit and looked at Lizzie. "It concerns me that he's spending time with Evelyn."

"You worry too much."

Esther didn't have the energy to argue with Lizzie.

They were both quiet for a while, and the

121

dining room remained hushed.

After the group had retreated upstairs, Esther and Lizzie began to clear the table. "Let's save a plate for the boy." Lizzie gathered bacon, biscuits, eggs, and fruit, piling an ample amount on a plate for Jayce.

Once the dishes were piled on the counter, Lizzie began to run warm water in the sink. "What was all that about yesterday? When I was showing Jayce how to handle Poppy and the buggy, I saw Gus talking to Mr. Clarkson. It looked like they were pretty friendly." Lizzie cocked her head to one side, scowling. "And we both know Gus isn't friendly to anyone."

Esther grinned. "I suppose we should give Mr. Clarkson his due credit."

"What does that mean?" Lizzie lowered a stack of plates into the soapy water.

"He offered Gus a role in his movie." Esther chuckled.

Lizzie turned to face her, water dripping from her hands above the sink. "What in the world for? What kind of movie person would want Gus in their film?"

"I don't know, but Gus is quite proud of the fact, flaunting it actually. And I bet it was Mr. Clarkson's way of keeping the peace with him, instead of hearing constant complaints about how loud the generators are." She winked at her sister. "Smart man, I'd say. Although Gus strutted around like a movie star, so I'm not sure which will be worse — grumpy Gus or Gus the movie star."

"*Ach,* I know we're not supposed to see movies, but I'm going undercover to see any movie Gus is in. I'd have to see it to believe it." Lizzie flinched, shaking her head as if scrambling her brains. "Ick. Gus in a movie."

Esther laughed. "I can't picture it either."

They'd almost finished the dishes when Esther asked, "How concerned do you think we should be about Jayce spending time with Evelyn? Since he's been in jail."

"You don't think he murdered anyone, do you?' Lizzie gasped. "Or maybe he robbed a bank?"

Esther groaned. "Lizzie, of course he didn't do anything like that. He'd still be in jail."

"Someone slipped me a file in a cake, and I escaped."

Lizzie and Esther jumped and spun around to see Jayce standing in the kitchen, grinning at them.

"I guess I missed breakfast." His eyes searched the room and landed on the plate on the counter. "Unless that's for me?"

"Ya, ya." Esther shuffled to the counter, picked up the plate, and set it on the table. "We saved you some."

"Are you sure I'm worthy? I mean . . . I'm a criminal."

Esther and Lizzie stood staring as Jayce lowered his head in prayer. *A praying criminal.* Esther was speechless, and for once in her life, Lizzie was quiet too.

Jayce finished a slice of bacon, wiped his mouth with his napkin, then looked up at Esther and Lizzie, the smile gone. "I'm not proud of what I did, but I assure you, I'm no murderer or burglar. You don't really think that, do you?"

Esther and Lizzie exchanged glances, but neither said anything.

"I got in a fight." Jayce picked up his biscuit and began slathering it with butter. "I don't really think the guy had issues with me. He hated my father for firing him. But stuff was said, and I punched him. The guy filed assault charges, and my dad wanted to plea bargain to avoid the press. So he spent a bunch of money to keep things on the lowdown." He paused as he looked somewhere past them, seemingly lost in thought.

After a few long seconds, Jayce went on. "Like I said, I'm not proud of it. But when he started saying things about my mom . . .

I guess he hit a nerve."

Esther had never been in such unfamiliar territory. She and Lizzie remained quiet.

"I was mad at my mom when she left. In hindsight, I don't know how she stayed with him as long as she did." Pausing again, he lowered his eyes to his plate, but mostly just moved his eggs around with his fork. "No matter what happened, I love my mom, and I couldn't let that guy stand there and say such awful things about her." He lifted his eyes to Esther's. "Right?"

She could see the longing for approval, for someone to agree with him. But she shook her head. "I don't fully understand things in your world, *sohn*. But we don't believe in violence, no matter what situation might present itself."

"Maybe it's just different for women." He continued to push his eggs around. "Men are expected to stand up for the people they love — to protect them."

Jayce was only going to be here a month. Esther wasn't going to change his beliefs within that time frame, nor was it her place to do so.

"Can I just say this?" He set his fork down and looked them both in the eyes. "Evelyn is a nice person. I can see that. I know we live differently, but she will always be safe in my presence. If we become friends, well, that's great. Maybe we'll write letters or something after I leave. I've never known anyone like her, so maybe we'll learn things from each other. But I don't want you to worry for one moment that she isn't safe or that I won't behave like a gentleman."

Esther's heart warmed. It was such a sincere and seemingly truthful statement. Lizzie was back to batting her eyes at him.

"We are in no place to judge you for what you did, Jayce. Only *Gott* can do that. And as long as you're remorseful about your actions, you should put it in the past," Esther said.

"I'm remorseful." He lowered his eyes to his plate again. "I probably shouldn't have hit him so hard. But if you'd heard what he said . . ."

Esther was glad he didn't finish his sentence. She wanted to tell him that he shouldn't have hit the man at all, but she didn't want to fuel a situation they already didn't agree on. Jayce seemed like such a gentle soul, but he was also a young man fiercely protective of those he loved. But did it end there? Would he have hit Gus during their confrontation? How often did he use his fists in anger?

She reminded herself again that he'd only

be here a month. She glanced at Lizzie. Her sister wasn't batting her eyes anymore, but she also wasn't glaring at Jayce. Esther recognized her expression, one of pained tolerance. Lizzie liked the boy, so she'd likely try to change him, even though ministering to outsiders wasn't their way. Lizzie didn't always follow the rules.

"Thank you for the breakfast." Jayce stood and laid his napkin across his plate, still half filled with food.

After he left the room and was out of earshot, Lizzie looked at Esther. "I think he's more remorseful than he lets on."

Esther nodded. "I think you're right."

Jayce slipped into his jeans, then pulled on a blue T-shirt with short sleeves. Half his tattoo showed, but he didn't care. If Evelyn hated the artistry, then so be it. He wasn't going to change himself for an Amish woman he didn't even know.

He lay on the bed and threw his arms behind him. How did Esther and Lizzie find out about his stint in jail? They would be shocked to know it hadn't been his first rodeo. He'd been arrested twice before for similar outbursts. Both of those events felt justified at the time. Looking back, he should have avoided the fights.

But for the sisters to question Evelyn's safety left Jayce feeling sour, and a bad attitude had snuck into his psyche. He liked Lizzie and Esther, and he wanted them to respect him for the man he wanted to be. It made sense they would worry about Evelyn, but it stung to hear them voice their concerns. He almost wished he could cancel the outing, but the alternative would be worse. Spending the day totally alone, or being forced to be around his father and some of the other crew members he could do without.

He almost dozed off but jumped when he heard horse hooves coming up the driveway. He pushed his feet into a pair of flip-flops and headed downstairs, thankful the living room was empty. He wasn't in the mood for conversation with anyone, and he was already feeling sorry for Evelyn because of it.

He crossed through the front yard and waited for her to pull up. This buggy didn't have a top on it.

"It's such a beautiful day, I thought I'd bring the spring buggy." She smiled before she glanced at her horse. "Millie seemed to like you the other day. Do you want to drive?"

"Nah, that's okay." He walked around to

the other side and climbed in beside her, hoping his bad mood would take a hike.

They rode mostly in silence with a few more comments about the weather. The night before hadn't felt awkward. Today did.

Evelyn turned on the next road, a dirt road not much wider than a walking path. She pulled back on the reins and the horse came to an abrupt stop. Then she twisted to face him. "You're not acting normal."

"You don't know me, so how do you know what normal is?" It was a mean response, and he regretted it right away. He opened his mouth to apologize, but horror gripped him when her eyes filled with tears.

"I'm so sorry!" she said. "I have no idea what came over me. I've never been that forward with a man." She covered her face and shook her head, sniffling. "I'm so embarrassed, and I won't blame you if you want me to take you back to the inn." She finally uncovered her face and met his stupefied gaze. "You must think I'm . . . trampy."

Jayce covered his mouth to stifle a grin. He felt awful that she was crying, but if she thought a quick kiss was trampy . . . Wow. She'd think some of the women he knew were downright ladies of the night.

He uncovered his mouth, still struggling

not to show his amusement. "Evelyn." He stared into her eyes. "I do not think you are trampy." It was an odd word, and he laughed. "Not at all."

"But I kissed you!" she shrieked. "And it wasn't even a *gut* kiss." Throwing her arms up, she shook her head. "I don't even know you."

"Nope. You don't." More tears pooled in her eyes. "Evelyn, listen." He reached over and clutched her hand, a little surprised she didn't pull away. "Are you attracted to me?"

She didn't move. Jayce wasn't sure she was breathing. He took a deep breath. "I'm attracted to you. Very much. And you seem like a nice person. I can tell you all of that because once you find out who I really am, you're never going to want to hang out with me again. So don't give the kiss a second thought." He paused, smiling. "Although, that kiss is pretty much all I thought about last night." He was happy to see a small smile from her, but it was going to fade quickly. "I was in jail recently. I beat up a guy because he talked bad about my mother. And that wasn't the only time I've lost my temper or been in jail."

Her mouth hung open.

"So there's no need to worry about a spontaneous kiss. You're not . . . trampy."

He still fought a smile when he said the word. "Your reputation is fully intact. Unless you keep hanging out with the visiting bad boy. Then there might be talk among your people."

He waited for her to let all that soak in. Millie kicked at the dirt like she was ready to go again.

A slow smile spread across her face. "You thought about the kiss all night?"

Jayce laughed. "I just told you that you're hanging out with the visiting bad boy, but you want to know about the kiss?"

She continued to smile as she nodded.

"It was unexpected. It was nice. And you shouldn't feel bad about it." He paused as her expression shifted to a more serious one he couldn't read.

"It wasn't a *gut* kiss. I know that. I practically slammed my mouth into yours, then ran to hide like a young girl." She chewed her bottom lip.

Jayce's sour mood had fled. This woman amused him. "What are you saying? You want to try again?"

She shook her head, eyes wide. "*Nee. Nee.* It was inappropriate the first time. I'm just saying that's not how I would normally kiss a man. Or how he would kiss me. Not that I would let a man kiss me on a first date.

I'm not like that. I've never —"

"Evelyn."

She took a deep breath and let it out slowly.

Jayce pushed his hair out of his face. "Do you want to take me back to the inn now that you know I'm tarnished?"

She shook her head. *"Nee."*

"Like you said, it's a beautiful day. I'd like to spend it with you, but when Lizzie and Esther heard I'd been in jail, they showed some concern about your well-being, and it left me feeling weird. So if you want to take me back, I'll totally understand." At that moment, he realized how disappointed he would be if she chose to take him back to the inn. And she seemed to be taking a long time to answer.

"I'd like to spend the day with you too." Her eyes gleamed with interest. "There's just this one thing."

Jayce waited.

"Can you maybe not beat up anyone today?" She pressed her lips together as she narrowed her eyes. The expression was so serious and cute all at the same time. She wasn't just gorgeous. She was witty too.

"I don't just go around beating up people. But if it'll make you feel better, we can avoid the general population today."

She nodded, the hint of a smile playing on her beautiful lips. "*Ya.* That might be best." Then she flicked the reins, and Millie bolted into action.

Jayce clutched the side of the buggy. He held on tight, his mood having shifted from cranky to hopeful. This might not turn out to be such a bad day after all.

SEVEN

Esther carried a basket of wet clothes down the porch steps, Lizzie on her heels with another load. Esther's back was aching.

"I don't think I realized how much Naomi did when she was working for us." Lizzie dropped the basket and turned to Esther. "We underpaid that *maedel.*"

Esther dug two clothespins out of her apron pocket and clutched one between her teeth as she picked a towel out of the basket. After she clipped the second pin, she said, "I think we paid her well, but we just don't have the energy she has."

Lizzie blew a strand of hair out of her face as she nodded to Gus. "What in the world is that man wearing?"

Esther scooped up another towel but watched Gus as he sauntered from the cottage toward the main house. "He has a hat on, which is no reason for you to pick at him. Leave him alone, Lizzie. Just let him be."

Lizzie dropped the towel she was holding in the basket and slapped her hands on her hips. Esther's words had fallen on deaf ears.

"Who are you supposed to be?" Lizzie's tiny frame looked even smaller facing off with Gus.

"Mind your business, woman. I ain't here to see or talk to you. As a matter of fact, I wish I had a magic wand I could wave in your direction and — poof! — you'd disappear." Gus tipped his hat toward Esther. The man was intolerable at times, but he was nicer to her than anyone else he encountered. She eyed his hat. It was dark brown and flat on top with a rim similar to a baseball cap. He'd also trimmed his gray beard, though his hair was in its usual ponytail.

"Well, if *I* had a magic wand, I'd wave it at you and turn you into a worm. Then I'd squash you until you were one with the dirt." Lizzie snorted as if she'd said the funniest thing ever. It was pointless to remind her they were supposed to be passive. At least when it came to Gus.

"It won't be long until you treat me with the respect I deserve." He glared at Lizzie.

She bent at the waist laughing. "Never,

never, never."

Esther just shook her head and reached for another towel, hoping Lizzie would do the same so they could get this chore behind them and hopefully take a nap before they had to start supper.

"I've come to have a chat with Brandon. Is he available?" Gus's formality was so out of character that Esther was having trouble keeping a straight face.

"I saw him head over to the motor home on the right earlier." Esther hadn't noticed the loud humming lately, so she must have gotten used to the noisy generators. She wondered if Gus had, too, or if he was just enduring it now that Mr. Clarkson was giving him a part in the movie.

Gus spun around and started back in the opposite direction without another word. He beat on the motor home door, and after a few minutes a pretty blonde woman answered. She motioned for him to come in.

Lizzie finally picked up a towel and pinned it to the line. "We're never going to hear the end of this, you know. Gus's head will be the size of a bowling ball, along with his ego."

Esther smiled. "Maybe if he's happy, life will be easier for all of us. An oversized ego might be a big improvement over the man he is now."

Lizzie shook her head. "I don't see how. I shiver to think about it."

Esther's thoughts drifted away from Gus. "I hope Evelyn and Jayce are having an enjoyable time."

Lizzie pinched her lips. "It's hard to believe that boy's been in jail. But even though it isn't our way to be physical, I can't help but wonder what that fellow said about his mother. It must have been awful for him to react the way he did."

"It doesn't matter," Esther was quick to say. "Violence is never the answer."

"*Ya, ya.* I know."

Esther knew what Lizzie was thinking because her own thoughts mirrored it. Jayce seemed like a nice fellow who had grown up in a world they were unfamiliar with. His relationship with his father wasn't what it should be, and he'd gotten into some trouble.

She and Lizzie were both good at judging a person's character, and Jayce seemed like a good man stuck in a life he didn't want. But only he could change his circumstances, his reaction to his situation, and his journey. He and God. She said a quick prayer that things were going well today for him and Evelyn.

A person could never have too many friends. Esther also prayed that the young people would be wise enough to keep things friendly and pursue nothing more. It was the smart thing to do. But Esther still felt a familiar itch to play matchmaker. She needed to squash the thought and certainly not mention it to Lizzie. Her sister was already smitten with Jayce — jail time or not — and she'd likely jump on any opportunity to fuel a romance between Evelyn and Jayce.

But the boy wasn't Amish, and that left too much room for broken hearts. Still, something prodded at Esther. For now, she'd watch and wait. And pray about it.

Evelyn stayed on the dirt road and kept Millie at a steady trot. "I packed a picnic lunch. There's a park at the end of this road if you want to eat later."

"I always want to eat." Jayce's sunglasses were on top of his head. Evelyn was wearing hers, mostly to sneak glances at him without him noticing. The sun shifted behind the clouds as if in hiding, then presented itself full force, the process repeating continually. With a nice breeze, it made for perfect weather.

"Thanks for doing that," he said. "But I would have taken you to lunch." He rubbed his hands together. "What are we having?"

"Chicken salad on homemade sourdough bread, potato chips, pickles, and red velvet cake."

Jayce smiled. "You're kidding, right? Did you make all of that?"

Evelyn fought the urge to swell with pride, but it overtook her just the same. "*Ya,* I did. And I brought tea."

"It sounds great. At home we eat out most of the time. Dad doesn't cook, and he doesn't like me messing up his kitchen." Jayce rolled his eyes.

"So, before this job, did you have another job?" Evelyn had tried to envision Jayce's life in Los Angeles. Surely he lived in a fancy house with his father, and he probably drove an expensive car.

"I haven't had a real job for about a month. Not since my father got me black-listed."

Evelyn didn't know what that meant, so she waited for him to go on.

"My dad and I have never really gotten along. On my eighteenth birthday, he turned over a trust fund he and my mother had set up when I was a kid. It was a substantial amount of money, and my dad had a long list of opportunities he wanted me to pursue, all related to the film industry." He paused to take a deep breath. "I didn't want anything to do with his business. It's a shallow world filled with cutthroat people competing to write the best screenplay or get hired by the best directors and so on. I had something else in mind."

Frowning, he turned to Evelyn. "So I went against my dad's wishes and opened a deli. Not just any deli. It was upscale in a nice part of town." He stopped again and shook his head. "Dad hated that I wasn't following in his footsteps, so to speak. He refused to eat there, encouraged others not to, and the place ultimately failed. To be fair, I can't blame it all on my dad. He didn't support me, and he certainly spread the word about how horrible the food was, even though it wasn't. But I made some business mistakes too. So I have to shoulder part of the blame."

Evelyn had never met a man who was so open about his life. His vulnerability was visible even though he didn't seem to realize it. The men Evelyn had dated before always started out trying to impress her. Then little by little, their personalities revealed themselves. In the end none of them had completely meshed with hers. She enjoyed hearing about Jayce's life. It offered her the freedom to share about her own in ways she wouldn't normally. Maybe that was why she'd acted so spontaneously when she kissed him. Admittedly, his looks played a part in her bold move. But he also made her feel comfortable.

"If you and your *daed* don't get along and you don't want to work in his business, why did you choose to make this trip?" It was a rather nosy question, but she was curious and didn't think he'd mind, based on everything he'd already told her.

"He's paying me a lot of money for this job. Neither of us have admitted it, but we both want me to get my own place. In a month that's exactly what I'm going to do."

"Why did he sabotage your deli if he wants you to move out? It seems to me he would want you to succeed, to make enough money on your own." She was afraid of overstepping, but she was having a hard time understanding Jayce's relationship with his dad. He sounded like a cruel man.

"You would think so, huh?" There was a faint tremor in his voice as though some raw emotion were pushing to the surface. "My childhood was no picnic. But despite everything, I always wanted my dad to be proud of me. He wanted me to succeed in the movie business. When I chose not to, our relationship got even worse."

"I'm sorry about that — and about your deli." Evelyn couldn't imagine such a relationship with her father, who was a stern but fair and supportive man. "What will you do for work when you get home?"

Jayce shrugged. "I don't know yet, but it won't be a deli or any type of eatery." He paused, glanced at her, then sighed. "Whatever I choose to do, I'm going to give it a lot of thought. The first priority is to get away from my father. He drags me down, and it's just not a healthy relationship."

Evelyn didn't know what to say.

"Okay, so that's my sad story. What's yours?"

Evelyn thought for a few seconds. "I'm sorry. I guess I don't have a sad story."

"Oh . . . Don't apologize. That's refreshing to hear." He scratched his head. "But I thought everyone had some sort of sad story."

"Hmm . . ." She looked his way and smiled. "Do you want me to make something up?"

Laughing, he said, "No, that won't be necessary. But can I ask you some questions?"

She stirred uneasily as she considered what he might want to know. "*Ya,* sure."

Evelyn slowed the buggy when she saw the park up ahead. She was nervous about what he might want to know but pretty sure she'd answer anything he asked. She recalled some of her dates in the past. She'd tried to impress her suitors in the beginning too. She didn't feel that way with Jayce. Maybe because she'd already broken the ice with the kiss. But it felt . . . different. Like he wouldn't judge her.

"Okay." He rubbed his chin and stared at her. "Why do you all dress the same?"

She'd expected a more personal question, but this one was easy. She'd been asked before by outsiders. "We don't compete with each other. We keep everything universal so no pride is displayed. Our clothes are the same, along with our buggies, and we follow a uniform code set forth in the *Ordnung.* It's a code of conduct we know by heart and live by."

He nodded. "Why no electricity?"

Evelyn had been asked this plenty of times too. "We try to stay detached from outsiders. Not because we believe ourselves to be better than others, but because we are secure in our faith and try not to involve ourselves with others who might be unequally yoked."

He cringed. "It kinda *does* sound like you believe yourselves to be better. What do you mean by 'unequally yoked'?"

She thought about the best way to explain their beliefs. "Let's see. Okay . . . for example, I know for sure that everyone in our community is faith-driven and committed to *Gott.* But when I meet new people, I don't know if they share my beliefs."

He stared at her for a while. "But it's not up to you to judge whether or not someone is worthy. Only God can do that."

Evelyn wasn't prepared for this conversation. "I didn't say worthy. That's not the right word. I'm just saying that we stand together as a group that believes the same way, so detachment from the outside world is encouraged."

"But . . ." He stroked his chin. "I heard Quinn and Hal talking about a restaurant they ate at that is run by Amish people. How is that being detached?"

"I-I . . . don't know how to explain it. Someone like the bishop or even *mei daed* could give a better explanation."

"Sorry, I'm not trying to knock your religion. Not at all. I'm just curious about how you live because it's so different. I'm not saying different is better or worse."

Evelyn tugged Millie to a stop when they reached the park.

"There's just one more thing." Jayce paused, long enough to make her nervous about what he might ask her. "How long is your hair?"

She smiled. "Long." Then she stepped out of the buggy, reached into the back seat, and retrieved the basket of food.

They walked to a picnic table, and Evelyn set down the basket. She faced Jayce, folding her arms across her chest. "You're a believer."

"You say that like it surprises you." He raised an eyebrow.

Evelyn tried to corral her thoughts. "I guess it doesn't. Or it shouldn't. But you're very passionate when you talk about God. That's nice."

He shrugged, then pointed at the sky. "Me and God are on good terms. I just have a lot of questions, mostly about organized religion."

Evelyn began unpacking the basket, hoping he didn't ask her any more questions about God. She didn't feel qualified to provide answers. But her curiosity about that last comment was too strong to ignore. "Like what kind of questions?"

"I wasn't raised as a believer, at least not

145

by my parents. When I visited my grand-parents as a kid, they took me to church. Some of it stuck, but it wasn't until I was older that I really learned about a relation-ship with God. I guess you could say a friend introduced me to Him." He scratched his cheek. "I guess it's confusing to me how different religions interpret the Bible in vari-ous ways. I've gone to a lot of different churches over the years, but none of them seem to be a fit for me. It's left me with questions."

Evelyn smiled. "I don't think any of us have all the answers. It's a journey, and we learn along the way. I don't think He cares how we find Him, just that we do."

"I'm willing to go with that." He sat on the bench at the picnic table, eyeing the of-ferings. Evelyn sat opposite him.

"Hmm . . ."

Evelyn set out two plates, then stilled her hands. "Hmm, what?"

He shrugged again. "It's nice to be able to talk about God so openly and without judg-ment."

It was the last topic of conversation Eve-lyn could have expected, but she was glad Jayce had a relationship with God. Espe-cially since she'd sensed that he might be lost. Something in his eyes spoke to her, but maybe she'd misread him.

She lowered her head in prayer, and Jayce did too.

After they filled their plates, Jayce stared at her from across the table. "Okay, here's a question about God for you."

Uh-oh. "What's that?" She expected him to ask the question she'd first asked her parents about God. *Why does God let bad things happen to good people?* It was a common question, and Evelyn could remember her father's answer clearly. *"We don't question* Gott's *will."* She wasn't sure Jayce would accept that answer.

"So . . . regarding organized religion." He raised an eyebrow. "Who's right? I mean, you've got your Protestants, Catholics, Muslims, Mormons, Amish, and a bunch of other religious organizations that believe theirs is the right way to heaven. Who do you think is right?"

After a few seconds, when she didn't answer, he said, "I'm sure you believe that being Amish is the best religion and the most surefire way to get to heaven."

Evelyn opened her mouth to say something, but words weren't forming any sentences that made sense. "I, uh . . . I don't know that I would say that. It's not *mei* place to judge other religions."

147

Jayce was quiet for a while. He was on his second sandwich before Evelyn had eaten even half of hers. "Ironically, I don't know anything about yours," he said after taking a drink of tea.

Evelyn would have to agree with that. His studies must not have taken him anywhere near the Amish way of life. But she wanted to shift the conversation in another direction before she rattled off something that didn't make sense or was untrue in the eyes of God. He was starting to confuse her. She'd been taught not to question her upbringing or relationship with God.

Since he hadn't posed a direct question, she pointed across the field adjacent to the park. "When we were young, we used to run that way about a half mile. There's a cave. Not a big one like people tour. It's a small one, just big enough to crawl inside. We used to get on our hands and knees and go about ten feet to a space the size of the living room at *mei haus.*"

His face went white. "Oh no. You didn't bring me here to force me to conquer my fears, did you?"

"*Nee,* of course not. I'm just pointing out a landmark from my childhood." She giggled. "I wouldn't do that to you. Each person has to face their own fears in their own time."

The color still hadn't returned to his face. "Now, don't freak out or anything." He had a mouthful of food that he slowly swallowed.

Evelyn's chest grew tight. "Freak out about what?"

He slowly pointed to her left arm. "I've never seen a butterfly actually land on anyone, and —"

She jumped up, tipping over her plate and sliding her hand along the picnic table, knowing right away she'd pulled back a splinter. But she kept going, waving her arms in the air, spinning around and around to get the creature off. "See, I told you! All things that fly find me."

Dizzy, she finally stopped and caught her breath, and when she looked at Jayce, his eyes were wide.

"Wow. You really are afraid of anything that flies." He wasn't smiling or making fun of her like so many others had. "Come here. You're bleeding."

Edging toward him, she held out her throbbing pinky as drops of blood trickled to the ground. "I'm not as brave as Millie," she said softly.

He stood, gently took her hand in his, and moved his face closer to her finger. "I'm going to guess you don't have any tweezers handy?" His eyes met hers, and she shook her head, flinching.

Tenderly, he held her hand and drew his face even closer. "I see where it went in. It's deep. I think I can get it out though." He looked up at her, his beautiful eyes seeming to feel her pain. It was odd and wonderful, and it caused her heart to flutter. "Do you want me to try?"

"*Ya.* It will stop hurting so much once it's out."

As he applied pressure on the deep end of the splinter, Evelyn squeezed her eyes closed, not wanting to watch. "Ow," she whispered.

"Sorry, I've almost got it." His voice was deep and low but filled with the same compassion he'd had with Millie.

A few seconds later, the pressure was gone and Jayce had a napkin wrapped around her finger, still holding her hand. "Better?"

"*Ya, danki.* I mean, thank you."

"*Nichts zu danken.*" He smiled, still applying pressure to her little finger.

"That sounds like 'you're welcome' in our dialect. Very close. How did you know that?"

"I took a semester of German in college." He offered her hand back. "I feel up for an adventure."

"*Ach* dear. I'm afraid to ask." She laughed. "Wasn't my dancing around like a crazy woman enough adventure?"

"I'd like to see your cave."

Evelyn's jaw dropped. "You're kidding, *ya?*"

"I didn't say I want to go in it." His body stiffened. "I'd just like to *see* it. I can't imagine crawling through a hole and not knowing where it led." He shivered. "No way."

"We were kids, invincible." She shrugged. "There are small caves all over southern Indiana."

"Feel up to it?" He wiggled his eyebrows up and down.

"*Ya*, sure. I haven't been there in years. Let me just give Millie some water and make sure she's tethered securely." She walked to her horse and poured some water in a bowl, then checked that the reins were sufficiently taut. "Ready," she said when she walked back to the table. He'd already put the container of chicken salad back on the ice block in the small cooler.

"You kinda lost half your sandwich. Do you want to make another one before we go?" He pointed to the bread, then to the chicken salad he'd just stowed.

"*Nee,* I'm fine."

They started their trek toward the cave.

"It's so cool you can just leave your horse there with no worries of someone stealing her." Jayce shook his head. "It's not like that where I come from."

"I guess there are a lot of people where you live?"

"Yep. Too many." He took long strides, so Evelyn tried to keep up. She could see the tip of his tattoo showing and wanted to ask what it was. But she feared it might embarrass her. Or him.

When they finally reached the small cave with an opening the size of a Hula-Hoop, her childhood memories began playing through her mind. "It was our secret spot. We used to place weeds around it to cover the entrance, hoping no one else would find it. There were three of us, all girls." The space was clearly visible now. "I'm sure others have been down there."

"You know I'm not going in." Jayce ran a hand through his hair. "I know I'd have the freedom to get out, but that's just too tight a space for me."

"I know. I would never ask you to." She thought about how he didn't make her feel bad about the butterfly incident.

"Well, I might have considered . . . following you in there."

"Really?"

"Yeah. Maybe. But aside from my being uncomfortable in small spaces, there's something else that would worry me." He lowered his head dramatically, then lifted his eyes to hers, smiling broadly. "I'd be scared to death you'd try to kiss me."

Evelyn gasped but couldn't stop laughing. When she finally caught her breath, she said, "I'm going in."

"No. Don't do that." Jayce became visibly concerned, his expression twisting into fear. "It's been a long time since you've been down there. What if something happened to you? I'd be forced to save you." His expression lifted. "Then you'd be forced to kiss me . . ." He shrugged. "I don't know. It might be worth it."

Evelyn sank to her knees and started crawling inside the hollowed rock.

"Seriously, please don't do that. How are you going to see inside?"

She kept going, turning only briefly to pull out a flashlight she'd left in her apron pocket. It was no bigger than a fountain pen. She clicked it on. "Never leave home without it." That wasn't exactly true. She'd just forgotten to take it out of her pocket early this morning.

Maybe she'd stay in there a while, but

close enough to the entrance that he wouldn't be too uncomfortable to slip inside. *And maybe he'll kiss me.*

EIGHT

Jayce stood rigid, his heart hammering against his chest, his fists clenched at his sides. "Are you okay in there?"

"*Ya.* It's just like I remember. Although it seemed bigger when we were *kinner.*"

Her voice echoed when she spoke. He assumed *kinner* was her word for kids.

He dropped to his knees and thrust his head inside, keeping the rest of his body out of the cave. "Seen enough?"

Her head popped out, almost bumping into his. "*Ya.*" He jumped back to give her room to crawl out and stand, wishing he'd taken the brief opportunity to do as he'd threatened and kiss her.

"Your thing on your head, your, uh . . . prayer covering. It's lopsided." He was tempted to help her straighten it, but when he reached out, he stopped suddenly, unsure if touching her head was allowed. Although, apparently kissing was.

She adjusted the covering and tucked loose strands of hair back beneath it. Then she brushed the dirt from the black apron she wore over her maroon dress. Her attire reminded him of *Little House on the Prairie* reruns. He'd never admit to anyone that he liked the old sitcom. Aside from the simpler way of living, it was about a big family in a house filled with love. If Jayce ever had a home and a family, he was going to strive for that kind of atmosphere.

"Okay. So aside from caves, what else do you have to show me in this part of the world?" Jayce raised his arms and stretched. Her eyes landed on his tattoo, so he lowered his arms and raised his short sleeve so she could see the entire thing. "I'm going to guess tattoos aren't allowed?"

She shook her head but put a hand over her mouth as she took in the multicolored design. "It's a dove," she finally whispered. "And . . ."

He kept his sleeve raised, eyeing the artistry. "Yeah, of all things, I have a tattoo of a bird." He suspected she was thinking about something beyond her fear of winged creatures. "You're wondering why it's so many colors and abstract?" He waited for her response.

When she finally nodded, he continued,

"Because peace isn't easily attainable, and you can't have it all the time. Life isn't perfect, and it never will be. But . . ." Jayce traced the outline of the bird. He'd chosen various shades of blue for the dove, blended with hues of black and purple in the background. "Even though the lines aren't defined, the meaning is."

She reached up and gingerly ran her finger along his arm, sending a shiver down his spine. Her eyes glowed as if the tattoo held some special meaning for her. It was almost weird the way she looked at him, but there was a mysterious warmth in her expression as well.

"It's beautiful," she whispered as she eased her hand away.

Jayce glanced at the artwork. He could still recall the night he'd had it etched into his skin. He'd been at a point in his life when things could have gone very badly if he hadn't found a way to cling to hope, to God, and to the promise of peace. If not always, at least some of the time. And that strength had given him the courage to keep putting one foot in front of the other, even on the darkest days.

He stared into her eyes, still teasing him with mystery. There was more to this girl than she was letting on. But there was a

157

time and place for everything. He got in step with her when she finally started walking back to the picnic tables. As the clouds parted, sun rays flooded the space around them, slowly at first, then shining as far as Jayce could see. A gentle wind ruffled the few leaves on the ground, and as fate would have it, a cluster of birds fluttered and fled as he and Evelyn walked near an elm tree. She moved closer to him, almost shoulder to shoulder.

"Tell me about Los Angeles." She reached into her apron pocket and took out her sunglasses. What else did she keep handy in those pockets? Like her purse, it seemed to be a purposeful yet curious hiding place.

"Like I said before, lots of people. Traffic all the time." He glanced at her. "It's busy. Always something going on. Lots of restaurants, businesses." Shrugging, he tipped his sunglasses from his head to his nose. "The polar opposite of this." He waved around the park as a horse and buggy galloped by in the distance.

"I don't think I'd like a big city." She briefly looked up at him before shifting her gaze to another buggy turning a corner not far ahead.

"I don't think you would either." He couldn't envision this sweet woman, dressed in her calf-length dress, black apron, and head covering, walking the streets of LA. She'd be out of place, stared at, and probably made fun of. Then he'd have to defend her honor and would probably end up back in jail. He wasn't proud of his temper, even when his intentions seemed honorable. But he'd never admit that to his father.

They were quiet for a while as they walked, but it didn't feel awkward. It was as if it was okay just to be.

"Do you ever want to leave here?" Jayce scratched his head. "I mean, you might not like a big city, but are you ever curious about what's out there, away from here?"

"Believe it or not, I have been to other places."

"Like where?"

"Florida. We've vacationed there twice. *Mei bruders* even surfed."

"Really?" Jayce raised an eyebrow. "Did you like it?"

"I liked the ocean," she said softly. "It's one of God's biggest wonders, I think. Huge masses of water that can be calm and soothing or ferocious and dangerous. We were there once when a hurricane was coming. I'd never seen such big waves."

As they approached the picnic table, Jayce realized he wasn't ready for the day to be over, but he didn't know the area well enough to suggest something else to do.

Evelyn blew out a big breath. "It didn't seem like such a hike to the cave when we were *kinner.*" She popped her hands on her hips as she eyed the cooler. "We're out of tea. There's a place up the road that has sandwiches, snacks, and drinks. The best lemonade ever."

Jayce smiled. "I could go for some lemonade." He tried to remember the last time he'd had a glass of lemonade. His past dates would have been more inclined to order a beer or a glass of wine.

He stood beside her as she untethered the horse. They'd made the walk to the cave and were probably both a little sweaty, but he caught a whiff of lavender swirling in the space around her. He'd noticed it earlier too. And it wasn't overpowering like the vanilla smell in Lizzie's buggy. It was heavenly.

"I don't really care what we do." He stuffed his hands in the pockets of his jeans. "I'm just enjoying spending the day with you. And you smell good, too, like lavender."

She didn't look at him as she gathered the reins in one hand, but he caught her smile. *"Danki."*

■ ■ ■ ■

Esther refilled coffee cups, happy Naomi had come for a visit.

"It's not the same here without you." She eyed Naomi's growing belly with two new lives forming inside. "But Lizzie and I couldn't be happier for you and Amos." She peeked out the kitchen window. "Are those generators bothering the two of you? We didn't know they would be bringing those big vehicles."

Naomi shook her head. "Not anymore." Laughing, she said, "Amos had some earplugs from when he used to go to the shooting range years ago, when he was first learning how to handle a gun. We've been using those. And I might keep using them long after your guests are gone. I can't hear Amos snoring when I'm wearing them."

Esther didn't like guns, but if you were going to eat deer and other animals, then it was best to know how to use the weapons correctly. She reached over and touched Naomi's hand. "Pregnancy agrees with you. You're glowing and seem so happy."

"I am." She smiled dreamily. "I had planned to use a midwife, but since I'm having twins, even she thought it best that I see a doctor in Bedford. The doctor has me on limited activity. I just wish I were able to do more to help you and Lizzie."

Esther shook her head. "*Nee*, now don't you give it another thought. When I said we missed you, I meant your sweet smile and company."

"I know, but it's a lot of work running the inn with just the two of you doing all the work, especially when you have such a big crowd. Are you having any luck finding help?"

"Not yet. But we will find the right person." Esther was beginning to doubt that. It seemed like the bulk of young people had grown up overnight and started lives of their own. Everyone was either old, like she and Lizzie, or starting a family like Naomi and Amos.

The sound of feet pounding like a herd of cattle began to descend the stairs.

"It's the movie people." Esther rubbed her tired eyes. "They have meetings in the dining room. You might want to go. Some of the words in their vocabulary aren't fit to be heard, let alone spoken aloud. The boss, a man named Mr. Clarkson, is the worst." She stood. "I should probably offer them some snacks."

Naomi waddled around the table and

hugged Esther. "Give Lizzie *mei lieb.*"

Esther nodded. "Speaking of Lizzie, I haven't seen her in a while." She glanced toward her closed bedroom door. "Napping, I suppose."

Gus walked in the door that led directly into the kitchen just as Naomi was leaving. "*Wie bischt,* Gus," she said as she brushed by him.

Their grumpy renter mumbled a response, but Naomi was just as accustomed to Gus's unpleasant demeanor as Esther and Lizzie were.

"I need some sugar." He was still wearing his movie hat as he held out a bowl. "Tea ain't no good without sugar. And I need some paper plates. Otherwise I'll be forced to wash dishes."

Esther slapped her hands to her hips. "Gus, this isn't Walmart or the Bargain Center."

Gus looked toward the dining room, then back at Esther. "What's happening in there?"

"I guess they're having a meeting. I heard them talking about going back to Bluespring Monday, something about reshooting a scene." Esther cringed when she heard Quinn challenge something Mr. Clarkson had said. Then, after some expletives were

163

thrown her way, she was quiet. The movie producer always addressed Esther in a respectful way, but he wasn't nice to his employees or his son. Esther was glad Naomi had gotten out the door before the conversation became heated.

"Well, I don't know why I wasn't informed about this meeting." Gus straightened his hat and stomped toward the dining room.

Esther shook her head as she gathered her and Naomi's coffee cups. After setting them in the sink, she began to prepare a plate of snacks for her guests. Giovanni and Hal seemed to enjoy the pretzels and cheese sauce Lizzie had made. Esther filled a plate and walked into the room, quietly setting the tray in the middle of the table.

"Best pretzels ever," Hal said as he reached for one.

Gus hovered near one empty chair, presumably reserved for Jayce, who wasn't present. "I didn't realize we were having a meeting today," Gus said.

Esther glanced around the room as eyes darted in every direction. Quinn leaned back in her chair and grinned, raising an eyebrow at Mr. Clarkson.

"Gus. You've met everyone." The man in charge waved an arm around the room. "Actually, we were just talking about a scene we need to redo."

"What will my part be? I wasn't there for the first shoot." Gus's indignance could be heard in his voice.

Esther left the room, returning a moment later with a platter of full tea glasses. Quinn's arms were folded across her chest as she stared into her lap. Hal and Giovanni busied themselves with the pretzels while Jesse stared at Mr. Clarkson.

"Uh, no worries, Gus," Mr. Clarkson said, followed by a smile. "We'll get you in the scene on Monday when we revisit the cavern. Right now, we're just discussing some technical issues, things that didn't turn out exactly as planned."

"What time should I be ready to go?" Gus helped himself to a pretzel. "And what part will I be playing?"

Quinn covered her mouth with her hand, still staring at her lap. Esther finished her task and continued listening from the kitchen.

Mr. Clarkson cleared his throat. "Um . . . you'll be playing a man named John. We'll give you more instructions on Monday. But we'll pull out around eight. It's not necessary for you to be present in this meeting. Mostly lighting problems, and some of the scuba equipment malfunctioned, which wasn't pleasant for our leading lady."

"I'll be ready."

Gus passed back through the kitchen with the pretzel between his teeth and picked up his bowl of sugar and a stack of paper plates Esther had placed next to the bowl. He didn't offer any thanks, but Esther learned long ago not to expect any.

After the screen door closed behind Gus, she quietly pulled her chair out and sat, tempted to catch a nap, but worried her guests might need something.

Quinn chuckled. "John? Since when do we have a character named John?"

"Yeah, news to me too," either Hal or Jesse said. Esther wasn't sure.

"The guy's cranky as —"

Esther put her hands over her ears and flinched when Mr. Clarkson began cursing again. She could still hear him despite her best efforts not to.

"It was the only way for me to get the guy to shut up about the generators. We'll just stick him in the background somewhere."

"He smells," Quinn said. "Maybe you can make up a reason for him to take his own vehicle."

Esther couldn't dispute Gus's lack of personal hygiene. Although, when he had taken her to her doctor and hospital appointments a little while back, he'd made an effort to clean himself up. And some days he'd even left his gruff demeanor behind. Those glimpses into the man Gus might have been at some point in his past were always welcome, but rare.

"Just put up with him Monday, and we'll tell him we don't need him anymore," Mr. Clarkson said.

"Where do you want him in the background, and how do we explain who he is? Only the key players are in the cavern." Giovanni laughed. "Is he going to be some ancient caveman's ghost?"

Quinn was the one chuckling now. "I don't think cavemen had big fat bellies."

"What are you people even talking about?" Mr. Clarkson wasn't laughing. "We're not actually putting him in the movie. Just stick him somewhere and make him think he's in the background, just to shut him up. I'm telling you, he was driving me crazy about the generators, and I can't listen to that for an entire month."

Esther couldn't help feeling sorry for Gus. She stayed quiet and continued listening.

"Well, he seems to think he's part of our group now," Quinn said. "Speaking of our group, I haven't seen Jayce today."

"He's running around with an Amish

girl," Giovanni said. "Billy told me he had dinner with her Friday night and was spending the day with her today."

Mr. Clarkson grunted. "You've got to be kidding. He doesn't get enough at home, so he has to go poking around for it here — in an Amish community?"

Poking around for what?

"Billy said he talked to him. Let him know these girls are pious," Giovanni said.

Jayce's father laughed. "Like that would stop my son from going after her."

Esther gasped, quickly covering her mouth with her hand as Mr. Clarkson's words took on meaning. But then a chair scraped across the floor.

"I hate the way you always assume the worst about your son, Brandon. Maybe if you took the time to get to know him —"

"Oh, I know him. And here you are once again defending him." He paused. "Maybe you and Jayce had a thing, Quinn?" There was mockery in his voice. Esther didn't believe the claim could be true. Quinn was a lovely woman but considerably older than Jayce.

The woman called Jayce's father a name that Esther wished she hadn't heard. Then her heels clicked across the room and up the stairs.

"She's too sensitive. I was just kidding."

Esther didn't hear any remorse in the comment. But all was quiet afterward.

She would be counting the days until this group went back to Los Angeles.

Jayce took in his surroundings as Evelyn guided the buggy down a gravel road. There were homesteads on both sides of the road, most with farmhouses, barns, and silos. Jayce felt like he'd stepped back in time to a place where life was slower, where simple pleasures were appreciated, and girls were happy with hot dogs, popcorn, and lemonade. Evelyn probably had no idea what saltimbocca was and probably hadn't feasted on caviar, enjoyed seared lamb chops dusted in mint sauce, or tasted a host of other foods Jayce had grown up with. To this day he preferred a slow-cooked roast with potatoes and carrots like his grandmother used to cook. He still missed his grandparents.

They passed a small white building. "Is that a church?" It didn't resemble a church. There was no cross or stained glass, but it didn't look like a home either.

"It's a school." Evelyn clicked her tongue, gently slapped the reins, and picked up the pace.

"It's not very big for a school." He saw a

hand water pump outside. "I guess there's no electricity either."

"*Nee,* no power. It houses grades one through eight for this district." She slowed Millie to allow another horse and buggy to turn in front of her.

"What do you mean grades one through eight? Through the windows it looks like one big room."

"*Ya,* all the children are together in one room. Lessons are tailored to each child's age until graduation, which is after we complete eighth grade."

"Then where's the high school?" Jayce lifted his sunglasses and scanned the mostly open fields around them.

"No high school. We are only schooled through the eighth grade."

"Wow." Jayce lowered his sunglasses and relaxed against the seat. A whiff of Evelyn's lavender aroma wafted his way but was quickly overridden by Millie when the horse decided to do her business en route.

Evelyn guided them into a small parking lot, and a few minutes later they were seated across from each other inside a sandwich shop, drinking lemonade.

After a few gulps Jayce set his Styrofoam cup on the table and gazed at Evelyn. "I could live like this."

"*Nee,* you couldn't." She spoke with an authority that surprised him.

"Why do you say that? My favorite times were with my grandparents on their farm. It's slower here like it was there, quieter, peaceful. And from what you've said, there's no performance pressure or desire to be better than someone else. There has to be peace in that way of life."

Evelyn frowned. "We're still human, Jayce." She nodded toward the window. "Widow Byler, down that road, makes the best banana pudding around. She won't share her recipe, and believe me, she prides herself on that pudding."

"That's just a small thing."

"*Mei* own *daed* insists his corn crop is the healthiest and tastiest in the district." She grinned. "And I agree, but he's been known to brag about it. Both *mei bruders* flex their muscles anytime they're around a woman they're interested in."

"Yeah, but no one is striving to have a better car, house, job, or more money than someone else." Jayce sighed. "I'd buy a farmhouse, have a garden, and ride around in a buggy anytime rather than go back to the life I have."

"Jayce . . ." Evelyn's expression sobered. "You're basically here on vacation. I know you're working, but this is still just a change of scenery for you. After a month, you'll be ready to get home, back to what you're used to. And our way of life isn't just about simplicity, even though that's a large part of it. The simple living is symbolic of our literal translation of the Bible."

Jayce thought about what was waiting for him back home. He'd find employment, move out of his father's condo with the money he'd made on this job, and strive to be everything his father didn't want him to be. Not out of spite, but because his father's lifestyle had never suited him. But Evelyn had hit a nerve.

"You're wrong." He knew the moment he said it that he meant it. "I tend to interpret the Bible literally. Maybe that's why I've had a hard time committing to any religion. I'm living a life that doesn't represent how the Bible tells us to live. Other religions all have varying translations. I'm not saying that's wrong. I'm just saying that the literal interpretation as written makes the most sense to me."

She took another drink of her lemonade, then met his eyes. "So you wouldn't mind living without electricity? No more fancy house, cars, television, or regular visits to the movies?" She shook her head. "It would be even harder for someone like you to convert to our ways."

The jab stung. "What do you mean, 'someone like me'?"

"Privileged." She spoke softly. "I suspect you've enjoyed far more luxuries than the average *Englisch* person. *Englisch* is what we call non-Amish people." Shaking her head, she said, "It would be too much of a stretch."

Jayce loved a challenge, but if Evelyn had any idea how much he despised the life he was living, she wouldn't think overhauling his life was such a stretch.

"I guess you don't gamble. I mean, you're not willing to lay down any money on your convictions." He raised his eyebrows as he stroked his chin, already stubbly with an afternoon shadow.

"*Nee,* no gambling either." She paused. "You haven't even been here a full three days yet. You think you've stumbled upon a lifestyle you would find pleasing, an escape from whatever ails you back home."

Jayce leaned back against his chair. "It's more than that, but now you're starting to get the picture."

"But those things like not having electricity, no cars . . . They're tangible things." She placed a hand on her chest. "You have

173

to find out who you are in your heart first. And even if you ultimately chose to live a slower-paced life, you don't just buy a buggy and start riding around in it or purchase a house with no power and call yourself Amish. It's about our beliefs, our relationship with *Gott.*"

"You're doing it again. You're presuming that your relationship with God is more solid than mine." He tried to keep the edge out of his voice, but he'd worked hard to establish his relationship with God. "You look at me with my long hair, tattoo, and the luxuries I've had, and you believe that my way of life makes my relationship with God less than yours. Just because I have electricity, drive a car, and so on . . . You can't judge my relationship with God any more than I can judge yours." He smiled so she would know they were just having a friendly debate, even though it was starting to feel a little heated, which hadn't been the intent. "You said your people don't hang out with non-Amish people because they could become unequally yoked. I could say the same thing about you. I have no way of knowing you're solid in your faith, other than you've said so."

"Wow. As you said earlier" — she was quiet as she tilted her head slightly to one side — "I've never had a conversation this serious with an outsider."

Jayce sat taller, rubbed his fingers on his shirt, then blew on them, grinning. "I'm not just *any* outsider."

"*Nee* . . . I guess you aren't."

There was something playfully seductive in her voice. More and more, he wasn't as interested in what was beneath the baggy clothing as he was in her mind. With every word this woman spoke, he wanted to get to know her better in other ways.

"I have one more day off tomorrow, and then it's back to the cave for me on Monday." He rolled his eyes. "Care to spend more time with me tomorrow?"

She shook her head. "*Nee.* We have worship service tomorrow."

"Oh yeah. It's Sunday." He hesitated. "Can I go?"

"*Nee,* you can't." She rose from her chair, so Jayce did too. "I probably need to get you back to the inn so I can get home in time to help *mei mamm* make supper."

It was only two o'clock. Jayce tried to read her expression for the couple of seconds before she turned toward the door. He got nothing, but something had changed.

On the way back to the inn, she was quiet and kept her eyes straight ahead.

When they pulled into the driveway, Jayce thanked her for lunch.

"You're welcome." She tried to smile, but he could tell it was forced.

"Did I, uh . . . say something to upset you?" He'd thought they were simply having a healthy conversation about God, but he must have pushed a button or something.

"*Nee,* not at all." She made another attempt at an awkward smile.

Jayce stepped out of the buggy, but before he closed the door, he said, "I enjoyed today."

"*Ya.*" She avoided his eyes. "Enjoy your stay."

He closed the small door when she began to back up Millie. He watched her ride away, wondering what he'd done. Things weren't the same, for sure.

NINE

Evelyn had never met a more misguided English person in her life, regarding her way of life. Jayce was incredibly handsome, compassionate, kind . . . and utterly clueless about Amish beliefs and traditions. He'd left Evelyn feeling frustrated, even though she had to question why. She was attracted to him physically, but some of the things he said had given her a headache.

As she rode home she pondered why she was upset. She'd been brought up one way, taught what to believe, and she'd never had someone challenge her beliefs or doubt them. Jayce put her on the defense about God, and she shouldn't have to defend her relationship. Then why did she expect him to defend his? Was she judging him — doubting his faith? What right did she have to do that? And how had she allowed a handsome English man — whom she'd even kissed — to get under her skin the way he had? Was she so unconfident about her faith that Jayce had triggered a barrage of doubt she hadn't even known existed?

By the time she walked into the house, her mood had taken a bad turn, and it must have shown.

"What's wrong with you?" Lucas was sitting on the couch. He dipped his hand into a bag of chips, his socked feet propped up on the coffee table.

"Nothing." She scurried past him toward the kitchen. Something was already simmering on the stove.

"How was your outing?" Her mother opened the oven door and slid in a loaf of bread.

"It was okay." Evelyn picked up a chocolate chip cookie from a platter on the table. She was surprised her brothers hadn't gobbled them all up.

Her mother turned, leaned against the counter, and wiped her hands on the kitchen towel hanging over her shoulder. "It doesn't sound like it was okay."

"It's just . . ." She wasn't sure her mother would understand what she was feeling, but it seemed too personal to discuss with anyone else. "You know how we try to stay detached from the *Englisch*?"

"Do we?" Her mother's eyes grew openly

178

amused.

"*Most* of the time," Evelyn said as she sat at the kitchen table. "And we've always been taught to use caution, that those outside our community might not share our faith. But today, I felt like the one on the outside . . . like Jayce was questioning *mei* beliefs as much as I was questioning his. And it bothered me that I didn't have answers for some of his questions. I didn't know how to explain in a way he'd understand."

Her mother pulled out a chair and sat across from her. "I'm surprised you had such a serious conversation with this boy when you barely know each other."

"*Ya,* but he doesn't like the life he's currently living in Los Angeles. He's attracted to our way of life, but he has no real understanding about it." She took the last bite of her cookie and chewed on it the way her mind was chewing on Jayce's comments.

"It's not your job to minister to him or to defend or explain why we live the way we do." Her mother sighed. "Although, it won't be the last time you're tempted to give explanations to the *Englisch.* You wouldn't believe some of the questions I've been asked over the years." She shook her head. "I once had a complete stranger ask me if I knew I was going to hell for not believing in Jesus."

Evelyn straightened. "What did you say?"

"*Ach,* it ruffled *mei* feathers for sure. I wanted to tell her that I believe in Jesus and that I look forward to joining Him some-day." She shrugged. "But instead I smiled, said a silent prayer for her, and kept walking across the Rural King parking lot." She found Evelyn's gaze and held it. "Because that is what we are taught to do, not to engage about such subjects. And that's what you should do in the future and with that boy. Don't allow yourself to be swept into a conversation about our beliefs."

"*Ach,* well, first of all, he's not a boy. He's a man, a few years older than me. And I doubt I'll see him again." It was true, but saying it aloud stung a little.

"That's for the best." Her mother gave a taut nod, then grinned. "Especially since he is a nice-looking fellow."

Evelyn felt her cheeks turning red. "*Ach,* he's nice looking. Just challenging."

"Oh dear." Her mother folded her arms across her chest. "*Gut* looking *and* challenging. That sounds exactly like someone you'd fall for. Definitely best to avoid him."

"Why do you say I would fall for someone like that?" Evelyn wasn't sure if her feelings should be hurt. It felt like it.

"*Mei* sweet *maedel.*" She dropped her arms to the table and leaned forward, a sympathizing smile starting at one corner of her mouth. "It's one of the many things I love about you, but it's also the reason you've rejected most of the fellows around here. You love a good debate. You thirst for knowledge, and you embrace challenge. You haven't met your match, the intellect you seem to crave."

She paused. "Maybe *intellect* isn't the correct word. *Understanding* might be a better description. Telling you and showing you isn't enough. You long to understand things on a level most of us don't strive for. And there's nothing wrong with that. You'll eventually bond and fall in love with a man who shares your curiosities." Her expression grew somber. "And in light of what you've told me, it would be best to stay away from the *Englisch* boy, or man as you called him." She pulled the kitchen towel from her shoulder, then stood and walked over to the oven to set the timer. "Now, I am going to spend some time with your father down by the creek."

Evelyn knew her parents had been meeting at the creek like teenagers their entire lives. When they were younger, Evelyn and

181

her brothers had made fun of the fact that their parents were still in love enough to want privacy. Now she found it to be sweet.

Her mother laughed. "Your father likes to debate things and have a well-rounded understanding of a subject, be it our faith or something else. You get that from him."

After her mother left the room, Evelyn thought about her comments. Her mother might be right about Evelyn's thirst for knowledge and understanding. But right now, she needed Jayce to understand her feelings. *Or is it more than that?*

Jayce sat in a rocking chair on the front porch. He could hear the meeting of the great minds in the dining room through the open screened windows.

By great minds he meant his father, Quinn, Hal, Giovanni, and Jesse. Out of the entire bunch the only true great mind was probably Quinn. She was the art director, probably the lowest on the production team totem pole, but she was smarter than all the men in the room. Too bad his father couldn't recognize that. Someday Quinn would tire of his treatment and leave. She wasn't one to cling to his diamond-studded coattails. Neither was Veronica, but even though their leading lady had cut personal ties to Jayce's father, she still had a contract to fulfill.

Since arriving, Jayce hadn't spent much time with Veronica and the others who had taken up residence in the motor homes. They were the lesser evil of the two groups right now, and he had to do something to get Evelyn off his mind. It bothered him that she judged him. Or did she?

He pushed himself out of the rocking chair and walked over to the motor homes. Veronica would be in the larger one, rooming with Kate, her hair and makeup person. There were also Jodi, Pam, and Lindsey, the part of her entourage who enjoyed a place on the payroll, although Jayce didn't think they really had titles. Kind of like him. This job was a farce, a means to an end, an opportunity for Jayce to move on with his life. As the thought crossed his mind, it stung. Despite his desire to move out, he wished things were different between him and his father.

Jodi, Pam, and Lindsey were Veronica's party buddies. Jayce had liked Veronica the first time he'd met her at a party. She'd been nice to him from the beginning, and later when she began to date his father, she'd often defended Jayce. She was like Quinn in that regard, though the women were opposite in every other respect. Quinn worked out, stayed away from booze and drugs, and focused on her job, determined to be the best at what she did. And she was.

Veronica partied. Way too much. Somehow it didn't seem to affect her beauty or acting abilities. She was stunning on-screen and had a talent most actors only wished for. Maybe it was because she wasn't much older than Jayce that she didn't bother with vigorous exercising like Quinn, who was in her forties. Several people thought Quinn was more suitable for his father, but Jayce knew otherwise. Quinn would never put up with Brandon Clarkson in a personal relationship. Even Veronica had eventually tired of him and his overbearing, bullying ways.

Jayce recalled their split and how his father acted like losing Veronica was comparable to losing at the blackjack table — just a bad day and better luck would come along soon in the form of another woman. His father hadn't dated anyone since they broke up. Jayce suspected the loss was more than his dad let on. Sometimes he caught his father looking at Veronica with regret and remorse, like maybe he realized what he'd lost.

The other motor home was the temporary housing for the camera crew. Jayce didn't really know them. This was their first film to work with his father. So he tapped on Veronica's door. Jodi opened it and stood in a pair of jean shorts with a white tank top. In Jayce's opinion, all three of Veronica's playmates showed off more skin than necessary. Ironically Veronica, the star of the show, downplayed her physical assets.

He thought of Evelyn and her overly modest dress. Seeing women in this type of clothing would embarrass her, he was sure of it. His new friend had a level of modesty Jayce wasn't familiar with, but he appreciated it.

"Hey, Jayce." Jodi stepped aside, a martini glass sloshing in her twenty-five-year-old left hand. "Come in, sweetie."

Jayce was only three years younger than Jodi, but she referred to everyone as sweetie, regardless of age or gender. He trudged up the steps, knowing he wouldn't stay long. The smell of recently smoked pot hung in the air. He'd given all that up a long time ago, and while the smell didn't make him want to gag or anything, it brought back memories of a time in his life he'd rather not think about.

Veronica sashayed into the room wearing jeans and a pink T-shirt. She could wear anything and look good. And despite her stardom — she was a big name in the business — she was always kind. He'd heard she panicked when her scuba equipment had a glitch on Friday, but he doubted she made a big scene or blamed anyone. Veronica was high maintenance on several levels, but she kept a cool head during a crisis.

"Jayce, hey," she said as she pointed to the kitchen area. "Want a drink? We've got the usual. Red wine for Lindsey, martinis for Jodi and Pam, and of course the ever-popular vodka and diet cranberry for me."

"Thanks, but I'm fine." He glanced around the luxury RV his father had rented for the trip. The purchase price was probably well over a million dollars. It was nicer than most apartments in LA. He'd taken a tour when they first leased the forty-five-foot-long vehicle complete with three bedrooms, a cozy den area, and a roomy kitchen with an island. There were two bathrooms, three televisions, and recessed lighting along the floor and above the cabinets, not to mention the two electric fireplaces. The other motor home was a lot smaller but equally elegant.

"I saw an Amish woman pick you up earlier and drop you off a little while ago." Veronica settled into a spot in the corner of the tan leather couch and set her drink on the table beside her. Jodi had retreated behind a closed door, presumably her bedroom. A flash of humor crossed her face. "Was that like a *date*?"

"Maybe." Jayce felt a flush creeping into his cheeks. He caught Veronica's gaze. She seemed to be waiting for more, but he wasn't sure he wanted to talk to her about Evelyn. He sat in a recliner across from her and crossed an ankle over his knee.

Jayce was more age appropriate than his father when it came to dating Veronica, but their relationship had never been that way, even before she started sleeping with his father. They'd been friends, casual friends who didn't know each other well. Then somewhere along the line, the relationship had grown and shifted. She was like a big sister. He recalled the sympathetic look she'd thrown his way at the cave.

"Well, since you don't want to share about your date, how are you and your dad getting along?" Veronica picked up her drink and took a sip. Jayce appreciated her not pushing the issue about Evelyn.

"Same as always." He shrugged. "They're having some meeting in the dining room. I could hear him bellowing, so I decided to hide out here." He forced a smile. "I'm sure it's about how to fix the equipment that failed Friday."

The color drained from Veronica's face. "Um, yeah. That didn't go so well. I was at least twenty feet underwater, and something went wrong with the scuba gear. I couldn't breathe." Pausing, she took two gulps from her glass. "But I made it out okay."

"I hope my dad was sympathetic." Jayce grunted. "Doubtful."

"Actually, I think he was terrified. When I eventually surfaced and Hal got me out of the scuba equipment, I couldn't stop gasping for air." Pausing, she looked somewhere over Jayce's shoulder. "Your dad was so comforting. It made me remember all the reasons I fell in love with him."

Jayce knew that side of his father, but he rarely showed it. Unless he was scared, and that didn't happen often.

"But then he started yelling at everyone, more than they deserved . . ." She sank into the couch. "I remembered the horrible fights we had, the way he talked to me sometimes. I just couldn't live like that, you know?"

Jayce nodded. "You're too good for him. You'll find someone better."

She flashed her award-winning smile. "I think I already have."

He wasn't surprised. "Anyone I know?"

"No, he's not in the industry. It's still new. We're keeping it pretty quiet for now." She shivered. "And definitely until after this film wraps. Your dad would go nuts if he knew."

Jayce was happy for Veronica, but she was right. His dad would go off big-time if he knew she was dating another man. No one needed to rile him up any more than he already was. Jayce decided to shift the subject back to work.

"You scared about Monday, about diving again?"

Veronica shifted uncomfortably, then took another swig of her drink. "You know what they say." She took another sip. "When you fall off the horse, you have to get back on."

Jayce knew what fear could do to a person, and he could see it in her eyes. "Can't you get them to call in a stunt double?"

"Probably." She sat quietly. "But I want to do it myself, just to prove to myself that I can." Her head snapped in his direction. "But, Jayce, that's just me. I'm not saying you should do that. I'm sorry if it sounded like that."

Veronica had known about Jayce's claustrophobia since he'd met her. His father made sure to let everyone know. "Oh, I know." He waved a dismissive hand. "No problem." Even though it was a problem for

Jayce. He'd like nothing better than to get on that boat Monday, to show his father he could do it, but also for himself. So, ironically, he said, "Just don't do it to prove anything to my dad."

She chuckled nervously. "Oh, I quit doing anything for your dad's benefit a long time ago." She slapped a hand gently to her leg. "Okay, I can't stand it anymore. Tell me about the Amish woman. I don't know much about these people."

"Apparently I don't either," he mumbled as he thought about his conversation with Evelyn. "But I'm not sure they're quite so different from us."

Veronica raised both eyebrows. "I beg to differ. They live like pioneers — even dress like them. How did the world pass them by?"

"Their choice. They choose to live like this." He shrugged. "I think it's kinda cool."

Scrunching up her face, she said, "I couldn't do it."

Jayce was sure of that. Veronica was sweet as she could be, but he couldn't begin to imagine her without her cocktails, often starting at noon, her hair and makeup person nearby at all times, and her tendency to bask in the spotlight she'd earned.

She twirled a strand of her long blonde

hair between her fingers and grinned. "Do you like her? You went out Friday night too."

"She's interesting." Evelyn was much more than that, and Jayce liked everything about her. But he was sure Veronica wouldn't understand.

"Hmm . . ." She ran her finger around the rim of her glass. Usually her nails were long and painted a bright color. Now they were trimmed short and plain, presumably for her role in the movie. " 'Interesting,' huh?"

Jayce rested his elbows on his knees and perched his chin atop his hands. "Yeah, she's deep, likes to talk about things." He sat back in the chair and ran a hand through his hair. "So I guess that makes her interesting."

"I can't imagine the two of you having anything in common." Veronica twisted her hair into a knot on the top of her head, then picked up a clip from the table beside her and secured the long tresses.

"You'd be surprised." Memories of the movie, popcorn, and lemonade rose to the surface of his mind.

"Well, well . . ." Veronica's mouth twitched with amusement. "I think you have a crush on this girl."

He laughed. "A crush? Isn't that some eighties word? I said she's interesting."

"That's how it starts." She picked up her drink and chugged the last of it. "Although, to fit into your world she'd have to ditch those frumpy clothes and the horse and buggy."

"She'd never fit into our world." Jayce couldn't tell Veronica how much he longed for the lifestyle Evelyn lived. "Besides, I don't even know her. Not really."

Then why did it feel like he'd known her a lot longer than a few days?

Veronica lifted herself from the couch and strolled straight to the vodka bottle on the kitchen counter. She was unscrewing the lid but paused to look out the window. "Hey, I think your girl is back."

Jayce peered out the window.

"Is that her in that buggy pulling in?"

He waited a few seconds to be sure. "Yeah, that's her."

Veronica grinned before walking back to her glass. "Better go see what she wants."

Jayce had no idea. She'd been rather cold when she dropped him off. Maybe she was here to see Lizzie or Esther.

Only one way to find out.

"Yeah, I guess so." He scratched his cheek as he walked to the door, but before he opened it, he turned to Veronica. "Hey. Don't do anything you're not comfortable with on Monday — during the dive. They can get someone else to do it."

She shrugged but didn't look at him as she filled the glass with vodka. "It'll be fine," she said as she added a splash of cranberry juice.

"Okay." Jayce stared at her for a minute, but she didn't look up. "I'll see you around tomorrow, or for sure on Monday."

He left the motor home and strode to Evelyn's buggy. She was just sitting there, making no attempt to get out.

When he got to the buggy, he took in her olive skin, her high cheekbones, and the way her green eyes twinkled. She was gorgeous in all the ways Veronica wasn't. It was a weird comparison, but Jayce had seen Veronica without makeup. This girl didn't have a smidgen of anything on her face. She was just naturally radiant.

"You here to see me?" He felt a flutter in his stomach.

"*Ya,* as a matter of fact I am." She reached down and lifted Jayce's sunglasses from the seat beside her, then pushed them toward him. "You left these. I didn't know if you had another pair."

He had several, but he took the sunglasses. "Thanks." Pausing, she sat with a curious expression on her face. "You wanna come in?" He nodded over his shoulder at the inn. "Although, my dad and his group are having a meeting in there that you might find offensive. Their language isn't always the best."

She shook her head. "*Nee,* I'm not staying. But I am offended about something."

Her eyes changed color right before him, slowly losing the twinkle and darkening as her lips thinned. Jayce wasn't good at reading women, but there was no mistaking Evelyn's expression. She was mad.

"Uh-oh," he said, cringing. "What did I do?"

She raised her chin slightly, but her bottom lip trembled. "I-I feel like you judged me. And you don't know me well enough to judge me."

He stuffed his hands in his pockets, his emotions flitting about in an unusual way. "That's funny, because I felt like you were judging me."

"I wasn't judging you." Her lip stopped trembling, but her eyes retained their green color, void of twinkle. "Only *Gott* can judge us."

"I think we both agree on that." He rocked back and forth in his flip-flops, hands still in his pockets. "I think we're bothered about the same thing. I know you got me thinking about things. Sometimes a healthy debate or conversation can be good."

Her eyes softened a little. Jayce waited for a response.

Evelyn recalled what her mother had said in the kitchen. Jayce was proposing the exact thing her mother said to avoid — more conversation about God and relationships. Now that she was confronting Jayce, going as far as to say he had offended her, she couldn't find the words to back up her statement.

"Look . . ." He ran a hand through his gorgeous long hair. "The last thing I want to do is offend you or hurt your feelings."

"Jayce! We need you in here."

They turned toward the porch.

"Be there in a minute." Jayce held up a finger, then turned back to Evelyn. "I have to go."

"That's fine. I said all I came to say" — she nodded to the sunglasses he'd tucked into the collar of his T-shirt — "and to bring your shades."

"No. It's not fine. I want to talk about this some more." He spoke with such a sense of urgency, it touched her. "I know tomorrow is church for you, and I have to work on

Monday. Can we talk Monday night?"

Everything logical in Evelyn's mind told her to say no. "Okay."

Jayce's eyes brimmed with eagerness, and Evelyn knew she was in dangerous territory.

He nodded past the inn. "There's a pond down there. Watch the sunset?"

It sounded too romantic to pass up, and the fact that she'd thought about romance should have prodded her to say no.

But again she said, "Okay."

TEN

Monday morning brought a flurry of activity to The Peony Inn, and Esther hoped a nap would come early for her and Lizzie. Not only were Mr. Clarkson, Jayce, Hal, Jesse, and Giovanni present for breakfast, but other members of their group came in and out. Each time Esther went into the dining room, platters and bowls were empty. Some of them carried toast, eating as they passed from the dining room through the living room. Others stood around sharing plates, as if that were proper protocol.

"This is craziness," Lizzie said when Esther walked back into the kitchen for the third time. She was cracking more eggs into a bowl.

"They are like wild animals in there." Esther pulled a stack of extra plates from the cabinet. "Might as well give them all something to eat off of."

She carried the plates back into the room,

handing them out to those standing and apologizing that there wasn't enough seating. It was hard not to stare at some of the people, especially the women — young ladies in their twenties, made up with far too much makeup, but still so striking that their looks drew her in. Men were a minority in this crowd. She shuffled back to the kitchen.

"Craziness," Lizzie said again as she stirred eggs over a flame that was much too high. Esther sure hoped her sister didn't burn the eggs, but they were completely out and needed to get more on the table. Lizzie was making sure she cooked them as fast as possible. *Can you even burn eggs?*

Esther took out two more jars of jam, strawberry and apple butter. "They'll be gone soon enough." Pausing to rest, she sighed. "Then we can take a nap."

"You can. I can't." Lizzie turned to her and lifted up on her toes. "I found us some help, and I'm going to pick her up as soon as everyone leaves."

Esther held the jars to her chest and looked up. "Praise God." She turned back to her sister. "Who?"

"Her name is Rose Petersheim, and she just moved here from Ohio. She's kin to Big Roy and Katie Marie." Lizzie turned up the heat another notch until smoke was rising from the skillet of eggs. Seconds later, she dumped them in the empty bowl.

Esther carried the bowl into the chaotic dining room, many of the guests talking over one another. Jayce stood quietly in a corner eating. With a mouthful, he nodded at Esther, then winked. She supposed that was a signal that the food was good. Although at the moment, it was more about quantity than quality.

"Why did the girl move here?" Esther asked Lizzie when she returned to the kitchen. "Why would she leave her family?"

"I don't know her story, and I don't care." Lizzie dabbed at the sweat beads on her forehead with a napkin. "She can cook and clean, so she's hired."

Esther nodded in agreement. She and Lizzie could not keep up this pace. "Do you want me to go with you to pick her up? Will she live here like Naomi did?"

"*Ya.* Big Roy and Katie Marie don't have room. And no, you don't need to go. Get a nap in. One of us should." Lizzie spat her dentures into her hand, surprising Esther. Her sister rarely complained about them anymore. "Stupid teeth are giving me fits again."

It had taken Lizzie a long time to get used

to the dentures. Not wearing them or spitting them out in front of people had been a common occurrence. Esther hoped this problem was temporary.

"We don't have room right now either." Esther pressed a hand to her forehead, which was also sweating. "All of our rooms are full."

"I figure you and me can bunk together. She can have *mei* room until this rowdy crew is gone." Lizzie frowned before wrestling the dentures back into her mouth.

Esther thought about Lizzie's snoring, but it was the only option. "Be sure to take out all those romance books you read and hide under the mattress." Lizzie's jaw dropped. "*Ya,* I know about them. Naomi too. She changed the sheets and, on occasion, so did I."

Lizzie raised her chin. "There is nothing wrong with reading about love between two people."

Esther tucked her chin and scowled at her sister. "I hope they are clean books and not filled with things you shouldn't be reading."

Lizzie huffed, then walked into the dining room. Esther chose not to follow in case her sister acted in character and told them all to hurry it up or keep the noise down, or something similarly inappropriate.

Esther set to making an apple pie since those seemed to go the quickest. These guests were midnight scavengers. By morning all kinds of food had been eaten. But at least it was being consumed and not going to waste.

Jayce crossed the front yard toward the two waiting limos. Everyone was packed in, and even though the drive wasn't very far, he hoped he could choose the car without his father in it. Unfortunately, there was no way to know with the tinted windows.

Then he saw the grumpy old man, Gus, climbing into a rusty black pickup truck. He stopped and took a few moments to decide on the lesser of the two evils. He turned to Gus's truck. He'd heard the cranky neighbor would be joining the crew. Apparently, Jayce's father had promised him a part in the movie so the guy would stop complaining about the generators. A promise Jayce doubted his father would make good on.

"You ain't riding with me," Gus bellowed when Jayce opened the passenger door. The crazy man flicked his arm at him, almost catching the side of his face. "You go with your people in their fancy cars. They already said they only have enough room for one more, so I'd have to take my truck. I'm guessing you're the one more." He scrunched up his face until his gray eyebrows almost touched in the middle of his forehead. "So get out."

"You go ride with them, and I'll drive your truck." Jayce pushed his hair out of his face and grinned. "You've probably never been in a limo anyway."

"As a matter of fact, you snot-nosed kid, I have been in plenty of limousines. And you got yourself a deal." He pushed open the rusted door, causing it to squeak and whine.

"Oh, wait." Jayce eyed the stick shift on the floor. "I don't know how to drive a standard."

Gus pulled the door closed, glowering at Jayce, his jowls moving back and forth as he shook his head. "Well, ain't it my *un*lucky day." He waited. "Get out. Go with your people."

"Look, man. You've got on enough Old Spice to suffocate a small child, but I'd rather hitch a ride with you than ride with my dad, and I'm not sure which car he's in. I'm sure someone saw me get in your truck, so they'll know I'm not left behind. But oh, how nice it would be to avoid this whole charade and not go at all."

Gus stared at him long and hard. "Your

pop seems like a fine fellow to me. And you strike me as an ungrateful brat."

"Whatever. You don't know him." Jayce got in and leaned his head back against the seat, wishing the conversation with this man would just end.

Gus finally started the truck, grinding the gears as he shifted, and followed the limos. Jayce did his best to breathe as little as possible. Luckily both windows were down.

"So what's your dad done that makes you hate him so much?" They both bounced on the bench seat as the old truck caught a few ruts along the driveway.

"I don't hate him." Jayce slid on his sunglasses, hoping to avoid a conversation about the many reasons he despised his father. *Hate* was too strong a word.

They were quiet. Gus continued grinding each gear until they were on the highway at a steady, bouncy speed. By the looks and sounds of it, Jayce was surprised the truck even ran.

"I got a daughter who hates me too." Gus's mouth was set in annoyance when Jayce glanced over at him.

Jayce chuckled. "Gee, how could that be? You're so friendly and likeable."

"Kid, I'll drop you on the side of the highway if you don't lose the attitude." He tossed a seething look in Jayce's direction, and Jayce was pretty sure the man was serious.

"Okay, I'll bite. Why does your daughter hate you?"

"None of your business." Gus coughed so hard that the buttons on his red-and-white plaid shirt separated slightly. He was wearing suspenders that draped over his big belly to hold up his black trousers. Jayce couldn't imagine what his father must have promised him. A speaking role? Just someone in the background? Most likely he'd lied, since there wasn't a place in this movie for a big fat guy with a long ponytail sitting in the background.

"So, I've got another question for you." Jayce turned to him. "Aside from your likeable personality and polite demeanor, why do you rent a cottage from two Amish women? You're clearly not Amish and the place doesn't appear to have electricity. Why live like that if you're not one of them?" Then he snapped a finger. "Ah, they must let you live there for free." He laughed. "Although, I can't imagine why."

Gus's face turned as red as the barn back at the inn. "I pay those widows rent every month. And while your kind needs electricity and television and all those fancy things,

I'm content to just get up and exist each day."

"Well, you could be nicer to them. They're sweet ladies." Jayce yawned, knowing it was going to be a long day.

Gus roared with laughter. "The words *Lizzie* and *sweet* don't go together. Esther is okay." He turned to Jayce, sneering. "That wicked and crazy sister of hers is another story. She's actually kicked me, more than once."

Jayce tried to picture the tiny woman popping Gus with one of her black loafers, or maybe her bare feet since these people didn't wear shoes all the time. "Hmm . . . I can't imagine why she would do something like that."

"Are you always this sarcastic? You're on my last nerve, and we still have a ways to go before we get there. Maybe zip it up, sonny." Gus coughed again, a deep, throaty wheezing that sounded like asthma or whooping cough, if that still existed. Jayce's dad was a germophobe. If old Gus started coughing like that on set, good ol' Dad would probably shove him in the water.

He thought again about Veronica having to make the dive.

He decided to stay quiet. No decent conversation was going to ensue with this miserable man.

When they arrived at Bluespring Caverns, they were greeted by three enthusiastic kids, clearly excited to have the film crew back. The boats were lined up and ready. Jayce went through the same drill as on Friday, trekking up and down into the cavern with most of the equipment, staying at water level, the sunshine against his back.

Gus strutted around like he was the star of the show. Jayce's father barked orders like he always did. When Jayce carried the last of the scuba gear to the dock and handed it to Hal, he heard his father talking softly to Veronica.

"Listen, the equipment has been checked and double-checked. We won't have the problems we had Friday, okay?" His voice sounded comforting, reassuring. Kind. "If you have any problem at all, we'll pull you up right away. You okay?"

Jayce watched as Veronica nodded.

His father pushed back a strand of her hair, then kissed her tenderly on the cheek. "I won't let anything happen to you."

Jayce blinked a few times. *Wow, he still loves her.* He thought briefly how much it would hurt his dad to know Veronica was seeing someone else. It was a rare emotion for Jayce, sympathy toward his father.

But within seconds the man was back to firing off orders. He never spoke to or looked at his son standing on the dock as the boats pulled away. The only person looking at Jayce was Veronica, and she was white as a ghost, her eyes almost pleading with him to go with them.

Never before in his life had he wanted to conquer his fear of enclosed places as much as he did right now. But every muscle in his body trembled at the thought.

Esther relocated Lizzie's personal items from her sister's bedroom to her own, remembering to snag the books between the mattresses. Lizzie had at least fifty items on her nightstand — a dozen pill bottles, many of them herbal remedies for various aches and pains. There were also bottles of Tylenol, ibuprofen, and low-dose aspirin. A box of tissues, two gardening magazines, a lantern, and a flashlight were also on the table next to the bed.

As Esther began to stow pill bottles in her apron pockets, she noticed the container Lizzie kept her teeth in. She hesitated to open it. Esther was already worried about Lizzie making a good enough impression that Rose would be willing to take the job. Her sister had a big heart, but she did not have a filter when it came to saying what was on her mind. Esther hoped she'd speak kindly to this new young woman, and she hoped it would be with her teeth in place.

She sighed when she opened the container and found the dentures inside. Lizzie talked with a lisp when she didn't wear her teeth. Esther said a quick prayer that Rose would accept the job.

She had just finished putting fresh sheets on Lizzie's bed when she heard her sister's buggy pull into the driveway. Thankfully, she had a passenger. Esther brushed the wrinkles from her black apron, adjusted her prayer covering, and walked outside to greet their new employee.

Rose carried a small red suitcase and had a black purse strung over her shoulder, and at her feet was a larger brown suitcase. Esther wasn't sure any of them could carry the bigger piece of luggage up the porch steps.

"Welcome to The Peony Inn." Esther extended her hand. Rose had a firm grip.

"*Danki* for having me and employing me. I'm looking forward to helping out." She smiled, which only added to her beautiful features. Rose was a tall, slender woman with big brown doe eyes. She was rather dainty looking but easily lifted both suitcases, so Esther motioned for her to follow.

"Can you get that up the stairs?" She looked over her shoulder. Lizzie was trailing behind Rose, staring at the ground, quiet. Esther hoped she hadn't already said or done something she regretted. But the girl was here, and she seemed anxious to be employed.

"*Ya, ya.* No problem." Rose marched easily up the porch steps. Esther's knee popped on the third step, and she was acutely aware of her age. Thank goodness God had sent them Rose.

Lizzie walked directly to the kitchen as Esther showed Rose to her room. "This is normally Lizzie's room," she said as they walked through the door. "But we have a large group of guests staying until the end of the month, so I hope this will be suitable for now."

"*Ya, ya.* This is fine." Rose set down both suitcases, still smiling, her eyes wide as she took in her surroundings. "I'm going to love living here. I know it already. *Danki* again for having me."

She might not feel the same when she saw the enormous pile of laundry in the basement. The workload wouldn't always be so heavy, but until they weren't catering to a full house, things were busier than usual.

Hopefully Lizzie had explained that on the way here.

"We are thrilled to have you here, Rose. I'm going to help Lizzie get lunch started and give you time to unpack. Please let us know if you need anything."

"I'm sure everything is perfect." Rose bounced up on her toes, clasping her hands together in front of her.

Esther met up with Lizzie in the kitchen. She was frying the fish Amos caught the day before. Only she, Lizzie, and Rose were there for lunch, and the fish would certainly smell up the house. But she didn't say anything about it. She'd bought some air freshener at the market recently. Their mother used to make a spray from scratch that smelled of lavender. These days Esther chose her battles, and a 99-cent can of air freshener did just fine.

"She seems like a sweet young lady." Esther took ketchup and horseradish from the refrigerator and set them on the table. "A pretty young gal too."

"Uh, *ya*." Lizzie didn't look up from the pan of sizzling fish.

Esther waited for details, but her sister stayed quiet. "You forgot your teeth," she finally said.

"*Ach ya*. I remembered after I was on *mei*

way. They're bothering me again."

Esther sighed. "Well, instead of choosing not to wear them all the time, maybe go back to the dentist so he can adjust them and make them more comfortable for you."

"*Ya, ya.* I will."

Esther set the kitchen table for three while Lizzie continued to cook in silence.

"Lizzie, is everything all right? What did you and Rose talk about on the way here?" Her stomach clenched. "She seems very bubbly and happy, but you didn't say anything to upset her or make her not want the job, did you?"

Lizzie mumbled something under her breath.

"What did you say?" Esther stepped closer to her sister.

"She did most of the talking." Lizzie cleared her throat. "I'm sure she'll be just fine."

Esther turned toward the living room when she heard footsteps. Rose skipped into the kitchen with the spring of youthfulness. What a breath of fresh air she would be. She was probably around twenty. *I wonder why she isn't married.*

"I'm so happy to be here." She bounced up on her toes again. "I'm very *gut* at cleaning. *Mei mamm* said I will make an excellent *fraa* someday. At first when I was young, I didn't like to clean bathrooms, but they don't bother me at all now. I used to scream if I saw a spider, but I've conquered that fear as well. I'm *gut* with mending, especially hemming trousers. I have three *bruders,* so I've done lots of that." She took a breath. "Do you have chickens? Of course you do. I saw a chicken coop. I'll diligently remember to collect the eggs every morning. I've only dropped one in *mei* life. I don't eat carrots, though. If it's all right with you, I'd rather not cook them either. But I can prepare anything else you like. Are your horses for riding, or just for pulling the buggies? We had bats in our barn back home. Do you have bats here?" She pointed to the pan of fish. "Do you want me to finish preparing the fish? Or maybe I should complete my unpacking like Esther suggested. I'm about halfway done, but I thought I would check to see if I could be of assistance with lunch."

Esther's mind was awhirl as she stared at the girl. "Um, *nee.* I think we are fine in here, dear. You go ahead and finish unpacking."

She bounced up on her toes for the third time. "*Ya,* of course. I'll be back soon. The fish smells *gut.* I'm hungry. I didn't eat much breakfast this morning. I've been so excited about this new phase in *mei* life . . . There won't be carrots for lunch, will there? I mean, I know I mentioned my dislike for them just now, but I thought I would —"

"No carrots," Lizzie said without turning around.

"Okay, then I'll go finish unpacking. I'm so happy to be here! I'll see you soon for lunch."

Esther didn't realize her mouth was hanging open until Lizzie turned around and raised an eyebrow.

"I'm sure she's just nervous and excited. She's in a new state with a new job. Surely the *maedel* doesn't always talk that much."

Lizzie scowled, shaking her head. "You ain't seen nothing yet."

ELEVEN

After walking all around the area surrounding the caverns, Jayce occupied his time by browsing through the gift shop, not that he had anyone to buy a souvenir for. He'd been told the film team might be in the cave two hours or all day. It seemed a waste of his time to be loitering around, but even if he had gone in the boats and into the cave, he would have been in the way. At least that's what he would keep telling himself.

"They're back." A guy who worked there walked in from outside with an apple in his hand. "I heard the boat motor." He took a large bite and headed behind the counter to a room in the back.

Jayce began walking down to the river, then took a right and descended the rest of the way to where the boats were. Once again, Bluespring had given exclusivity to Jayce's father and the crew, offering free tour coupons for another day to the people who showed up to purchase tickets. School was in session, and it was Monday, so only a handful of people had left disappointed.

Near the parked boats, he waited until the guide docked the boat with his father, Veronica, and the more important players. He was surprised to see Gus in the boat with them. Following close behind was the second boat with everyone else.

Jayce started gathering equipment as soon as the boat docked, but he paused when Veronica got out. "You okay?" he mouthed as he tried to read her expression. She nodded but quickly cast her eyes downward. She was still wearing her wetsuit but had a blanket wrapped around her. Jayce had unloaded several pieces of equipment before he noticed that Gus was dripping wet. He laughed.

"What happened, big guy? You fall in?" Jayce reached for a box of odds and ends — camera lenses, extra batteries, cables, and various other items.

Gus opened his mouth like he was ready to unload on Jayce, but the old man glanced at Jayce's father and must have thought better of it because he stayed quiet, jostling the boat from side to side as he lifted himself onto the dock.

"My gear malfunctioned again," Veronica

whispered as she eased up to Jayce. "That man, the big one, Gus . . ." She blinked back tears. "He jumped in. I guess everyone was trying to figure out what to do. I was panicking because I couldn't breathe." She glanced at Gus, standing off to the side by himself. "Gus jumped in and pulled me to the surface. I was kicking, fighting him, and . . . It was horrible, much worse than Friday." A tear rolled down her cheek. "He saved my life, Jayce."

Jayce glanced at Gus, the unlikely hero, shaking and dripping as he gulped from a bottle of water.

"That's twice the equipment has failed, and I don't know if I'm cut out for a movie where some of it is filmed underwater."

He hated seeing her so upset and wrapped her in a hug. "You tell my dad to get a stunt-person and to find some reliable equipment if there are any more scenes in the water. Be firm, Veronica." Jayce stepped back and caught her gaze. "You okay otherwise? Are you hurt?" He eyed her up and down, but it was impossible to see if she was injured beneath the wetsuit.

"I'm okay, just shaken up." She glanced at Gus, then told Jayce she'd be right back.

Jayce had plenty to carry, and it was going to take a dozen trips, even if the crew took mercy on him and helped. When Veronica reached up and wrapped her arms around Gus's neck, Jayce stood watching. Gus lifted one arm and barely patted her back. She spoke to him for another minute or so. Gus just nodded, then abruptly walked away.

Jayce got back to work. His dad passed by him without a word. Surprising. Usually he took out every bad thing in his life on Jayce.

It was an hour later before everything was loaded. Veronica was in dry clothes. Everyone was unusually quiet.

Jayce opened the door to Gus's truck and got in. He waited a full five minutes before Gus walked out of the gift shop, presumably having gone to the bathroom.

"So, I hear you're the hero of the day," he said when Gus opened the door and stood there scowling.

"I forgot I'd have to listen to you gab all the way home." He climbed in. He was missing his suspenders and his shirt was untucked. His gray hair, no longer pulled back in a ponytail, was a matted mass that hung around his shoulders like a worn mop.

"Hey, I just paid you a compliment. No need to be nasty." Jayce pushed his sunglasses up on his head. "So, what happened anyway?"

"Your father has a bunch of idiots working for him." Gus growled. "I was only supposed to be going along for this one scene, but I can see that I'm going to have to travel everywhere they go, just to make sure everyone is safe."

Jayce pressed his lips together to stifle a smile. His dad would despise having Gus around constantly.

"Most of them are pretty good at what they do." Jayce felt he should defend the crew, at least a little.

"Then they need to stick to doing what they do well and not put a woman's life in danger, which is exactly what they did today. And from what I heard, it was nearly as bad on Friday." He shook his head. "Idiots."

"Veronica said you saved her life." Jayce kept his eyes on the old guy, curious how he'd respond.

"Somebody had to." He snapped his head to the right and glared at Jayce. "Why weren't you in the boat, by the way? You two seem close. Didn't you want to make sure she'd be all right?"

Jayce wasn't going to fess up and give Gus anything to fuel his scorn.

"Not close the way you might think. She dated my dad until recently. You're not going to say anything bad about him, are you?

You might get booted from the film." He grunted. "Like everyone else, you have to kiss up to Brandon Clarkson no matter what. Did he even make a move to go in after Veronica?"

Gus stared straight ahead. "Kid, can you just shut up until we get back? I've had a traumatic ordeal, and you're giving me a headache."

"I'll take that as a 'no.' Dad didn't throw himself in harm's way to save the woman he loves, or at least used to love." Jayce was pretty sure his father still loved Veronica, but he wasn't sure he loved anyone more than himself. Putting himself at risk seemed unlikely.

Gus was quiet for a while, so Jayce kept silent as well. No matter what, he'd saved Veronica, and the man deserved respect for that.

"You know, you kids don't know a thing about raising kids. There ain't no handbook." Gus's jowls jiggled when the old truck hit a pothole. "Maybe you oughta give your dad a break and quit acting like a little punk."

"Watch it, old man." Jayce felt a familiar rage bubbling to the surface, but he would never hit an elderly person, not even someone as obnoxious as Gus. "Don't act like

219

you know me or my father. You don't know him." He huffed. "Trust me. You don't know him."

"Maybe you don't know him either."

It seemed a strange thing to say, but Jayce recalled Gus saying he had a daughter who hated him. "Does your daughter know *you*? You said she hated you."

Gus rattled off a string of curse words, ending with, "You're just a punk kid."

They turned onto the driveway at the inn. "And you're a grumpy old man who treats people like dirt. But you did save Veronica's life, and for that . . . I am very grateful."

Jayce got out of the truck and headed for the main house. He was ready to spend a quiet evening watching the sunset with Evelyn.

When he opened the door and stepped into the living room, the aroma he'd begun looking forward to didn't waft up his nostrils. Instead, something smelled burnt. He rushed toward the kitchen.

Esther had the stove open and was using a dustpan to fan smoke toward the open window. Lizzie's head covering was falling off her head as she knelt on the floor picking up what appeared to be charred loaves of bread. An Amish woman Jayce hadn't seen before paced the kitchen, crying.

Instinctively, Jayce went to the woman crying. "What's wrong? Are you okay?" He glanced at Esther and Lizzie, but neither one looked up, only stayed busy with their tasks.

"*Ya, ya.* I'm fine. Except I almost burned the *haus* down on *mei* first day of work." The woman covered her face with her hands. "Lizzie and Esther went to take a nap. The timer was set for the bread. All I had to do was take it out of the oven when the buzzer went off. But it didn't go off!" She uncovered her face. "So I waited a while. But then I needed to use the facilities, so I did. Then I remembered I needed to collect the towels from the guest rooms upstairs. I saw all the pretty clothes on the racks, and I was just looking at them as I gathered the towels. I guess I stayed up there too long." She drew in a breath before swiping at her tears. "By the time I came back downstairs, I was winded and decided to rest. All I did was sit on the couch and lay *mei* head back. *Mei mamm* calls them power naps. You sleep for five minutes and wake up feeling refreshed. I must have slept longer than five minutes. Maybe I was tired from my trip." She lifted her shoulders and raised her palms. "And the bread burned."

Jayce was speechless.

Esther finally closed the oven, and Lizzie threw the charred bread in the trash can. "Everything is fine," Esther said. "Jayce, this is Rose, our new employee. Today is her first day, and she's just having first-day jitters."

"You two go out on the porch." Lizzie motioned toward the living room.

"Rose, gather yourself, dear. Everything will be all right. Jayce, where's everyone else? I didn't hear them come in." Esther coughed. How smoky had it been? A strong stench still lingered.

"Actually, they stopped at a restaurant. I was riding with Gus, and he didn't want to stop." Jayce cringed. "Do you need me to do anything in here to help?"

"*Nee*. Just take her outside." Lizzie waved to shoo them away again. Jayce saw her roll her eyes and did as she asked.

Esther held her head in her hands and sighed.

"I don't want to hear it. You told me to find someone to help us, and I did." At least Lizzie's teeth were back in her mouth. "I don't know what to do about her."

Esther was more exhausted than she'd been before Rose joined them earlier in the day. "Can we train her not to talk so much? I'm sure she's a sweet *maedel* and all,

222

but . . ."

"Well, thank the Lord the others stopped to eat somewhere and didn't walk in on this." Lizzie lifted her apron and wiped her face with it, a habit she'd formed as a child. Only now there was no one to reprimand her about it except Esther, and she'd tired of saying anything a long time ago.

"She cooked the hens, right? She said she knew how to stuff them." Esther opened the refrigerator and breathed a sigh of relief. "*Ach, gut.* There are six hens in here. And I see she made a salad. And the potatoes are peeled, cut, and ready to be boiled and mashed." She breathed a sigh of relief. "She's prepared supper, and it will still be *gut* if our guests want lunch tomorrow, or we can make more side dishes and reheat the hens. The four of us can dine on one tonight, assuming Jayce plans to eat." She grinned. "And I haven't seen that boy turn down a meal."

She heard horse hooves crunching against the gravel driveway and walked to the window. "Is that Evelyn Schrock?"

Lizzie joined her. "*Ya,* sure is. I knew there was a spark between her and Jayce. I think they're sweet on each other."

Esther recognized the dreamy way Lizzie spoke. As much as she would love to nurture a budding romance, this wasn't one to encourage. "Whether they are or not, Jayce leaves in a few weeks. You've already caused them to almost vomit by overwhelming them with vanilla in your buggy."

Lizzie pushed her bottom lip out. "I made a mistake." She pointed to the small house the couple lived in. "Amos didn't live here when he became smitten with Naomi. And now they are married and expecting twins."

Esther put her hands on her hips and sighed. "Lizzie, Amos was Amish, even if he was from somewhere else. Jayce isn't just from somewhere else. He might as well be from another planet." She shook her head. "They are too different for us to intervene in any way. Encouraging a romance would only end with one or both of them hurt. We've already talked about this."

"Maybe." Lizzie continued staring out the window. "Stranger things have happened." She leaned closer to the glass, craning her neck to see Jayce and Rose sitting on the porch. "And speaking of stranger . . ." She lifted her eyes to Esther's. "I hope that girl settles down, because she'll put me in an early grave if she talks that much all the time." She tapped a finger to her head. "And I'm wondering if maybe a few marbles are missing. I know I set that timer for the bread."

"In her defense we've both burned bread before. It's her first day, so we will see how it goes."

Lizzie huffed. "Here's how it's gonna go. She's going to quit talking so much, or I'm going to lose *mei* mind." She ambled barefoot toward the living room. "Your shift. I'm taking a nap."

Esther watched Evelyn tether her horse and walk toward the house. Some days, when her arthritis was bothering her or her stomach ulcer flared up, or even when she was just exhausted, she longed for youth. But age brings wisdom, and when she thought about it carefully, she realized she'd never want to go back to those early years.

Yes, she'd fallen in love and gotten married, but a person in his or her twenties was still finding their way. Esther prayed that the three young people on the porch would make wise choices. Especially Evelyn and Jayce. She had no idea what to think about Rose. She also prayed that she and Lizzie hadn't worsened their already stressful situation with this new hire.

Evelyn slowly approached the porch since Jayce had made no effort to come to her.

Instead, he sat on the porch swing beside a crying woman, his hand on her arm. It looked intimate enough that Evelyn had been tempted not to get out of the buggy but to just head back home.

"Should I leave?" she whispered as she stood at the bottom of the porch steps. "I don't want to interrupt."

"*Nee, nee,*" the woman said as she swiped at tears and stood up. "I'm Rose, Lizzie and Esther's new employee. I've been hired to cook, clean, and help them run the inn. I've made a horrible mess of *mei* first day." She held her arms stiff at her sides as she winced. "I wanted to make a *gut* impression. I think I'm overexcited. I just arrived here from Ohio. I don't know anyone, and I just . . ." She covered her face with her hands, and Evelyn walked up the steps to her.

"Please don't cry. Lizzie and Esther are wonderful people and very understanding. They know you'll need time to adjust." Evelyn touched the girl's arm. Jayce slouched on the porch swing, one hand to his forehead.

Rose sniffled. "Are you here to see Lizzie or Esther?" She glanced over her shoulder. "Should I go get them?"

"Um . . ." She glanced at Jayce, who stood up.

"She's here to see me," he said before he yawned.

"If you're tired, we can reschedule." Evelyn didn't mean for the comment to sound snappy when it left her mouth.

"Nope. Let's go." Jayce turned to Rose. "Everything is going to be okay. Don't worry."

Rose nodded. "I'll just go inside and try to make amends with Lizzie and Esther."

Jayce cleared his throat. "Maybe just let them rest for now. Having so many guests is wearing them out."

She nodded, then Jayce motioned for Evelyn to follow him.

"Nice to meet you, Rose." Evelyn waved before she got in step with Jayce.

"Oh wow," he said once they were far enough away from the main house. He shook his head. "That is one sweet girl, but . . ." He turned to Evelyn. "She's nuts."

Evelyn playfully slapped Jayce's arm. "That's a terrible thing to say." Oddly, a surge of relief coursed through her. At first glance Jayce had looked cozy with Rose.

"Yeah, you're right. *Nuts* is a bad word to use." Jayce shook his head. "But she talks a lot." He raised both eyebrows. "I mean, a *whole* lot."

Another wave of relief washed over her. Then she saw a bench ahead facing the pond, and her stomach swirled with anticipation. Fear and excitement combined to form an emotion she didn't know how to process. All she knew was that she'd been looking forward to spending time with Jayce.

"Hopefully everything will work out for Rose. Lizzie and Esther don't usually have this many guests at one time, so I'm sure things are somewhat disorderly right now."

Jayce sat on the bench and Evelyn took a seat beside him.

"I don't bite," he said, grinning.

She noticed the large space she'd put between them and scooted over a little.

"In case you get the urge to kiss me again, I don't want you to strain your neck." A big smile spread across his face.

Evelyn chewed her bottom lip, partly from nerves, but also so she didn't start laughing.

"Go ahead and laugh." Jayce pressed his lips firmly together as he shook his head. "But you're a very aggressive Amish woman."

Evelyn burst out laughing. "Don't say that. I don't even know why that happened." In part, that was true. But it happened because she was attracted to him and had been nervous at the time.

"Do you want to kiss me?" His dark eyes held her gaze, as if searching her face for permission.

"No," she said softly.

"Really?" He spoke with a heavy dose of sarcasm, back to his playful self.

"That's right. I no longer succumb to such urges." She raised her chin and attempted a serious expression.

Jayce lowered his head. "Well, that's a bummer."

Evelyn was smiling broadly when he finally looked up. "Maybe we just see how it goes."

He grinned. "I can live with that."

"You have got to be kidding me!" A loud voice came from behind them, causing them both to jerk their heads around.

"Hey, hero." Jayce waved at Gus.

"Oh no," Evelyn whispered. The grumpiest man on Earth was walking toward them, toting a tackle box and a fishing pole slung over his shoulder.

"First it was Naomi and Amos coming down here to paint their pictures and smooch." He lowered the fishing pole to his side. "Now I've got to deal with you two? Is this Lovers' Lane or what? And do you have to do your canoodling during the best fish-

229

ing time of the day?"

Evelyn could feel her face turning red.

"Gus was a hero today." Jayce looked back and forth between her and Gus. "He saved our star actress from drowning."

Evelyn didn't have to feign shock. Her dropped jaw happened naturally as she tried to picture Gus as a hero. She'd only known him to be obnoxious and rude. "Really?" she managed to say.

"Oh, whatever." Gus growled. "How long you two going to be down here?"

Jayce shrugged. "I don't know. The canoodling hasn't officially started, so it could be a while."

Evelyn elbowed him as she put a hand over her mouth, horrified and amused.

"She's Amish, ya know. She ain't used to your type." Gus threw the words at Jayce like big rocks.

"You'd be surprised," Jayce said, grinning.

Evelyn laughed. She couldn't hold it any longer.

Gus let out a heavy sigh. "This day is getting stranger and stranger." He did an about-face and stomped off.

"Bye, Gus!" Jayce yelled, but the man kept going.

When Jayce's eyes locked with hers, she reminded herself not to let her gaze travel to his lips. "I don't canoodle," she whispered as the sun settled close to the horizon.

"I know." His expression was serious. "And I'd never do anything to disrespect you. You know I was teasing, right?"

The strange surge of disappointment ran the length of her spine this time. "I know." She forced herself to smile.

"This has been a weird day." He shook his head and then told her what happened at the caverns, how Gus really did save Veronica's life.

"That doesn't sound like Gus." Evelyn thought about all the times she'd avoided the man. "Especially since there were so many others who could have jumped in to help."

Jayce twisted slightly, rested his arm on the back of the bench, then propped up his chin and stared into her eyes. "Back home, I used to be a master at faking the person my father wanted me to be. It was exhausting. When I quit trying to be that person, that's when all the problems started." He paused for a while. "I've been trying to find myself ever since. Maybe Gus isn't really the horrible person he tries to be. Maybe he's just unhappy with his life, and his offensive behavior is a defensive move to protect him from getting hurt."

Evelyn cringed. "I don't know about that. I've seen him show a few kindnesses over the years, but mostly . . . he's been terrible to folks." She paused. "But it's interesting that you think that. You must be someone who tries to find the good in everyone." She smiled. "And that's nice."

"Maybe it's because I want people to see the good in me. I've done things I'm not proud of. But God forgave me. I think I'm still searching for the good in myself, the person I want to be."

Evelyn stared into his eyes for a long while. "I see that good in you, Jayce."

He smiled a little. "Do you?"

She nodded. She'd never wanted anyone to kiss her more in her life than she did in this moment. But Jayce turned to face the pond as the sun became one with the water, glazing the surface with orange hues, descending faster than Evelyn wanted it to.

TWELVE

Esther made the trek to Gus's cottage much later than she'd meant to. It was well past dark, so she held a flashlight in one hand and carried a pie tote in the other. Her knees had given her fits all day, which usually meant bad weather was coming.

"What do you want?" he asked when he opened the door.

Esther hung her head, willed her blood pressure to stay within range, then looked back at him. "Gus, why is it that you must address a guest like that right when you open the door? Here." She pushed the chocolate pie at him. He took it. "I heard you did a good deed today, and I thought you would enjoy this pie."

"Yeah, you don't bring me pie as often as you used to." Gus scratched the top of his head. He looked freshly showered and shaved, his hair pulled back neatly in its ponytail. Beyond his broad shoulders she could see the squalor he still lived in. Whiskers, his cat, was stretched out on the couch, seemingly unbothered by the clutter. His only attempt to better his conditions was the time his daughter had come to visit, and that hadn't gone well for either of them.

But he was right about the pie. At one point Esther had promised to bring him pie for the rest of his life. The more she'd thought about it, the more unreasonable it seemed, especially since he'd bullied her into it. The man was already guaranteed life in the cottage, and for minimal rent. So Esther had broken her promise and asked God to forgive her.

"I don't know why everyone is making such a big deal about today." He spat the words before he lowered his arm to his side. "That woman . . ." He pointed toward the larger of the motor homes. "She brought me a huge box of chocolates, said it didn't seem like nearly enough, and then she hugged me for the second time today. I don't need all that, Esther, but I reckon I'll be traveling with them on their other shoots. People ain't safe otherwise, because Brandon's got a bunch of idiots working for him."

Esther thought Gus could use hugs. "Saving a life is a big deal." She turned to leave, too tired to carry on any more conversation with him. She was also afraid she might slip about Mr. Clarkson having no intention of actually including Gus in his movie. It was a dishonorable thing the film producer was doing, but Esther was going to stay out of it. Maybe it was best that Gus was on-site with the crew. It did sound like danger had found them twice already. "Good night, Gus."

"Wait. We need to talk about something else." Gus set the pie on the chair on the porch and took a few steps toward her.

She hadn't even made it to the bottom of the stairs. Looking up, she whispered, "*Gott, give me strength.*" This had been an exhausting day.

"I don't know what kind of place you're running over there . . ." He waved his hand toward the main house. "But it seems like another couple has taken to my fishing spot. First it was Naomi and Amos playing all smoochy-smooch on my bench. Now you got Brandon's kid and Evelyn Schrock down there playing kissy-face."

Esther brought a hand to her chest. "Did you actually see them kissing, Gus?"

"Well, no. But that's how it starts, romantic sunsets and all that other baloney. And it interferes with my fishing time." He raised

235

his chin, though his jowls hung low and sad.

Esther was one to keep her cool, even on her weariest of days, but Gus was about to push her over the edge, as he'd been known to do in the past.

"Gus, you rent the cottage. You do not rent the entire property. The pond, the bench, and the sunset are for all to enjoy."

"You and Lizzie are up to no good encouraging that Amish girl to get involved with that kid." Gus puffed his chest out as if to make a bigger point. "I know how you two operate."

"I assure you neither Lizzie nor I are playing matchmaker with Evelyn and Jayce. We foresee it as an explosive situation and are praying that they remain friends." She turned to leave again, squeezing her eyes closed for a few seconds, fearing Gus would call out to her again.

But all he said was, "Thanks for the pie."

Esther smiled. In a day consumed by obstacles, a small miracle had occurred. "You're welcome," she said without turning around.

Lizzie was in bed reading one of her romance books when Esther returned.

"Don't say anything," Esther said as she climbed into bed with her sister. She and Lizzie were good at reading each other's minds. "Gus deserved the pie."

"Whatever you say." Lizzie already had her teeth out, but she pushed her gold-rimmed reading glasses up on her head, her long gray hair flowing well past her waist, the same as Esther's once she pulled her scarf from her head. "But that old grump would have let me drown."

"I doubt that." Esther yawned, fluffed her pillows, then lowered the flame of her lantern, just as Lizzie turned up the flame on her own. "Lizzie, I need sleep," she mumbled.

"I know, and I'm tired too." Lizzie sighed. "But what are we going to do about Rose?"

"We show patience and give her time to learn how we do things." Esther snubbed out her lantern completely and hoped Lizzie would get the idea.

"How much time? She could have burned down the *haus* today. And she never stops talking. Never. And I'm telling you, there was something in those hens, the stuffing, that shouldn't have been in there. I couldn't even identify the ingredient." Lizzie grumbled. "I've been a nervous Nellie all day today. Esther, the girl makes me feel on edge. I think *mei* blood pressure was off the charts today."

"The hens were all right." Esther cringed

a bit. The birds were edible, but that was about it. "You think everything makes your blood pressure go up, and every time we've checked it, even during stressful situations, it's fine. Go to sleep. Or go back to reading your nasty book." Esther settled beneath the covers.

"I don't read nasty books. They're love stories. Speaking of . . . is something blossoming between Jayce and Evelyn? They were down at the pond. Alone."

"*Ya*, I heard from Gus." Esther yawned. "We will keep an eye on it. As I said before, we can't get involved. Those two are not meant for each other. Only heartache would follow."

"I guess we'll see."

Esther heard Lizzie open the book. Finally, she could close her eyes and sleep. After she prayed about the events of the day. Unsure exactly what to ask for, she just prayed that God's will would be done.

Evelyn was sitting on her bed brushing her hair when there was a tap on the door.

"Can I come in?" Her mother peeked her head inside the door. "I saw the light shining under the door. I thought we could talk."

"If this is about Jayce, *Mamm,* please don't worry. I know we can only be friends, and I won't let things escalate to anything more." Evelyn stowed her brush in the drawer of her nightstand.

Her mother wore the same white robe she'd always worn. Her salt-and-pepper hair was knotted on top of her head, and her tentative smile revealed her worries like a secret code mother and daughter had always shared. She sat on the bed.

"*Mei maedel,* the heart wants what the heart wants." She cupped Evelyn's cheek in her hand. "We can't control our emotions. Even if you know a situation is dangerous, it can still be difficult to walk away. And you are spending a lot of time with this boy."

Evelyn could only remember telling her mother one lie in her life. She once watched television at an English friend's house even though her mother had asked her not to. Evelyn had denied watching the movie. She was about to tell her second lie.

"We are just friends, *Mamm,* and there is nothing to worry about." She knew she was in over her head — she had an enormous crush on Jayce. The night had ended with a hug and no attempt at a kiss good night. But she'd longed for Jayce to kiss her.

Her mother's expression grew tight with strain. "There is everything to worry about." She kissed Evelyn on the cheek, rose from the bed, and shuffled toward the door, turning around before she left. "You can talk to me about anything. You know that, right?"

"*Ya,* I know, *Mamm.* I'm fine. I really am."

Her mother blew her a kiss and closed the door. Evelyn had always been close to her mother. Maybe it was because she was her only daughter. There was a part of Evelyn that wanted to tell her mother how much she liked Jayce, and not just because of his looks. There was something real and unpretentious about him. He spoke what was on his mind and didn't filter anything out.

Evelyn had never been one to discuss her personal business with her girlfriends. Montgomery's Amish community was small, and no matter the good intentions of confidants, word always seemed to get out. Like it had about Jayce. It seemed that everywhere she went, someone questioned her about the English man she'd been seen with at the Bargain Center. Perhaps Widow Byler was partly to blame. But a lot of people saw Jayce leaving that day and telling her he'd see her later.

She pulled her damp hair to the top of her head and bobby-pinned it in place so it wouldn't soak her pillowcase. After lying down she left the lantern's flame on low and watched the shadows dancing on the ceiling the way she'd done for as long as she could remember. It was her form of cloud watching, as images came and went, depending on which way the flame flickered. Tonight the movement reminded her of the twinkling stars overhead when she'd said good night to Jayce.

Her mother was right to be concerned and correct about not always being able to control your feelings. As Evelyn tossed the thoughts around in her mind, she reminded herself Jayce would be leaving in a few weeks. Would they remain friends? Would they write letters? Or would he return to his world with only fond memories of an Amish woman he met in Montgomery, Indiana?

A crash against the window caused her to jump. *A bat.* It had happened before. One of the winged creatures had flown into her upstairs window. Lucas had found the dead bat on the ground the next day. She squeezed her eyes closed. As much as she disliked anything that flew, she didn't like to think about any of God's creatures dying.

Then it happened again — another crack against the window. Two bats hitting the glass pane in one night would be too much of a coincidence, so she tiptoed to the window, which she'd closed earlier when the wind picked up.

Her chest felt like it might explode when she saw Jayce on the front lawn, shining a flashlight at his face. A thrill of frightened anticipation wound its way up her spine as she lifted the window.

"What are you doing here?" He'd obviously thrown rocks at her window. She said a quick prayer that her parents and brothers wouldn't see or hear him.

"Can you lower your ladder and come down?" He spoke in a loud whisper.

"*Mei* what?" Evelyn's heart fluttered and pounded against her chest.

"You said you had a ladder you could drop down out of your window." He still had the flashlight shining so she could see his eager expression. "Can you come down?"

Evelyn's jaw dropped as she leaned closer to the screen. "I was teasing. I don't have a ladder." She was a bit floored he'd truly thought she did. It was an easy walk from the inn, but she never would have expected this.

He shined the flashlight at her window, and she blocked the bright light with her hand. Turning the light back on himself, he winked. "I didn't think nice Amish girls lied."

"It wasn't a lie. I was teasing, and I thought you knew that." Fear he'd get caught twisted her insides into knots. "You have to go before *mei* parents or *bruders* catch you out there."

He hung his head, the light at his feet.

"Is everything okay?"

As he lifted his head and grinned, Evelyn practically swooned in her bedroom, then realized she didn't have her head covered, not even with a scarf. At least her hair was pinned up.

"Is everything okay?" she asked again.

"Yeah. I just found myself thinking about that kiss again." He shrugged. "Next thing I knew, I was here." He scratched his head, the light back where she could see his face. "I'm disappointed about that ladder story."

Evelyn laughed, then quickly put a hand over her mouth. "Go back to the inn before you get us both in trouble."

Smiling broadly, he saluted. "See you soon."

As he turned and walked away, Evelyn was sure her mother was wrong. She hadn't just dipped a toe into a dangerous situation. She was drowning in it, totally smitten with Jayce Clarkson, a man from the big city, from a world she knew nothing about.

And he'd leave here in a few weeks.

Esther awoke from a deep sleep, looked at the clock that read 2:00 a.m., then nudged Lizzie. "Wake up." She turned an ear toward the noise she'd heard, which sounded like it was coming from the kitchen. "Do you hear that?"

Lizzie didn't even lift her head. "It's one of those Hollywooders." Lizzie had taken to calling their guests by the nickname even though none of them were from Hollywood. "They eat at all hours of the night."

"I know. But I never hear them." Esther was on her feet. "It sounds like someone is singing."

"Maybe they're practicing for the movie." Lizzie pulled the covers over her head.

"It's getting louder. Whoever it is, they are going to wake up the entire household." She nudged Lizzie's arm. "Get up. We need to go see what's going on for the safety of all our guests."

Lizzie groaned but rolled out of bed. They hustled into their robes and threw scarves over their heads before they tiptoed out of the bedroom, then crossed through the living room. Esther saw movement coming from the dark kitchen, lit only slightly by the propane light in the yard beaming in through the window. The singing grew louder, so they picked up the pace.

Esther reached for the flashlight on a shelf in the living room and hurried to follow Lizzie.

"Hush!" Lizzie yelled in a loud whisper.

Esther shined the flashlight in Rose's face, but the girl didn't seem to notice. She only sang louder as she wiggled her hips from side to side, her fingers pointed at the floor as her arms bounced up and down to her rhythm.

"This *maedel* is crazy as a loon." Lizzie stomped her foot. "Rose, what in the world are you doing?"

"Lizzie, stop." Esther pointed the flashlight at the ceiling, lighting the space around them. "She's sleepwalking."

"And singing?" Lizzie's eyebrows shot up. "We don't *sing*. And that sounds like that loud music Mr. Philips used to play after he bought that car without the top on it."

Esther stood next to Lizzie, equally stumped. "Where do you think she learned to dance like that?" Esther cringed. Rose's dance moves were inappropriate at best.

Lizzie shook her head. "Should we lock her in the basement?"

Esther gasped. "Of course not. I once read

245

that you are supposed to just walk a sleep-walker back to bed, that it can be bad to wake them up, make them feel confused and frightened."

Lizzie's eyes widened. "If anyone should feel frightened, it's us."

Esther walked toward Rose, and when she touched her arms, the girl stopped dancing. "Time for bed," Esther said softly as she studied the girl's dazed expression. Esther waved a hand in front of her eyes, but Rose didn't even blink.

She allowed Esther and Lizzie to walk her back to Lizzie's bedroom. After she was tucked in, the sisters tiptoed back to Esther's room.

"We fire her first thing tomorrow," Lizzie said as soon as they were back in bed.

"We will do no such thing." Esther set the flashlight on the nightstand, lay down, and put a hand across her forehead.

"It's no wonder that girl doesn't have a husband and her family shipped her to Big Roy and Katie Marie. Thinking back, Katie Marie practically pushed Rose out the door when I picked her up. We return her in the morning."

"She's not a package to be returned." Esther wondered if she would ever have a good night's sleep again, but firing Rose and shipping her back would leave her with sleepless nights as well. "Let's talk about this in the morning."

"It *is* morning," Lizzie snapped. But within a few minutes, she was snoring.

Esther stared at the ceiling, thinking what a peculiar day it had been. Gus had risked his life to save another. Rose almost burnt down the house. Evelyn Schrock and Jayce seemed too smitten for comfort, going out to the bench by the pond together. Esther's father used to call it the courting bench. It had been repaired and restained more times than Esther could recall.

They had a house full of English people, and more outside in big buses, who were as foreign as aliens. And now Rose was a sleepwalker. And she sang. And danced. Esther set herself to praying for all kinds of things, anxious about what the next day might bring. A body could only take so much.

THIRTEEN

It started raining before daybreak on Tuesday and hadn't let up by Friday afternoon. If the forecast was correct, the storms would continue off and on through the weekend. Esther's achy knees usually weren't wrong, but she hadn't anticipated this kind of weather. Or chaos.

"Giovanni went to Veronica's motor home to see if he could get the generator going again." Jayce held an armful of wet towels as he walked into the kitchen. "The roof is still leaking in my room, but I've got a pot catching the water now. What do you want me to do with these towels?"

"Can you please put them in the basement?" Esther took a deep breath. The inn had housed three generations, and it had certainly weathered some storms, but Esther didn't remember anything like this. Places throughout town that didn't usually hold water were flooded. The mail carrier said the East Fork of the White River was so far out of its banks near Williams that folks hadn't been able to get out most of the week.

"We're gonna need an ark." Lizzie shuffled into the kitchen looking as worn out as Esther felt. Lizzie had dark circles under her eyes and was wearing a wrinkled dark-green dress she'd fallen asleep in the night before. And she'd misplaced her dentures. "How are we holding up on food?" she asked with a lisp.

Esther usually made a run to the market on Thursdays, but the roads had been too bad to get out. "We'll have to make some adjustments to the menu, but I think we will get by."

Jayce stepped up from the last step of the basement into the kitchen, closing the door behind him. "Wow. There's a lot of stuff down there."

"*Ya,* someday we will get things cleaned out. We only go down there to bring up more food we've canned and to run clothes through the wringer." They'd also actually locked two young couples down there in hopes of solidifying a union. The first time was a failed attempt with Naomi and a man who was not right for her, but the second time she'd been with Amos, and that resulted in a patched-up argument, which eventually led to marriage. Esther wasn't about to share that with Jayce. She tried to offer the boy a smile, but all she wanted to do was go to bed and collapse.

Lizzie grumbled when someone knocked at the front door.

"I'll see who it is," Jayce said, his white T-shirt wet from the towels he'd carried. "Bound to be one of our crowd."

"Where is Rose?" Lizzie asked after Jayce left the room. "I'm surprised no one has complained about breakfast this morning. What was it anyway?"

Esther rubbed one of her temples, willing it to stop throbbing. "Some type of egg casserole — her *mudder*'s recipe, she said."

"I hope her *mudder* prepares it better than she did." Lizzie rolled her eyes.

"*Ya*, well, no one complained, and it got eaten. We will just need to see what she's *gut* at and maybe adjust the way we do things. If cooking isn't her strong suit, perhaps something else will be."

"Well, I checked the upstairs bathrooms earlier, and they're spotless." Lizzie paused. "Did you clean them today?"

Esther shook her head. "*Nee*, I didn't. Rose must have."

"She must have cleaned them and vanished. I'll go see if she's in her room." Lizzie nodded toward the dining room. "Those movie people must have no personal lives. All they do is meet in there and talk about that movie they're making. Don't they have families? I haven't heard a one of them on the phone, checking in with anyone, nothing."

"I'm sure they do that in private, Lizzie." Esther's lips thinned with irritation. "Have you thought about where your teeth might be?"

Amos came into the kitchen with Jayce behind him. "Naomi sent over these pies and two casseroles." He piled everything on the kitchen table. "She knows you shop on Thursdays and said you might need some extra food for all your guests. She would have come herself, but her feet are swollen, and I told her to rest."

"She needn't be getting out in this weather anyway." Esther eyed the gifts. "Please tell her we send our thanks. This will help a lot."

"Jayce said there's a leak in the roof. You still have that ladder in the barn, the really tall one?" Amos was soaked from running to the inn. "I'm going to get up there and have a look."

"I'll help," Jayce said as Esther handed Amos a towel to wipe his face and nodded about the ladder.

After they were gone, Lizzie leaned against the counter and attempted to straighten her prayer covering. "Well, the crops and flowers are going to benefit from all this rain if we don't float away."

Quinn emerged from the dining room holding an empty coffee cup. "Looks like we might be in our meeting for a while. If you'll show me where everything is, I'll make more coffee."

Lizzie took the woman's cup. "I'll handle it, hon." After Quinn left, Lizzie said, "I'm sure that woman has never percolated coffee before in her life. Probably has some fancy machine where she comes from."

"It was nice of her to offer." Esther stowed the casseroles in the refrigerator. "Bless Naomi for thinking of us."

"I miss that *maedel*." Lizzie started the coffee percolating and leaned against the counter again. "But I'm glad she and Amos stayed close by. Just think . . ." Lizzie smiled, despite her weariness. "We'll have two little ones running around soon."

A few minutes later, Amos and Jayce came back into the kitchen, both dripping wet. "We've got a tarp secured over the leak, but some shingles need to be replaced. I know lots of areas are flooded, but we had high winds too. When I'm able to get to the hardware store, I'll get the supplies to repair it." Amos turned to Jayce and shook his hand. "*Danki* for the help."

"No problem." Jayce turned to Esther after Amos left. "The new girl, Rose, must have cleaned upstairs because when I gathered up all the towels she'd piled in a corner, I peeked in the other rooms to make sure there weren't any other leaks. There weren't, and nothing was out of place. Even Quinn's room was straightened and organized. And she's more of a slob than the rest of us." He walked to the pitcher of tea on the counter and poured himself a glass, then turned to Esther. "I'm at your disposal." He nodded to the dining room. "They don't need me, and I don't want to be in there, so what can I do to help?"

"*Sohn,* you're not on the payroll. You're a guest." Lizzie sighed. "Unless you can help me find *mei* teeth."

Esther gasped. "Lizzie, those dentures are your responsibility. Jayce isn't going to help you find them."

Rose rushed into the room and handed Lizzie her dentures. "After I collected eggs, and I didn't drop any, I went to the barn to check on the animals." She bounced up on her toes. The girl seemed to be in perpetual motion. Esther felt even more tired just watching the girl's energy level rising. "I love the goats. They're probably *mei* favorite of all the animals. But I checked on the horses, fed them, and brushed them. I also filled up their water trough. *Mei* shoes are outside. It's very muddy. I dried off as best I could on the porch." She looked down and wiggled her toes. "Anyway, your dentures were on the workbench."

Lizzie snapped her fingers. "That's right! The broom handle broke, and I went to get another sweeper that was out in the barn. I set *mei* teeth down since they were bothering me again." She ran the dentures under some water before slipping them back into her mouth.

"I've cleaned the house top to bottom. There is some mud back on the living room floor from people going in and out, but that's to be expected. I'll wait until everyone is settled later tonight, then I'll make sure to clean the floors again. I'm wondering if this rain is ever going to stop."

Jayce sneaked out of the room. Esther couldn't blame him. The girl had the energy of a toddler loaded up on caffeine. Maybe this was a good time to talk to Rose about her sleepwalking and ask her if it was a normal occurrence.

"I also cleaned that man's cottage. I saw he was gone, so I thought it the best time to tidy up his place." She scrunched up her nose. "It was awful. Terribly dirty. He has a cat. Did you know that? I didn't know if that was allowed, but he was a sweet fellow — the cat, that is. Do we wash Mr. Gus's clothes? I didn't know, so I gathered them all up and put them in the basement. It was a lot of clothes, but I'll start on them shortly. And —"

"Stop." Lizzie blinked a few times as she held up a hand to shush Rose. "You cleaned Gus's *haus* and hauled all his dirty clothes here?"

"*Ya.* I didn't go to the *daadi haus* since you said a couple lived there. I assumed they take care of their own home."

Lizzie bent at the waist and laughed until Esther thought her sister might cry. Straightening, she looked at Esther. "I'll let you deal with Gus." Then she turned to Rose and winked at her. "*Gut* job, dear."

Esther eyed the pies. Suddenly talking to Rose about her nighttime adventures didn't seem appealing. But a large slice of pie did. She'd need strength when Gus showed up. She'd been surprised when she saw his truck was gone earlier. He'd be fit to be tied when he got home.

"*Ach,* and one more thing." Rose took a piece of paper from her apron pocket. "I hope I didn't take a liberty I shouldn't have, but I noticed while I was in the barn that the light on the answering machine was blinking, so I checked the message. There was only one. It was from a woman named Evelyn, asking for Jayce to call her." She handed Esther the number on a small slip of paper. "If it's the same Evelyn I met, she's really nice."

"*Danki,* dear." Esther turned off the burner under the percolator, feeling the weight of the world on her shoulders.

"Should I take the number to Jayce?" Rose's face radiated with spunk and energy, as if she hadn't missed a wink of sleep or had a worry in the world. But Esther had seen how quickly the girl could shift into another mood and break down in tears. Then again, almost burning down someone's house could do that to a person.

"*Nee,* you've done plenty. I'll get this to Jayce. You've been busy today. Why don't you go take some time to yourself." Esther slid a slice of pumpkin pie onto her plate.

"Are you sure? I can go into the basement to start running clothes through the wringer, although . . ." She tapped a finger to her chin. "We don't really have anywhere to hang them, do we? I wonder how long it's supposed to rain. Back home, me and *mamm* would drape clothes over the backs of chairs and even had a makeshift clothesline in the mudroom. But with so many people here, I'm not sure that's practical. But I can still start on the clothes if you'd like me to, or —"

"*Nee,* dear. You just go rest and take some time to yourself." Esther tried to smile before she forked a bite of pie.

Rose finally agreed and went to her temporary room, closing the door behind her. The good Lord was raining down mercy on Esther when Mr. Clarkson and his crew headed upstairs. All was quiet. Esther savored the moment and enjoyed her pie. She'd take Jayce Evelyn's message and number shortly, which added a layer of concern to everything else the day had brought.

Thankfully, with help from Jayce, Amos, and even Rose, things were beginning to calm down. Until Gus got home. Esther cringed when she thought about him walking into his clean cottage. He was going to go crazy. She flinched at the thought of Rose taking on the filthy task. Esther would explain to the girl later that housekeeping didn't include Gus's cottage.

She might not be able to cook, but so far, Rose appeared to be a tornado when it came to cleaning.

Jayce sat on his bed staring at the phone number Esther had given him and listening to the constant dripping of water into the metal pan. The tarp had helped, but the roof was still leaking. He set the piece of paper on the bed and went to the bathroom, returning with a small hand towel to put in the bottom of the pan. He hated to add more laundry to the growing pile in the basement, but the towel softened the sound so Jayce didn't feel like he was enduring some sort of water torture.

He dialed the number on the slip of paper and waited. After three rings, a man answered.

"Uh, I might have the wrong number, but I'm trying to reach Evelyn." Jayce studied the slip of paper, pretty sure he hadn't misdialed.

"*Nee,* you've got the right number. Hold on just a minute."

After about five minutes, Evelyn was finally on the phone. "Sorry it took so long," she said, sounding out of breath.

"I didn't think your people used phones. The only one Lizzie and Esther have is in the barn and strictly for business." Jayce stood, walked to the bucket, and pushed it to the left with his foot when the leak in the roof seemed to shift.

"It's *mei bruder*'s phone. David is *mei* oldest *bruder. Daed* doesn't like the use of mobile phones, or any phones, but he knows David needs one for his work. He does general contracting for a company in town, and the *Englisch* have to be able to reach him. Actually, *Mamm* has a phone, too, but it's only for emergencies." She paused. "It was her phone I had the day you helped me with Millie. *Mamm* wanted me to take it that day because the newspeople in the paper said it might storm. But it didn't." She chuckled. "But it was dead anyway. I decided to ask David to borrow his. *Mamm* wouldn't have thought *mei* calling you was an emergency."

Jayce smiled, remembering she'd had a phone the day they met. "She might have thought it was an emergency if you told her you missed me terribly and needed to hear the sound of my voice." He was blatantly flirting with an Amish woman he wouldn't see once he left here. But teasing her came naturally, and if she were there, her eyes would have taken on that twinkle when she blushed. She didn't say anything. "Hello?"

"I'm still here." She spoke softly, pausing. "I-I just wanted to make sure everyone was all right at the inn. I know Lizzie and Esther have a houseful, plus all those people in the buses."

She'd completely ignored his playfulness, but the way her voice trembled a little, he wondered if he'd hit the nail on the head. Maybe she had missed him.

"It's chaotic." He scratched his chin as he eyed the bucket in the middle of the room. "My dad and his group have kept the dining room occupied, sometimes with the entire crew, so there've been lots of people going in and out, everyone dripping wet. There are trails of mud on the floor, and there's a leak in the roof." He laughed, hoping to keep the mood light. "And, lucky me, the leak is in the room I'm in."

"Esther and Lizzie must be worn out."

Jayce sighed. "Yeah, I think they are."

"How's the new help working out?" She giggled. "The one you called nuts, which I still think was terrible for you to say."

"Well . . ." He sat back down on the bed, grinning. "She is never quiet. *Never.* And she can't cook at all. I have no idea what was in the breakfast she made today, but I was hungry, and I guess everyone else was too. It was some sort of egg casserole, but I think it had pimientos and something else in it. She baked hens earlier in the week that were terrible, with some kind of weird stuffing. Lizzie has done most of the cooking the past few days. She's been getting up super early — I think to beat Rose to the kitchen."

"*Ach* dear. I wonder if they'll keep her on. They've done everything themselves since Naomi left."

"Well, the woman can clean. She's got that going for her. The upstairs is spotless. She even cleaned Gus's house."

Evelyn gasped. "You're teasing, *ya*?"

"Nope. She admitted it was awful, but she thought it was part of the job."

Evelyn cringed. "I don't know Gus all that *gut,* but I'm surprised he allowed it."

"Apparently, he didn't. He was gone when she did it." Jayce laughed. "And get this. She hauled back all of his clothes to be laundered."

She laughed. "I could be wrong, but I suspect Gus won't appreciate Rose's *gut* intentions."

"Who knows? Maybe he'll be glad to come home to a clean place." He cleared his throat, wanting to get away from any more talk about Gus. "So have you been able to get to work the past few days? What's that place called, the Bargain Center?"

"*Ya,* that's the name. I went Wednesday, but I had trouble getting back home in the buggy. *Daed* was going to cart me back and forth, but even he had problems with his horse's hooves sinking in the mud when he tried Thursday, so we went back home. There are two women who live within walking distance of the store, so they are covering my shift."

"So you've kinda had a vacation." Jayce wished they were having a picnic out in the sunshine, or were back at the movies sharing popcorn. "Or are you bored?"

"I'm a little bored. *Mamm* and I have done a lot of baking. Lucas and David can't really work in this weather, so they've stayed upstairs. I think Lucas has a phone, too, even though he won't admit it. He works with David, but *Daed* said one phone was enough for their business. But I hear Lucas sometimes late at night, talking to someone. Both *mei bruders* have girlfriends. *Mamm* thinks they'll be publishing wedding announcements any day, which is our way of letting the community know when a couple is ready to commit to each other forever. *Daed* is praying that the weddings aren't too close to the same time." She laughed. "Weddings are big affairs here."

Jayce braced for thunder after a big flash of lightning lit up the sky outside his window. It was too early to be dark, but it was gray and dreary. After the rumble he decided to step up to the plate. "So . . . maybe you missed me just a little?"

"Maybe."

He tried to read into her one-word answer. "Hmm. I'll take a maybe, I guess." He hesitated. "I miss seeing you. Still thinking about that kiss. And I'm still disappointed you don't have a ladder to escape your bedroom."

She laughed. "I can't believe you really thought I would lower a ladder out of my window."

"It did make me wonder how often you had scaled down the thing to meet potential suitors." Grinning, he said, "I figured there must be a whole bunch of them."

She huffed into the phone. "*Nee,* not really. And since you've already brought up that dreadful kiss, I have something to say about it too."

"I didn't think it was dreadful at all. Just a bit rushed." Jayce smiled.

Evelyn squeezed her eyes closed, still embarrassed she'd behaved in such a way. She wasn't sure what bothered her more, the fact that she'd so boldly kissed him, or that it had been awkward and probably bruised his lips.

"Well, I just want to say, it won't happen again." She held her breath as she waited for his response.

"That's disappointing." He couldn't have sounded any more seductive if he tried. "Maybe if we spend more time together, you'll feel differently."

Her insides danced at the thought of being around Jayce. She recalled her mother's warnings again, and Evelyn knew she should heed them. Instead, she quietly said, "Maybe."

Then they agreed to have supper as soon as the weather cleared.

Evelyn would be counting the days. The minutes. And she'd do her very best not to think of how she'd feel when Jayce left.

FOURTEEN

It was after supper when Esther saw Gus's truck pulling onto the small gravel driveway in front of the cottage. Everyone, including Lizzie, had retired for the evening. Her sister was reading one of her romance books when Esther told her she was going to visit Gus. Lizzie didn't offer to go with her, and Esther was sure that was for the best. She didn't relish the thought of going to Gus's cottage, but she figured she'd better take the battle there before Gus brought his hostilities to the inn and disrupted what had finally settled into a peaceful environment. At least, for now.

She slipped into her galoshes by the front door, slung her black cape around her shoulders, and put on her bonnet. It wasn't raining at the moment, but that didn't mean it wouldn't start up again.

As she slogged her way to the cottage, dread filled her. By the time she arrived and heaved herself up the porch steps, her knees felt like lead. She was surprised Gus hadn't already come out and started yelling. Rapping lightly on the door, she closed her eyes and prayed for patience and tolerance.

The door opened slower than usual, and Gus was dressed quite presentably. It reminded her again of the times he had cleaned up to take her to her doctor and hospital visits. Even though her diagnosis had been a stomach ulcer, all the tests had terrified her.

Gus was wearing one of the same redcheckered shirts he'd worn during one of their trips to town. His black trousers were held up by suspenders, as always, and his hair was pulled back, but it appeared clean, and his beard had been groomed. Esther held her breath and prepared for his wrath.

He stared at her, narrowing his eyebrows. "Esther . . ." He paused to sigh. "I don't have any clothes. And there's only one person I can think of who would steal all my clothes, except the ones I'm wearing."

Esther was too stunned by his calm demeanor to know how to respond. She'd expected him to open the door ranting and cursing because someone had cleaned his house. She thought he might notice the clothes missing later. But then she thought about the way Gus smelled most of the time. Perhaps that was because he never went to town to use the laundromat.

"Why would your crazy sister steal all my clothes?" He scratched the top of his head, frowning. "That's a low blow even for Lizzie."

Esther tried to be discreet as she peeked around Gus. The cottage was clean, just like it had been when Esther helped Gus a while back prior to a visit from his daughter. The woman had made it clear she never wanted to see Gus again.

"And another thing . . ." He nodded over his shoulder. "Maybe the only reason she cleaned the place up is to spy on me. Or maybe she stole things from me." His expression soured even more.

Esther turned off the flashlight she was holding since the cottage was lit up with lanterns inside. "Lizzie didn't steal your clothes, and she didn't clean the cottage. Our new employee, Rose, did that. The girl didn't know any better, and she was just trying to help. We would have washed your clothes today and hung them to dry, but the rain prevented us from doing that. It won't happen again."

Gus folded his arms across his chest, resting them on his belly. "I guess I'll sleep in

267

this for tonight."

Esther didn't know what to say. Apparently, Gus really didn't own any other clothes besides the ones Rose had hauled away.

"Thank you for understanding." She turned to leave, wishing she'd brought a slice of pie to soften the double blow, but she was also stunned he hadn't thrown the fit she'd been expecting. "Good night."

"Can you stay for a few minutes? There's something I want to talk to you about."

Esther slowly turned around, uninterested in listening to Gus complain about something.

"Gus, I've had an exhausting day." She forced a yawn, which wasn't difficult, but she followed him inside when he ignored her comment and walked into the cottage.

She waited for him to wave his arms around and lambaste Rose for her efforts. But he sat on the worn corner of the couch, where it appeared he always sat, with the TV tray next to his spot. Even though there was no television or electricity in the cottage, the tray was a makeshift end table.

Esther sat on the edge of a rocking chair, hoping she wouldn't be staying long.

Gus scratched his chin and stared at the floor for a few seconds before he looked at her. "I went to see Heather today."

The name sounded familiar, but Esther couldn't place the woman.

When she didn't respond, Gus snarled, then huffed. "My *daughter,* Esther. I only have one daughter. You met her." He rolled his eyes. "Good grief."

Esther should have gotten up and left right then. She'd warned Gus about speaking to her in such a manner. But she was too curious about why Gus went to visit the woman. To Esther's knowledge, he'd only seen her the one time when they had harsh words.

"*Ya, ya.* I remember."

He eyed her a couple more seconds, as if to make sure she knew how disgusted he was that she hadn't remembered the name of a woman she'd met only once. "Did your visit go better than the last time? And why did you choose today, with this terrible weather?"

"I figured she would be home." He pulled his gaze away and stared at the floor again. "Everything's flooded, most people ain't getting out. My truck can get through anything. And I recently learned she retired from her job, but I can't remember what she did."

Esther heard the regret in the last part of his comment. "So you just walked up to her door, even after she said during her last visit to your house that she never wanted to see you again?"

"I know what she said, Esther." His mouth fell open like a cave, darkened by his jowls. "You don't have to rub it in."

At the time, Gus said he didn't care that his time with his daughter had gone badly. Esther suspected he'd been hurt more than he let on. "I'm not trying to rub it in." She crossed one leg over the other and cupped her knee with her hands.

He got up and began to pace the small living room.

Since Gus had lived there, Esther could count on one hand the times she'd been in the cottage. And this was the second time it was clean. The first time, Esther had cut Gus's hair in preparation for his daughter's visit. Maybe that's why he wasn't fussing about Rose cleaning the place. His daughter must be coming to visit again. But she waited.

"I figure now that I'm kind of a movie star . . ." He slowed his pacing and glanced at Esther. She did her best not to react. Being an extra in a movie was hardly a movie star. If he was even included in the picture show.

"I thought maybe she'd . . ." He cleared

his throat and avoided looking at Esther. "I thought maybe she'd like me more."

Esther thought it would make the woman incredibly shallow, if that were the case. And based on the vicious argument Heather and Gus had — part of it in front of Esther — she didn't think anything Gus did would change Heather's opinion of her father. But Esther had to tread softly. The fact that Gus had opened up this part of himself was proof that, whether Heather cared or not, Gus did. He cleared his throat again before Esther had time to respond.

"Brandon said he was going to have a private viewing of the scenes filmed here in Montgomery. They'd already done most of the movie off-site before they got here. He said these were unedited clips, but he wanted his investors to see them in case they needed to make changes while they're still here. Not everyone gets to go to a movie premiere, even if it's only to see an unedited clip. I wanted to ask Heather to come to the event."

Esther was scared to ask Heather's reaction, so she waited. Gus's eyes were fixed on her and he seemed to be waiting for her to say something. "Was she home?" she finally asked, thinking it might be best if she wasn't.

"Yeah, she was home." He sat back down on his spot on the couch, nervously tapping his fingers together.

Esther wanted to ask if the woman slammed the door in his face, but she just nodded.

"Anyway, she said she'd be there and to let her know when it gets scheduled." Gus kept his head down. A good thing since Esther was sure her surprise showed in her expression.

"Isn't that what you wanted?" she finally asked before stifling another yawn, a real one this time. But she was tired of holding her tongue. "I'm surprised she agreed to attend after the way things ended between the two of you."

Maybe she was provoking him intentionally. She wasn't sure. She just wanted to get home to bed.

Gus lifted his eyes to hers. "Maybe when she sees the type of people I hang around, she'll think me worthy to be in her life."

Esther thought her heart might crack. Her legs carried her to the couch somehow, and before she knew it she was sitting close enough to Gus to put a hand on his arm. "Gus, that is not a *gut* reason for her to want to be in your life. It shouldn't matter who your friends are."

He lowered his head again. Esther had never seen Gus this vulnerable. "I know, Esther." He slowly lifted his eyes to hers. "Will you come too?"

Esther smiled sympathetically. "I don't think I will lend any credibility to your circle of friends. I'm just an old Amish woman who rents you a cottage." She paused, slowly lowering her hand from his arm. "And you know our people don't watch television or movies."

Avoiding her eyes again, he cast his gaze onto the wooden floor. "I know you don't. And I'm not asking because of any credibility . . ." He shook his head and sighed before he locked eyes with her. "I'm going to be real nervous with her there."

This was a first, and Esther's jaw actually dropped a little.

"I just reckon I wouldn't be so nervous if you were there." He looked away again.

Esther had always suspected she might be Gus's only friend, even if their relationship wasn't a true definition of the word. If she asked the bishop to attend, he would likely say no. Esther wasn't a rule breaker. But when Gus looked back at her with such longing in his eyes, she said, "I'll be there."

Gus stood and started toward the door. Esther followed and stepped onto the porch when he opened the door. His jaw thrust forward. "Tell Rose Petal I can clean my own house. I don't need her snooping through my things. But I'm fine with her doing my clothes. That laundry place in town is expensive."

Esther was about to tell him Rose wasn't going to clean his clothes, but then reconsidered. Gus hadn't smelled good in all the years she'd known him. She'd never been sure if it was his personal hygiene or his clothes. Only one way to find out.

"I will tell her. But we don't call her Rose Petal. Just Rose." She narrowed her eyes at him to make her point.

"Yeah, okay, whatever." Then, in typical Gus fashion, he closed the door.

By the time Esther climbed into bed, Lizzie was snoring, and only a dimly lit lantern shone on Esther's side of the bed. She lay down, feeling like she should fall into a deep slumber right away. But she couldn't seem to lose the images of Gus floating around in her mind.

If Mr. Clarkson didn't include Gus in some capacity in his movie — and it had sounded like he wasn't planning on it — Gus would be humiliated in front of his daughter. If Heather was planning to attend the showing, it might be for all the wrong reasons.

Gus was a cranky old man who drove everyone crazy, a black sheep in their untraditional little family. But he was their black sheep, and she didn't want to see him get hurt.

Jayce had set the alarm on his phone Friday night, hoping to get up and downstairs before anyone else. With only 20 percent battery left, he'd have to remember to charge it at the cave. His father had scheduled everyone for work today since they'd lost so much time due to the rain.

Lizzie had been trying to beat Rose to the kitchen every morning, but Jayce knew the elderly sisters were spent. And if they had to eat another one of Rose's meals, he worried his father might come unglued. He was already a man on edge because of the weather delays.

Jayce had three pounds of bacon cooked and was scrambling eggs when Lizzie shuffled barefoot into the room, her head covered with a scarf, and still in her robe, minus her teeth.

"Go back to bed, Lizzie." He glanced at her before he sprinkled salt and pepper in the pan, then added a little shredded cheese he'd found in the refrigerator. "I got this."

"Step aside, Jayce." Lizzie nudged him with her elbow. "Do you even know what you're doing?"

He grimaced in good humor. "As a matter of fact, I do. And I know you've been trying to beat Rose to the kitchen the last few mornings." He added a small amount of cottage cheese to the bowl of eggs. It made them go further and added a fluffiness that complemented the effort.

"Who adds cottage cheese to eggs?" Lizzie shook her head.

"My mom did. I used to love watching her cook when I was a kid." He paused, thinking about those happier times. "Go back to bed." He glanced at the older woman, whose dark circles under her eyes were a testament to how tired she and Esther both were. "Just trust me. I used to own a deli, and believe it or not, I can cook. If Rose shows up soon, maybe she'll learn something. But I don't think any of us want to suffer through another one of her meals. I'll help you cook as much as I can."

Lizzie eyed him skeptically. "A deli sells sandwiches."

Jayce grinned. "Yeah, but we also provided hot meals. I took some cooking classes before I opened it. We even had a few breakfast items on the menu — gourmet eggs with chives, Parmesan cheese, fresh herbs —"

"Stop." Lizzie raised her hand. "Let's just see if everyone can tolerate that cottage cheese you've got going in there." She leaned closer to have a look, then sighed. "I'm too tired to argue. Have at it."

"Don't worry, Lizzie," he said as she shuffled back to her bedroom.

A few minutes later, Rose rushed into the room fully dressed. "*Ach nee.* That's *mei* job." She tried to pry the wooden spoon from Jayce's hand. "I wouldn't be earning *mei* keep, and why is there cottage cheese on the counter?" She gasped. "You didn't put that in the eggs, did you? That's not suitable for eggs."

He lowered the flame below the eggs and kept ownership of the wooden spoon. "Please let me do breakfast this morning. It might be a little different than you're used to, but I enjoy cooking."

Rose squinted at him. She was a beautiful woman, tall and slender, with gorgeous big brown eyes. And when she opened her mouth, she had perfectly straight white teeth. But then her mouth stayed open and never closed. Right now, though, she seemed a bit speechless, a welcome reprieve from her constant chatter. He convinced her to go set the table in the dining room.

Jayce turned when he heard heavy footsteps coming down the stairs and hoped it was Jesse, Hal, or Giovanni. But it was his father.

"Well now, there's a sight." His dad chuckled. "My son cooking breakfast in an Amish kitchen."

Jayce shrugged. "Esther and Lizzie have been getting up early to cook, so I decided to give them a break."

His father went to the percolator, poured himself a cup of coffee, then added enough sugar to wire him for the day. "I guess anything is better than what that new girl cooks. The older ladies make a great meal, but that new gal can't cook worth a . . ." His father rattled off words Jayce was used to, but when he lifted his eyes from the skillet, Rose stood at the entrance to the kitchen. Her eyes were watery, her bottom lip trembling.

"I just came to get more forks." She tucked her head as she moved toward the drawer where the silverware was stored.

When she left the room, Jayce glared at his father.

"Don't look at me like that. We paid for rooms and meals. The rooms are barely tolerable, so the meals should at least be decent." His father left the kitchen with his coffee cup and went back upstairs.

"Ignore him," Jayce said when a teary-eyed Rose came back in the kitchen. "He's a jerk." This was the quietest Rose had ever been, and while he wanted to enjoy the peacefulness of the morning, he didn't like that his father had upset her. "Come here."

She slowly made her way toward him. "People from all over the world cook all kinds of different ways. And not everyone has the same taste. But I can show you a few tricks to make a meal taste awesome."

Sniffling, she nodded. "I know I don't cook very *gut*. I'm worried Esther and Lizzie might fire me. But I try to do *mei* best even though *mei mamm* said cooking would never be *mei* strong suit. I do pretty well with pies. I mean, sometimes, but not always. I'm a *gut* cleaner, though, so I was hoping maybe I wouldn't get fired because of *mei* cooking. But they say food is the way to a man's stomach, and . . ."

Jayce took a deep breath, only half hearing as Rose rattled on. He found some fresh herbs, and despite Lizzie's warning, he doctored the eggs a bit more.

Half an hour later everyone was seated in the dining room. Esther and Lizzie were still sleeping. Jayce took a seat in the large room with the others. He would have preferred to eat with Lizzie and Esther in the kitchen, but he was glad they were getting some much-needed rest.

Rose served the meal, and everyone raved. When she nodded to Jayce and opened her mouth to say something, Jayce interjected. "Yes, Rose did an excellent job." He quickly turned to his father, who smirked. At least he didn't humiliate Rose in front of everyone.

Jayce ate as quickly as he could and excused himself. He'd be with his father and the crew most of the day, minus his time alone on the banks of the river cavern. He didn't want to spend a minute longer with the man than he had to.

Rose was sitting at the kitchen table eating eggs and bacon when he walked into the room.

"These eggs are very *gut.*"

He found a tablet of paper and a pen in the kitchen and scribbled down a recipe for chicken salad. "Follow this exactly, and you'll wow Lizzie and Esther at lunch. The rest of us will be gone, but I bet they'll like this recipe, if they have all the ingredients."

"*Danki,* Jayce. I want to cook better. I really do. It's something I'm working on, but it just doesn't come easily to me." She looked over the recipe. "But I can do this."

"I know you can." He pointed upstairs. "I gotta go finish getting ready. You okay?"

Smiling, she nodded. *"Ya."*

It was the briefest conversation he'd had with the woman. Thankfully.

After Jayce brushed his teeth and ran a comb through his hair, he rushed downstairs since he'd seen the others gathering outside already. It was barely daylight, but his father had been insistent they get an early start to film before Bluespring Caverns opened for business. Jayce liked the idea. Maybe he would be able to spend some time with Evelyn, depending on her work schedule. He'd been thinking about her way too much. They could never be more than friends, but her kiss, awkward as it was, consumed his thoughts.

He raced across the living room toward the front door. Rose stood in front of it, a broad smile on her face.

He waited for her to move, but she just smiled. "Hey. Everything okay?" *Please let it be okay.* He didn't have time for one of her lengthy conversations.

"*Ya,* I just wanted to thank you for helping me in the kitchen, and also for leaving me that recipe to try. I'm eager to make the chicken salad." Smiling more broadly, she

281

touched his arm. "Maybe we can spend some time in the kitchen together so I can learn more from you."

"Uh, yeah . . . sure." His eyes shifted to her hand still on his arm. "But right now I have to go. Everyone is getting ready to leave."

"*Ya,* of course." She slowly lowered her arm, winked at him, and stepped aside.

FIFTEEN

Jayce ran alongside Gus's truck as he was backing out of the driveway with both windows open. "Hey, you gonna let me in?"

Gus ground the gears and stopped. "Oh, that's right. I get the pleasure of your company again."

Jayce hurriedly climbed inside and didn't even have his seatbelt pulled across his lap when Gus started moving again. The truck was so old there wasn't a shoulder strap, but Gus's driving warranted the lap strap.

They were quiet for the first few minutes, but Jayce was bothered by Rose's actions. "Okay, so I need to ask your opinion about something." He shook his head. "I've known a lot of women back home, but I don't think it matters how many you know, they are just hard to understand."

"Oh, good grief. Please tell me you're not about to ask me advice about a woman." The old man scowled.

283

Jayce scratched his forehead. "Yeah, it's shocking even to me. But right now you're the only person I've got to ask." He told Gus about Rose touching his arm and winking at him. "I'm making too much of it, right?"

Gus laughed as the buttons of his red-and-white-checkered shirt threatened to pop. "Let me get this straight, kid." He chuckled again. "You're playing all kissy-kissy with the Schrock girl, and now you've got Esther's new help hitting on you too? How many hearts you planning to break before you leave here?"

"I don't want to break anyone's heart." He paused, his thoughts leaning heavily in Evelyn's direction. "Maybe I mistook Rose's appreciation for flirting. She's real bouncy and outspoken." Jayce grimaced as he looked at Gus. "Actually, she's more than outspoken. She talks *all* the time."

"Based on your expression, I'm guessing you don't like to talk. Which would be a surprise to me since you always seem to have a lot to say."

"Not like her," Jayce was quick to say. "She's a beautiful woman, but no way she'd ever be my type."

"Well, you'd best keep in mind the Schrock girl ain't your type either. She's

Amish."

"Really? I hadn't noticed." He grimaced as he rolled his eyes. "Amish or not, I want someone who can have meaningful conversations about things that matter. I have that with Evelyn, even though we haven't known each other very long. She's soft-spoken, but that's only because she thinks things through before she speaks. She gets this look, like a twinkle in her eyes, when she's deep in thought. I love to watch her. It's like you can almost see the wheels spinning in her mind. She's gorgeous, but that's not the only thing I look for in a woman." He paused, knowing he'd said way too much. "Anyway, we're just friends. Gotta be that way."

Gus stared at him long and hard. Jayce wished he'd get his eyes back on the road.

"You're sunk, kid. You already fell for the Schrock girl." He shook his head. "And you're deluded if you think she'd ever leave this place to go frolicking around with you in Los Angeles."

"I don't think that." He paused. "Never mind. I shouldn't have said anything."

"But you did." Gus's belly jiggled again, along with his jowls. He almost looked like a normal, happy person when he laughed. But it always seemed to be at someone else's expense.

"Why are you even going on this trip? I thought you were just an extra in one scene." Jayce was sure Gus was in for a big disappointment when he didn't show up the slightest bit in the film.

The old guy huffed. "Because people almost drown when I'm not there."

He had a point. Jayce ran a hand through his hair. With the windows open, it was blowing all over the place.

"You need a haircut." Gus ground the gears again, missed one, and landed in neutral as he made a turn, then coasted until he finally shifted into the right gear.

"So do you." Jayce eyed the gray ponytail that went a little past Gus's shoulders.

The man actually smiled a little.

Jayce let his thoughts drift back to Evelyn. Gus was right. He had no business getting involved with her romantically. But had the old man also been right about him having already fallen for Evelyn? Jayce had never fallen for anyone so quickly. Maybe he'd just never found the right woman. And that was a terrifying thought since he'd be leaving soon.

When they arrived at the caverns, it was the same drill as the other days. Jayce did almost all of the heavy lifting, and when the boats left the docking area, he stayed be-hind, wishing he had the guts to go with them. It was weird that he felt like Veronica would be safe because Gus, of all people, would be with them. Life had a strange way of twisting things into making sense when they shouldn't.

He sat on the dock. Billy would be in the car outside, likely napping or reading a crime novel. Jayce was going to enjoy some quiet time, then maybe he'd see if Billy wanted to get something to eat. Their other driver, Arlen, had come down with a bad cold not long after they'd arrived. Jayce preferred Billy anyway. Both men were about his father's age, but Arlen's personal-ity tended to mirror his father's. Billy was straightforward and an all-around nice guy.

Jayce studied his surroundings. Stalactites hung low as the river wound around the corner inside the cave. Giovanni had said there were crayfish in the water, and he'd even seen a few bats. But it was dark, only lit by handheld lights most of the time, until they reached the places they were going to film. There Jayce was sure everything was lit up like a baseball stadium.

He said a quick prayer that everyone would stay safe. Then he thought about Eve-lyn. Gus's warning merged with his own, but he couldn't control the way he felt. Or maybe he could. He just didn't want to.

Evelyn managed to sneak out of the house without a lecture from either of her parents. So far, her father hadn't said anything to her, but she'd overheard her parents talking. Her dad wasn't happy she was spending time with an English fellow. Her mother did her best to calm his worry, telling him the situation would phase itself out when Jayce left.

But that fact and her own worries weren't going to deter her from seeing him again. She'd convinced herself that they could remain friends when he went back home. Hopefully, they could write letters or have an occasional phone conversation. She was surprised when she pulled into The Peony Inn and the black limousines weren't there. Neither was Gus's truck, and Jayce had been riding with him.

She tethered her horse, unsure if she should wait outside or go in. The new employee, Rose, came out on the porch and waved, so Evelyn decided it would be rude not to go inside. Jayce had said to pick him up around four o'clock. She was a little early, but not by much. She waved back at Rose, crossed the front yard, and went up the porch steps.

"*Wie bischt*? Are you here to see Lizzie or Esther?" Rose smiled, and Evelyn was momentarily stunned by how pretty she was. She hadn't paid much attention the last time she'd seen her, but now, standing in front of her, it was impossible not to see. "I'm not sure where Esther is. Lizzie was napping earlier. She naps late in the afternoon sometimes. But I have *kaffi* if you'd like to come in. I also have muffins made. Lizzie put a roast in the oven earlier, a really big roast. It smells heavenly in the *haus*." She pushed open the screen. "Come in. I'm happy to have company. We didn't get to talk much when we met."

As Evelyn stepped into the living room she wondered how much anyone else got to say in Rose's presence. "I'm actually here to see Jayce." She kept her focus on Rose to see if the woman's expression fell, but she held her smile.

"Isn't Jayce wonderful? He's teaching me to cook. I'm not very *gut* at it." Her expression soured briefly before she was all smiles again. "He left a chicken salad recipe for me, and Lizzie and Esther were very impressed when I prepared it, so I'm hoping they will just be patient with me as I work on my cooking. I'm not sure how long Jayce will be here, but he's such a *gut* teacher. He puts cottage cheese in eggs. I wasn't sure how that would taste, but all of the guests enjoyed the breakfast." She paused to catch her breath. "And Jayce let me take credit for the meal even though he'd prepared it. Wasn't that nice of him?"

Evelyn nodded, thinking she sure was talking about Jayce a lot. Jealousy was a sin, but it had crept up on her somehow. And Rose lived under the same roof as Jayce.

"How nice to see you, Evelyn." Lizzie came from behind a closed bedroom door, yawning. She turned to Rose. "Hon, why don't you go take a look upstairs and make sure our guests have enough towels and that everything is in order."

"I already did." Rose gleamed. "I've cleaned the bathrooms, refreshed toiletries, and double-checked each room. And there are plenty of towels in the bathrooms."

"I thought I saw that we were running short on lavender soap. There's plenty more in the basement, but can you be a dear and go see if each bathroom has a *gut* supply? That woman . . . um, Quinn . . . mentioned how much she liked it. Maybe put some extras out for her to take home next time you go to the basement."

"Jayce likes the smell of lavender too."

Evelyn felt herself starting to blush. "I use lavender soap, and he mentioned something about it." As she tried to casually shrug, Lizzie stared at her, tipping her head to one side.

"I've been putting a spicier scent in the bathroom that the men are sharing," Rose said. "But I can put some of the lavender soap in theirs too."

"*Ach nee.* I didn't mean he would *use* lavender soap. That's probably a type of soap more for women. He just said he thinks of me when he smells lavender." Evelyn was sure her face was reddening even more. And she was ashamed of herself for being so deliberate, making sure Rose knew Jayce was spoken for, which was hardly the case.

"*Ya,* okay. I'll put extra lavender soap out in the women's bathroom." Rose hurried to the stairs. Once she was out of sight, Lizzie fell onto the couch, leaned her head back, and closed her eyes.

"I thought I'd better come save you." She lifted her head. "That is one sweet *maedel.* She can't cook, but that can be taught. She knows how to clean without a doubt." Moaning, she motioned for Evelyn to sit down on the couch beside her. "But I don't have a clue how to teach her not to talk so much. She wears me out."

"She said she made some chicken salad, a recipe Jayce gave her." Evelyn was fishing for information. She hoped it didn't show. Lizzie and Esther were known matchmakers. If they thought there was even a hint of love in the air, they'd be sharpening their cupid arrows. Maybe they already had hopes that Jayce would stay around for Rose. That seemed unlikely.

Lizzie straightened her prayer covering as she sat taller on the couch. Her bare feet barely touched the floor when she sat all the way back against the cushion. "The chicken salad wasn't bad. But it wasn't really *gut* either. And considering Jayce prepared a fine breakfast, I was surprised lunch wasn't better. But when I checked the recipe, I asked Rose if she'd followed it exactly. She said she'd miscalculated how much salt to use and forgotten the dill weed." Lizzie scrunched her face up, then leaned closer to Evelyn. "How do you miscalculate salt?"

Evelyn grinned.

"I heard her say that food was the way to a man's stomach." Lizzie huffed as she rolled her eyes. "She's going to be an old maid if that's the case."

Lizzie's comments squelched any worries

that she and Esther were playing match-maker between Rose and Jayce. Then Lizzie's eyes lit up. "Hon, I'm always happy when you visit, but are you here to see me or Esther?" She raised an eyebrow. "Or someone else?"

Evelyn cleared her throat and avoided Lizzie's inquiring gaze. "I'm having supper with Jayce." She glanced out the window. "He said four o'clock, but I'm a little early." She finally looked at Lizzie, and Evelyn felt like a fish caught on a hook.

"*Ach,* a date. I see." Lizzie twisted to face Evelyn. "He's a handsome boy."

Evelyn covered her mouth to cough, buying herself some time and hoping to deflect this conversation. "He's not really a boy. He's twenty-two." Her mother had called Jayce a boy too.

"At my age, dear, twenty-two is a boy." She twirled the string of her prayer covering. "He doesn't like his life in Los Angeles, and he doesn't fit in with the rest of them. He and his father don't get along at all. It's sad." She showed off her shiny white dentures. False teeth changed a person's smile. Sometimes for the better, but other times they seemed to distort a person's features. Lizzie's teeth lent cuteness to her unique personality.

Evelyn looked out the window again when she heard footsteps coming up the front porch. "Naomi is here," she said to Lizzie, happy to have a distraction from the conversation. Evelyn could tell where Lizzie was heading.

"*Wie bischt,* Evelyn. Nice to see you." Naomi had a box about twice the size of a shoebox under her arm. "This is for you and Esther."

Lizzie stood. "I hope it isn't heavy. You shouldn't be carrying anything that weighs much." She winked at Naomi.

Pregnancies weren't usually discussed, but prior to Naomi marrying Amos, and before Evelyn started working at the Bargain Center, she and Naomi had been close. Naomi had shared with her that she was having twins.

Naomi passed the box to Lizzie. "It isn't heavy. Amos and I have been cleaning the basement, and we found the box in a corner. I guess we'd never noticed it before, but it has your names on it."

"Goodness me. I don't know how a person would get into this thing. Look at all the tape around it." Lizzie pulled a pair of reading glasses from her apron pocket and looked closer at a small card taped to the box. "Hmm . . . It just says to Esther and

Lizzie. It has to be from our *mamm.*" She eyed the box a moment longer, then excused herself to the bedroom, closing the door behind her.

"Isn't that Esther's bedroom?" Evelyn asked Naomi.

"*Ya,* they are sharing the room for now. Rose is sleeping in Lizzie's room until all these movie people are gone." Naomi put a hand on her belly. With the type of clothing they wore, Evelyn could barely tell her friend was pregnant.

"How are you feeling?" she asked in a whisper, glancing upstairs.

"Rose knows." Naomi laughed. "Probably anyone who has come in contact with Esther or Lizzie knows we are having twins. I'm not sure who is more excited, Amos or the sisters. They will be like *grossmammis* to these *bopplis.*"

"Everything is perfectly ready upstairs," Rose said as she hit the landing. She pointed toward the window. "And just in time. They're back."

Evelyn's stomach flipped.

Lizzie shuffled out of the bedroom, the opened envelope dangling from one hand and the card in the other. "Evelyn, hon, did you see Esther outside when you came in? I haven't seen her in a while."

Evelyn shook her head. "*Nee*, I didn't."

Lizzie turned to Rose.

"She was on the other side of the *haus* earlier, pulling weeds in the flower beds. Do you want me to go get her?" Rose asked the question, but her eyes stayed on the activity outside. Everyone had gotten out of the cars, and they were all gathered in the yard. Gus and Jayce were in the circle as well.

"*Nee*, I'll find her later." She stuffed the envelope, card, and her reading glasses in her apron pocket. The color seemed to have drained from Lizzie's face. She was as ashen as the whitewashed walls.

"Is everything okay?" Naomi touched Lizzie on the arm.

"*Ach ya, ya.*" Lizzie attempted to smile. "Everything is *gut. Danki* for bringing us the package."

"Evelyn is here to pick up Jayce for a date." Rose made the comment with little emotion, void of her usual bubbly manner. It seemed to catch Lizzie's attention and, based on the smile that filled the older woman's face, it was a distraction from whatever was bothering her.

"*Ya*, I know." Holding the smile, she folded her hands in front of her.

Naomi hugged Evelyn. They hadn't seen each other in a while. "Stay away from the basement," Naomi whispered. Then they both laughed. Naomi had told Evelyn about the time Lizzie and Esther locked her and Amos in the basement before they were married. The two had a spat, and the sisters thought they needed time alone to sort things out, so they'd left food and coffee on the stairs and locked the basement door. And it wasn't the first time they'd done such a thing.

"What's wrong with the basement?" Rose raised her eyebrows.

Lizzie sent a look of disapproval at Naomi and Evelyn, who both smiled.

"Nothing, dear," Lizzie said to Rose as she patted her arm. She walked to the door and peered through the screen.

"I'd best go." Naomi eased around Lizzie after telling Rose goodbye. She crossed the yard not far from the group. Quinn and Veronica waved when Naomi did. The others were focused on whatever the man in the middle of the circle was saying. Evelyn assumed that must be Jayce's father. Jayce stared at the ground, his hands stuffed in the pockets of his blue jeans. Lizzie excused herself and went back to the bedroom, closing the door behind her.

Rose eased up to Evelyn near the window. "It's too bad Jayce isn't Amish."

Evelyn thought the same thing but never would have voiced her thoughts.

"But outsiders have been known to convert." Rose gleamed as she looked Evelyn straight in the eyes. Evelyn wasn't sure if she was encouraging her or warning her that she was interested in Jayce.

Of all the English people Evelyn had known over the years, Jayce seemed the least likely to ever convert. "I don't think Jayce would ever consider such an idea. He lives in a very fancy world in California."

Rose raised her chin, grinning. "You never know."

Evelyn didn't want to interrupt the film crew's meeting, but things were starting to feel awkward with Rose. Or maybe she was imagining it. She was glad when Jayce left the group first and headed toward the house. By the look on his face, something was terribly wrong. Evelyn's stomach began to churn.

"*Ach,* it looks like someone's date isn't very happy." Rose rolled her lip into an exaggerated pout.

Lizzie peeked out of the bedroom. "Evelyn, enjoy your date." She smiled, but it looked forced as she turned to Rose. "I need to lie down. If you see Esther, can you tell her I need to talk to her?" Lizzie's face was drawn, and she was still pale.

Rose nodded. After the door closed again, Evelyn was tempted to knock and make sure Lizzie was all right. But Jayce entered the room with his own sour expression.

He didn't say anything to Rose, just nodded for Evelyn to follow him. "You ready?"

She waved at Rose, who barely waved back, and struggled to keep up with Jayce as he hurried ahead of her to the buggy.

She wasn't sure how such a happy environment had gone bad so quickly.

SIXTEEN

Jayce wanted to enjoy his time with Evelyn, but he couldn't shrug off the conversation with his father, although he wanted to more than anything.

"Do you want to drive?" Evelyn asked after she'd maneuvered the buggy out of the driveway. They'd agreed to take her horse and buggy so as not to leave Lizzie without transportation.

"No, I'm fine with you driving." He tried to smile as he slid on his sunglasses. "You're better at it." The eyes were the windows to the soul, or so he'd been told. Right now, he didn't want Evelyn seeing how he felt.

After a while she said, "Do you want to talk about it?"

No surprise she picked up on his foul mood, but if he could keep it at surface level, it would be better for both of them. "It was just a rough day filming." He attempted to force another smile. "At least

300

there weren't any technical equipment failures, and no one almost drowned."

"That's *gut*." She flicked the reins and picked up the pace.

Jayce waited for her to push him to talk more. *Because that's what women do.* But she remained respectfully quiet, as if just allowing him to stay within himself. A part of him was screaming to get out, to spill everything about his horrible day. He wasn't sure he could do it without crying. And he never cried.

But today his father had taken a chunk of his heart and squeezed so hard that Jayce felt physically ill from verbal abuse. Just thinking about it made him want to cry. He needed to focus on something else to get through this dinner, which now felt like a chore.

"How was your day?" It was generic, but maybe she had something to share.

"It was fine. Uneventful." She glanced at him and smiled. "Where would you like to eat?"

"You pick." He heard the distance, the snap in his tone, so he cleared his throat. "Anything is fine with me. Really."

"There's a pizza place that isn't far." She didn't look at him this time. Most likely she was regretting her decision to join him for

301

dinner, or what she called supper. He'd learned the noon meal was referred to as dinner.

"Pizza sounds great." Hard as he tried to sound chipper, he was failing.

He still expected her to pry, to ask what was wrong, but she remained quiet, and Jayce found the sound of the horse hooves striking the gravel in perfect rhythm to be soothing.

When they arrived at the restaurant, he waited while she tethered her horse to a post. He supposed when there were so many Amish people in the area, either you provided a place to tie the horses or you lost business.

Inside, they were seated at a booth and handed menus. After they chose to share a pepperoni pizza and each ordered iced tea, Jayce slouched into the seat and leaned back.

"I'm sorry. I know I'm not in the best mood." He raised an eyebrow, almost daring her to ask him about it.

"We can't be in a *gut* mood all the time." She smiled before taking a sip of tea.

This woman had more patience than any of the therapists Jayce's father had sent him to over the years. The appointments had usually ended with a quick diagnosis and a prescription that made him tired.

Surely some small talk was coming, something to break what was becoming an awkward silence. But Evelyn spread her napkin on her lap, took another sip of tea, and continued to be quiet with a saintly smile.

"My father said some horrible things to me today. But I didn't want tonight to be about my relationship with my dad. I wanted you and me to have a good time, to just chill and get to know each other." He pounded a fist against his chest. "But I am so uptight, and I've been so upset, I feel like I might explode. Or cry." He shook his head. "So instead of burdening you, I'm just apologizing, and I'm hoping you won't judge me by this one night."

Her eyes took on the twinkle he'd noticed before when she was contemplating what to say, as if putting all of her heart and soul into it. "Jayce, only God judges us. And all too often, we judge ourselves. I'm here because I choose to be. If you want to talk about your day, I will listen, but never judge. If you don't want to tell me about it, if it's too painful right now, I understand that too." She paused. "But friends take the *gut* with the bad."

He held her gaze. "Is that what we are — friends?"

"It's all we can be," she was quick to say.

He stared into her eyes. She felt safe, for reasons he couldn't explain. "I hate my life." It was blunt and to the point, but it pretty much summed things up. "If it were up to me, I'd just stay here and never go back to LA."

The waitress came and put a pepperoni pizza between them and handed out two plates. They each slid a slice onto their plates, but neither Jayce nor Evelyn made a move to take a bite.

"Only you can change your life," she said before she peeled a pepperoni off her pizza and nibbled on it. "But I don't think you would be happy here. It's too different from what you're used to."

"Exactly. It's different from all I've ever known and disliked." He took a bite, swallowed, and said, "I've been on vacations to all kinds of places. Even overseas. But that's what they were — vacations. This is a way of life. Simpler, slower, and somehow less confusing."

"You've only been here a week and a half. That's not long enough to get to know a place or the people." She finally quit picking at the pepperonis and took a full bite.

"You're right. But there seems to be a sense of family here that I've never known.

My relationship with my father is horrible, and my mother wasn't exactly the best role model either. I don't want to be a grown man who blames everything on his parents. I take responsibility for my own actions. I never should have hit that guy and gone to jail. I don't usually admit it, but in some ways I've become a pro at holding my temper. I can't even count the number of times I felt the back side of my dad's hand. Until one day I got older and strong enough to grab his arm before it made contact. Now he just lashes out at me verbally. I doubt that's how you grew up."

"It's not." She dabbed at her mouth with her napkin. "But I had to pick a switch plenty of times and was dragged out to the woodshed where spankings were carried out. We weren't spared the rod, as I've heard it said. But I grew up in a loving family. We work hard, we love deeply, and we worship *Gott.* I don't understand how you grew up, and I'm sorry for you. But even here many times *kinner* — children — showed up at school with black eyes or bruises in other places, and I know they didn't hit their head on the coffee table or fall down the stairs. Family abuse and sin are everywhere, and our community isn't immune. *Ya,* we probably live simpler, but not necessarily slower."

She shrugged. "Maybe in some ways. We aren't slaves to a lot of the modern gadgets people today have. But you can't assume a change in scenery alters what is in here." She laid a hand on her heart. "I think you have to reconcile your emotions with your environment."

Jayce stared at her. "How is it that you can be so wise with only an eighth-grade education? Because" — he set down his second piece of pizza — "I've been to therapists with nearly a decade of education, who charge hundreds of dollars per hour, and they haven't made as much sense as you have in the past ten minutes."

"Then pay up," she said around a mouthful of food. Then she smiled, and Jayce actually laughed. He was somehow lighter around her, as if all the burdens he carried like lead on his shoulders had lost their heaviness.

"I could just stay here, you know. Nothing is keeping me in California." It was true. He'd distanced himself from most of his friends who were living a lifestyle that wasn't attractive to him anymore.

"*Ya*, you could stay here. Just make sure you do it for the right reasons." She put her hand over her heart. "You have to fix this just as much as your physical surroundings."

"I don't know how to do that. My relationship with my father weighs me down more than anything. It seems like physical distance from him would help heal what's inside." He was finally ready to tell her what had happened.

"Usually my dad takes every available opportunity to embarrass or humiliate me in front of people. This trip, it's been the crew and actors. But today we weren't around anyone when he laid into me about not getting on the boat. They needed an extra set of arms to hold some lights above the deepest part of the water. They were a person short. He used words I'm not going to repeat, but it was the most demeaning he'd ever been to me, even since I was a kid."

He wasn't about to retell the conversation in its entirety. His father had used words that would really offend Evelyn, probably some she'd never heard before, and he certainly didn't want to have to explain the meaning. "And despite everything, I pray. I pray all the time. I believe in the power of prayer, but I'm wondering when God is going to give me a little direction about how to change my life. I'm not sure just moving out of my dad's place is going to do it." He shook his head.

Evelyn knew it was not her responsibility to minister to others, but Jayce's undeniable pain screamed for answers. Answers she couldn't give him.

"God answers our prayers in ways we can't foresee, in His time frame. I wish I could tell you what to do, or even say something to make you feel better. But it's your journey, Jayce." She gently tugged on her ear. "Listen for the voice of *Gott*. Sometimes His words are subtle, but the more time you spend in tune with Him, the easier it becomes to hear His wisdom."

Without realizing it she was ministering to Jayce, but the words weren't her own. God had led her into this man's life for a reason. They had little hope of ever being more than friends, no matter how attracted they were to each other. But Evelyn had small steppingstones on the path that was Jayce's journey. She wasn't going to abandon the trail.

"I am really going to try to do that." He reached for a third slice of pizza.

"On a positive note, you never seem to lose your appetite, no matter your situation or mood." She laughed.

"Ha-ha." He smiled. "I figure I'd better fill up in case Rose gets turned loose in the kitchen again. It's like a race for me, Lizzie, or Esther to get to the kitchen before Rose starts a meal."

"I spent some time with her today before you returned to the inn. I think she fancies you." She playfully batted her eyes at him, just to see his reaction.

"She can fancy me —" A flash of humor crossed his face. "That's a cute word, by the way. She can *fancy* me all she wants. She's not my type." He looked up at the ceiling. "Lord, forgive me." Locking eyes with Evelyn, he said, "She never shuts up. I mean, never."

"She does talk a lot, but she'll find her mate." Relief that she shouldn't have felt washed over Evelyn.

"Probably someone who never says a word or barely talks." He flinched. "I didn't intend for that to sound mean. She's just not my type. *You're* my type." His eyes widened, as did hers. "Oh wow. I can't believe I just said that. I mean, it's true, but wow." He shook his head. "Sorry. I guess it's because that awkward kiss still dances around in my mind."

Evelyn covered her face with her hands. "I'll never understand how I let that happen." She giggled. "I'm surprised you ever wanted to see me again."

"Are you kidding? I'm still waiting for a chance to perfect it, when we're both willing participants."

She wadded up her napkin and threw it at him before looking around to make sure no one saw.

Surprisingly, he caught it with one hand. "You know what?"

She waited, her heart pounding at the thought of kissing him properly. "I would do anything to be able to get in that boat Monday and prove to my father I'm not half the words he called me, just because some enclosed places freak me out." His face turned red. "I'd do anything to just step into one of those boats like it was no big deal."

"If you want to do it, do it for yourself." She paused. "I could go with you as a practice run, if you want. I have a friend who is a guide there. Hardly anyone goes on the morning tours, and I'm sure I could convince him to take us by ourselves. And I'd be with you. Maybe you wouldn't feel all that pressure with your father around and the entire crew. But, Jayce . . . if you aren't comfortable with the idea, please don't hesitate to tell me. I was just thinking we'd have *mei* friend there guiding us, so it wouldn't be like being on a boat with a dozen other people. He could turn the boat around and go back at any time. There would be no one to keep you inside the cave."

"Really?" He gazed into her eyes. Even though she was disappointed he'd veered from the conversation about the kiss, the way he was looking at her now felt even more intimate. "You would do that?"

"Of course."

"No." He shook his head hard. "We can't."

"I completely understand, and —"

"No. You don't understand. Giovanni said he saw bats in the cave today."

Evelyn's stomach began to churn. She'd always gone to the caves when she was younger during the heat of the summer because the bats were said to mostly be inside the cavern during the winter. It was spring, so she had assumed there wouldn't be anything that flew inside. She sat taller. "Then we face our fears together."

"No. I can't let you do that. You're not having near the issues I am at the moment. You'll face your fear of flying things when you're ready."

Evelyn knew she'd never be ready, and the opportunity was staring her in the face, with pleading eyes he probably didn't know he was showing. "Don't you think I get embarrassed when butterflies get near me and I go all crazy? Why not face the scariest of all the flying creatures that haunt me?" She cringed.

He stared at her and didn't say anything.

"We could go tomorrow. We don't have worship service. If it worked out well, you could surprise your father on Monday. But even more, you'd be proving something to yourself that might help you with enclosed spaces in the future." She shrugged. "And besides, I've been in the boats and gone through Bluespring plenty of times and never seen a single bat." Although the fact that Jayce's friend had seen bats today didn't bode well for tomorrow.

"We can do this." Jayce's expression was tight with strain, but his voice was filled with hope.

"*Ya,* we can." Evelyn knew she didn't sound quite as confident, but there was a bonus to the entire ordeal. Being mostly alone with Jayce in a dimly lit area. She would pray that everything went well for both of them. "But it's too far to go in a buggy. We hired drivers when we went as *kinner* — children, I mean."

"I can take one of the limos, but will your

folks be upset?"

"Well, Millie can't make the trip. They know it's too far for a horse. And it doesn't make sense to hire a driver when you have access to a car."

"Okay."

When she dropped him back at the inn, he hugged her and kissed her cheek. It seemed appropriate for friends. And that's what they were, she reminded herself.

Then she decided to start praying early that tomorrow went well.

SEVENTEEN

Esther and Lizzie sat propped up in bed, lanterns lit on both of their nightstands. They stared at the box Naomi had brought over, along with the envelope and card that had been taped to the outside.

"We're not meant to open that box." Esther shook her head. On the outside of the envelope, she recognized her mother's handwriting. *Esther and Lizzie.* But after they'd read the card, it didn't appear the contents were for them. The short note only said:

It is important to me that Gus be given this box after *mei* passing.

Leib,
Mamm

Lizzie pulled her long gray hair over her shoulder, twisting it into a wet rope that was dripping on the sheet. Esther gently slapped her hand. "Stop that."

Lizzie groaned as she released the mass of hair. "Of course we're meant to open it." She picked up the envelope and pointed. "See, here are our names."

Esther wanted nothing more than to tear into that box. Maybe there was a clue inside about why their mother had made them promise to let Gus live in the cottage.

"And that envelope was barely taped to the box, easy for us to pull off." Esther shook her head again, her wet hair pinned in a bun on top of her head. "Look at the amount of tape wrapped around the box. There are layers of it."

"That doesn't mean we aren't supposed to open it." Lizzie picked up the box and shook it. "It's not very heavy, but it's not files or papers. More like a football hitting the sides of the box, or maybe something a little heavier but about the same size."

"It doesn't feel right to open it." Esther's fingers itched to get a knife and start cutting through the packing tape that had yellowed over time. Even the envelope and card were discolored with a light brownish tint, making Esther wonder how long ago her mother had written the note and packed the contents.

"Maybe *Mamm* had an affair, and Gus is

our long-lost *bruder.*" Lizzie covered her face with her hands and moaned. "Just shoot me if that's the case. The thought of sharing the same DNA with that man makes *mei* toes curl."

"*Ach,* hush now. You've brought that up before, and we both know *Mamm* never would have done anything like that."

"Then why, oh why, have we been forced to tolerate that man for the remainder of our time here on Earth? These are supposed to be our golden years, but Gus tarnishes each and every one of them."

Esther recalled asking Gus about his arrangement with their mother. He'd said, *"If she wanted you to know, I reckon she would have told you."* Since Gus wouldn't reveal any information about their relationship, it was even more of a mystery.

"Gus isn't Amish, for one thing. And he's only been around for eleven or twelve years." Esther tucked loose strands of hair back into the bun on her head.

Lizzie sat straighter as her eyebrows arched mischievously. "Thus the term 'long-lost *bruder.*' He could have returned like a prodigal *sohn.*"

"He's not our *bruder.* There must be something else." Esther shrugged. "Or maybe it's just personal papers *Mamm* had been holding on to for Gus. Maybe it's his birth certificate, or a passport, or medical records." She raised and lowered her shoulders again. "Things like that. They could be inside another container inside the box."

"You're probably right." Lizzie lifted the box onto her lap. "So there's no harm opening it." She picked at the tape with a fingernail. "Go get a knife."

Esther yanked the box from her sister's lap and placed it at the foot of the bed. "We're not opening it. We will give it to Gus, and it will be up to him whether or not to tell us what's inside."

Lizzie glared at the box but didn't reach for it again. She rolled her lip into a pout, even more pronounced without her dentures in. "I don't like that idea, Esther."

"I'm as curious as you are, but it just doesn't feel right to open it." She thought for a few moments. "What do we know about Gus?" Before Lizzie had time to list Gus's bad qualities, she said, "We know he has a *dochder,* but do you know if he was ever married?"

"I think *Mamm* mentioned it once, but I don't remember for sure." Lizzie pointed to the box. "There might be a marriage certificate in there."

"The first year he had Thanksgiving with

us, he mentioned he'd worked at a meat market and said that was why he should carve the turkey." Esther tapped a finger to her chin. "What else do we know about that man?"

"That he's cranky, rude, and mean." Lizzie huffed. "And he only cares about himself."

Esther eyed the box as other memories came into her mind. "But he was also very *gut* to me during my medical tests and appointments." She turned to Lizzie and widened her eyes. "And just this past week, he saved that actress's life by jumping in the water to rescue her."

Lizzie fell back against her pillow and moaned again. "You give him way too much credit, and his *dochder* doesn't seem to care for him either."

Esther told Lizzie about Gus inviting Heather to the short screening of the movie clip. "I'm surprised she agreed to attend since they fought so badly during her visit last year," Esther said. She shivered as she recalled the vicious words father and daughter had thrown at each other.

"Maybe she thinks he's getting money for being a background person." Lizzie cackled. "We both know that mouthy boss man just gave Gus a role so he wouldn't whine about the generators on those buses."

Esther's heart hurt for Gus. "I overheard Mr. Clarkson say he had no intention of including Gus in the movie background. Gus is going to be humiliated if his daughter is there just to see him in a movie." She waited for Lizzie to laugh or make a snide remark, but her sister just twisted her mouth from side to side and stayed quiet.

"Maybe I should tell Gus what I overheard." Esther recalled the way he pleaded with her to attend, saying how nervous he would be without her there.

"Maybe." Lizzie pressed her lips together.

Esther was surprised Lizzie wasn't latching onto any information she could throw in Gus's face. Maybe there was a tiny soft spot for Gus buried somewhere in Lizzie's psyche, even if she didn't realize it.

"But what if I'm wrong or overheard incorrectly? I could be stirring up trouble for nothing." Esther eyed the box, her temptation bubbling to a boil, but she was compelled to do what she believed was right in her heart. "Well, we are going to give the box to him."

Lizzie groaned like she was in misery. "Whatever's in it might answer questions that have plagued us forever."

Esther rolled onto her side and extinguished her lantern. She reread the card in the light still shining from Lizzie's lantern, then put it and the envelope in the drawer of her nightstand. "I will give it to him tomorrow."

Lizzie grumbled, but she extinguished her lantern too.

Evelyn woke up around three in the morning swatting at something flying around her room. She opened her eyes and realized she'd been dreaming. In a few hours she'd be picked up by Jayce and going inside Bluespring Caverns. Jayce was surely a nervous wreck, and he probably thought she was silly for being afraid of flying creatures, even butterflies. Maybe she should have explained why they frightened her. She had enough stories to justify her fears.

She rolled onto her side and laid an arm across the bed, briefly picturing Jayce beside her. It was a vision that would never go full circle, and a tinge of guilt wrapped around her for having such thoughts. It might have been his handsome features she was attracted to first, but his vulnerability was refreshing as well. It couldn't have been easy for him to tell her about his claustrophobia. She said another prayer that he'd do okay today, because he'd surely be embarrassed if he panicked. She added another prayer for no bats too.

After finally drifting back to sleep, she ended up oversleeping and rushing to get dressed and downstairs. Her mother was cleaning the breakfast dishes when she walked into the kitchen. Her brothers had likely retreated upstairs, and Evelyn knew her father had climbed back in bed to read the newspaper, which he did every other Sunday when they didn't have worship service. Her family truly observed the day of rest. Although today wouldn't be peaceful for her or Jayce.

"Sorry, *Mamm.* I woke up in the middle of the night, and it took me a while to get back to sleep."

"It's Sunday. I suppose you're excused." Her mother stood by the sink and dunked a stack of dishes in the soapy water. "But I see you're dressed, complete with *kapp* and shoes and socks. Are you going out?" She glanced at the clock on the wall. "It's still early."

"Um, *ya,* I'm going out." She bit her bottom lip and waited for the questions to come.

"Hmm . . ." Her mother didn't turn around. "Are you off to see that boy?"

"*Mamm,* he's not a boy. I told you that.

And we're just friends."

"*Ya,* you told me. He's a man, and you're just friends. So where are you off to?" She turned off the water, eased around, and leaned against the counter.

"Bluespring Caverns."

Her mother raised her eyebrows. "The few times we went as a family were in the middle of the summer when there weren't any bats in the cave. I'm not sure about spring. Are you nervous about the possibility of seeing them?"

"A little." Evelyn didn't want to tell her mother about Jayce's fear. She would think Evelyn was putting herself at risk to ease his burden, not her own. And that might imply she cared more for Jayce than she was admitting to her mother. "But he's never been inside the cave, and he doesn't have to work today."

"I'll say it again." She pointed a finger at Evelyn. "Be careful."

"I know what I'm doing." Later she would ask God to forgive the tiny fib. She didn't know what she was doing at all. "And, *Mamm . . .* he's picking me up in a fancy car, but only because it's the only type of car they have with them."

"You'd best enjoy it then." Her mother

chuckled. "And hope your father doesn't see."

She gave her mother a quick hug, then left when she heard Jayce pull in. She'd told him not to come to the door, that she'd meet him outside, hoping her father would be in his bedroom reading.

Jayce opened her car door. After she sat down, she looked through an open window behind her. She'd never seen such luxury, and she was still gawking when Jayce got in the car. "Nice, huh?"

"*Ya,* it is." Something smelled good. She wasn't sure if it was Jayce or the car. It was a minty aroma.

Jayce was quiet, and Evelyn wondered if he wanted to bypass this challenge for both of them.

"You *can* change your mind, you know." A big part of her hoped he would.

He quickly shook his head. "Nope. I woke up in the middle of the night thinking about it, but I really think if I can push through this, maybe it will help when I find myself in, uh, well . . . an elevator." He chuckled. "I'm in pretty good shape, but climbing stairs going any higher than the tenth floor begins to wear on a guy." He waited until she looked at him. "I was just lucky my dad's place is only on the third floor. Are you having any second thoughts?"

She shook her head, and they were quiet again. Finally, she asked, "Why do you think you're afraid of being in small spaces? Did something happen to make you that way?"

He tugged at his ear. "Hmm . . . no. Not that I can think of. I've just always been uncomfortable. I guess that's kind of an understatement. What about you?"

She figured she would try to justify her fear, especially since it included butterflies.

"Do you really want to hear this? I have had a lot of things happen with flying creatures, mostly birds." She flinched, then took a deep breath.

"Only if you want to tell me." He cocked his head to one side, peering curiously at her before focusing on the road again.

"When I was young, *mei mamm* let me stay over at a friend's *haus*. There were four of us girls spending the night." She sighed. "The girl who lived there had a *bruder* who had two parakeets. It was late at night, and we only had one lantern lit super low. Buddy, her *bruder,* threw the birds in her room and closed the door. They were flying around hitting the walls, running into us, and I'm surprised the lantern didn't get knocked over and burn the *haus* down." She shuddered. "It was bad for us, but also for the birds." She glanced at him to see if he was smiling, but he was just listening intently. "It was all that flapping and the way they were bumping into us and the walls."

"I guess that could make a person uncomfortable around birds." Jayce said it more as a question than a confirmation.

"It's not just that. Other things have happened." She looked his way again, and he raised an eyebrow. "*Mamm* took me, Lucas, and David to McDonald's one time when we were pretty young. I was probably six or seven. We had hired a driver to go to Bloomington. I think *Mamm* had a doctor's appointment. It was a treat because we rarely went out to eat. We sat outside because it was a pretty day." She shuddered again as she recalled what happened. "A bird actually flew down and snatched one of my French fries. Not *Mamm*'s or *mei bruders'*, but mine."

He laughed. "Sorry, I know it's not funny."

Evelyn fought not to grin. "Another time at the zoo, a big huge bird was flying loose in the building where the birds were housed. It kept swooping down at me. And once I was minding *mei* own business walking down the street. There was a line of trees, some with branches hanging over the road.

A bird flew down and pecked me on the head."

Jayce chuckled again. "Sorry."

"I know it sounds funny. *Mamm* said I probably walked underneath a branch with a nest and babies, and that it probably upset the mama bird." Hearing how it sounded, she laughed. "Silly things, I suppose. But bees, wasps, and hornets also seem to find me." She thought about the bats she might see in the cave today, and her stomach roiled. She didn't feel like laughing anymore.

Jayce turned down the radio in the fancy car. It had been on low while they talked. Not smiling, he asked, "Why butterflies? They're so delicate and pretty."

"They flutter." She crinkled her nose. "I guess I just don't do well with anything that has wings."

"You'd better hope we don't see any bats." Jayce made the statement in a tone far too serious, which caused Evelyn's stomach to flip again. "Are you sure you want to do this?"

"*Ya.*" She wouldn't admit it, but she mostly wanted to do it for him. Even if there were bats in the cave, they'd be far away from her. For Jayce to make the journey, it could be life changing. "Don't bats just hang upside-down from the ceiling?"

"Yeah, I think so." Jayce slowed the car when the cavern entrance came into view. Evelyn had already spoken to her friend Adam, who worked there. Most people didn't take the early tours, but he'd assured her that even if other people were there, he would make sure it was just Evelyn and Jayce in the boat. She appreciated that Adam didn't make fun of either of them when she told him they both wanted to face a phobia. She'd known Adam all her life. He was two years younger than her, and one of two Amish people who worked at the caverns.

Evelyn took a deep breath.

Jayce put the car in park as he stared at the walkway leading to the entrance. He'd woken up this morning knowing this was a bad idea. He was pretty sure the bats would stay in place, hanging from the top of the cave. But he ran the risk of making a total fool of himself. He could already feel the sweat beading on his forehead. His stomach growled from being hungry, but he hadn't been about to eat breakfast this morning. The potential for it to come up was too great.

He liked Evelyn, probably way more than

he should. But the reality was, he'd be leaving and didn't ever have to see her again. No matter how humiliated he might be in front of her, he wouldn't have to face her again. And even though he wanted to do this for himself, if he was able to get in the boat tomorrow with the rest of the crew, it would prove to his father that he'd conquered this fear, at least this once. And hopefully, he would be helping Evelyn too.

They walked into the small gift shop and up to the counter. Jayce paid for two tickets, and Evelyn introduced him to Adam, their guide for the hour-long tour.

"I've seen you around," Adam said as they made the trek down the four hundred feet to get to the water's edge. Then they took a right, and he saw the four boats docked. "You've been with that film crew. Evelyn said the man making the film is your *daed*." He flinched. "*Mei* friend was the one driving the boat the day the big man jumped in the water to save that lady."

"Gus." He forced a smile and nodded as he wondered who he would be most embarrassed in front of — Evelyn? Or another man? "Did Evelyn tell you why we're doing this?" He stopped, a little breathless from the long walk, although the return trip going uphill was much worse.

"*Ya,* she did." Adam was a tall, lanky guy with a friendly smile. He had on the normal Amish garb. "No worries, *mei* friend. This is usually an hour tour — about a half hour down the river and a half hour back. But since no one else is in the boat, we can turn back in five minutes if you want."

Jayce tossed his head back, then ran a hand through his hair. "Man, this makes me sound like such a wimp." He shook his head, still eyeing the boat without making an effort to follow the guide onto the metal structure. Evelyn seemed to be waiting for him to take the lead.

Adam smiled in a friendly, sympathetic sort of way. "I've had to turn back with a dozen people onboard. You'd be surprised how many people have a problem with being so far underground and on a river. Most of them were surprised they reacted the way they did." He laughed. "And you wouldn't believe how many cameras and cell phones are resting on the bottom of the river."

Jayce had intentionally not looked up details about the cavern, particularly how deep the water was. As he finally stepped into the boat on shaky legs, he could see the bottom. The water here couldn't have been more than three or four feet deep. It was bound to be much deeper the farther in they went. And he could see ahead that it was only a few yards before the boat would turn and daylight would be out of sight. He'd watched his father and the crew make the turn, and he'd been able to hear them talking for about a minute more before it was quiet.

He turned to Evelyn when he realized she hadn't gotten on the boat and was still standing on the dock. Somewhere along the line, the color had drained from her face, and her green doe eyes looked bigger than normal.

"You okay?" Adam asked. Jayce wished he would have asked first.

"*Ya,*" she replied. Adam offered her his hand and helped her into the boat. She sat down when Jayce did.

"Ready?" Adam had his hand on the rope to untie the boat from the dock.

Jayce had never been more unprepared for anything in his life. Then he felt Evelyn slip her hand into his, intertwining their fingers. Maybe they would be okay after all.

EIGHTEEN

Esther delivered the last tray of appetizers to the crew. They had gathered in the dining room again and moved in extra chairs and two folding tables since the gatherings had become daily.

After she asked if anyone needed anything, she went to her bedroom and picked up the mysterious box. As she crossed through the living room, she almost bumped into Lizzie.

"Don't say a word," Esther said as she stopped to face off with her sister. "I firmly believe that it should be up to Gus whether or not he shares the contents of the box." She raised her chin, ready for a new round of squabbling with her sister.

Surprisingly, Lizzie just frowned and marched to their bedroom.

As Esther closed the distance between the main house and the cottage, she noticed the generators on the motor homes weren't running. Maybe the film people decided to save on propane while they were having their meeting in the dining room. Whatever the reason, it was a bright sunny day, and it was quiet. Maybe those factors would entice Gus to be in a decent mood.

Esther ambled up the stairs and knocked.

"What?" he said as the door flew open. Then he closed his eyes, gave his head a quick shake, and said, "I mean, hello, Esther. How are you today?"

Esther pressed her lips together, but it didn't stop her from grinning.

"So now I'm doing what you asked, addressing you like you want" — he paused, frowning — "and you're laughing at me."

Esther arched an eyebrow. "I'm not laughing at you, Gus. I'm laughing with you. *Danki* for remembering the proper way to speak to someone."

"I guess I'm supposed to ask if you want to come in." He grumbled, turned around, and left the door open.

Esther didn't want to go in, but she followed him, noticing the place wasn't as tidy as it was on her last visit. But it also wasn't the pigsty it had been before Rose cleaned it. Their new employee had the day off on Sundays.

"What's that?" Gus stood in his living room and pointed at the box.

332

It wasn't until she handed it to him that she wanted to change her mind, take it back, and rip into it. But she'd stick with her original plan.

"Naomi found it in the basement at the *daadi haus.* There was a card with *mei* and Lizzie's names on it — a card from *Mamm.* She'd written that this package was to be delivered to you. I'm sorry if it's been there since her passing. There was so much stuff in that basement. We just never went through it all." She folded her hands in front of her. "But now you have it."

Gus stared at the box, a grave expression on his face. "Okay."

Esther brushed invisible wrinkles from her apron, stalling for time. She'd expected more from Gus, at least a hint as to what might be inside, or if he even knew the contents. Gus's cat, Whiskers, stretched from where she was napping on a rug in the corner.

He set the box on the couch. "Anything else?" He looked at Esther as he folded his arms across his big belly.

"*Nee,* I suppose not." She chewed her bottom lip, eyeing the mysterious find again. "Maybe the package contains important papers?"

"No." Gus walked to the door, which was

still open. He stepped aside, motioning for Esther to step over the threshold.

"You're welcome," she said coolly as she shot him a fake smile.

"Oh. Yeah. Thanks." He looked around Esther. "One of the limos is gone. I saw the kid take off in it early this morning."

Esther had noticed a car missing. "I figured it was Jayce. He doesn't seem to enjoy the meetings the rest of them have in our dining room. It's a beautiful day for a drive, although I'd choose a buggy over a car. Jayce carted Evelyn to eat in one of our buggies not long after he arrived."

"I'm sure that's who he's with now. Or maybe the other gal that has the hots for him. Your new girl, Rose Petal."

Esther slapped her hands to her hips. "I told you not to call her that. And what makes you think she fancies Jayce?" She liked the boy a lot, but he'd be leaving soon and she didn't want to see either girl get hurt.

Gus laughed, his belly jiggling. "That kid actually asked me for my thoughts about women. Can you believe that?"

"In all seriousness, *nee,* I can't." She tried to envision Jayce questioning Gus about anything to do with females or relationships.

"Well, it ain't the new gal he's after. Said

334

she talks too much."

Esther grinned. "The *maedel* does have a lot to say."

"I wouldn't be surprised if those two — the Schrock girl and Jayce — end up together." Gus grunted. "He probably hasn't thought about everything he'd have to give up to be with an Amish girl. But he ain't like all those others." He waved an arm in the direction of the inn. "I had the misfortune to have to take him back and forth to the movie shoots in my truck. I think he'd prefer to live on a farm somewhere out here, and the kid probably has the money to do it." Gus laughed. "He'd probably change his mind in the summer months. Took me a while to get used to no air conditioning when I first moved in here."

"It would be nice if he stayed on, but a relationship with Evelyn would be a bit more complicated." Esther's wheels were already turning. A little matchmaking side project might be the distraction she and Lizzie needed to get their minds off what was in the box. Or provide some much-needed relief from hosting the film crew. She recalled Lizzie's ridiculous attempt to make the couple feel romantic by loading up the buggy with vanilla. Esther and Lizzie worked better as a team when a situation warranted their skills. "Evelyn is a lovely girl. And we like Jayce a lot."

Gus scratched his head. "You just said it would be complicated, but that hasn't ever stopped you and your crazy sister from trying to get couples together."

"*Ya,* I know." She smiled. "We like a *gut* love story. But only once have we ever successfully matched up a non-Amish person with someone here in our community. Most of the time, outsiders don't want to make the changes that would be necessary."

"I didn't say he'd ever convert to your religious stuff. I just said he don't fit in with the rest of them, and he's mentioned how he wished he could stay."

"Hmm . . ." Esther tapped a finger to her chin. She was surprised that Gus talked about Jayce as if he might actually like him. Conversations with Gus about others almost always included negativity. The boy must have grown on him a little too.

Her grumpy renter smiled. "Go get 'em, Esther." He shook a fist in the air. "Go get wacky Lizzie, and you two go do your thing. Might not be bad to have the kid around."

Esther's mouth was still hanging open after he closed the door. Gus didn't like anyone, but he clearly liked Jayce, which was completely unexpected considering the huge differences in their lifestyles and demeanors.

As she walked back to the house, she was a tiny bit excited to talk to Lizzie about the possibility of Jayce and Evelyn becoming a couple. It seemed like a long shot. But seeing the way Gus had acted today left her hopeful that all things were possible. And she knew that to be true. *Through Christ who strengthens us.*

Esther had been working on Gus, trying to teach him to be polite and civil to folks. The man had a long way to go, but today was proof of Esther's and the Lord's efforts. Gus was coming around.

As she walked up the porch steps, she thought about Evelyn and Jayce. The more she pondered, the easier it was to see them together. She hoped they were enjoying each other's company today, but she also said a quick prayer that no one would get hurt. She also prayed that she and Lizzie would follow the Lord's lead when it came to Jayce and Evelyn.

After she found Lizzie in the bedroom folding towels on the bed, she told her everything Gus had said. "It would be exciting if he stayed on, don't you think?"

Lizzie shrugged. "*Ya,* he's a nice kid. But he's not Amish, and that changes things up a little."

Esther blinked in surprise. Lizzie was the one always jumping on the romantic bandwagon, even if the odds of the couple getting together were slim.

Lizzie picked up the towels. "I'm going to take these upstairs while the movie people are still in the dining room." She frowned. "They eat a lot more when Rose isn't cooking."

Esther sighed. "I know."

Lizzie walked out, leaving Esther to wonder if maybe her sister was madder about the box than she'd let on. Then Esther walked to the window, closed her eyes, and prayed again that Evelyn and Jayce were having a good day, whatever they were doing.

Jayce couldn't believe how wigged out Evelyn was. They'd barely rounded the corner when she started trembling and squeezing his hand. It was fairly dark with only the dimly lit running lights on the boat and a small light attached to Adam's hat. He'd swapped out his Amish straw hat before they left. Twice Adam had asked if they wanted to go back, and Evelyn shook her head both times.

At some point Jayce's arm had found its

way around Evelyn, and he held her snug against him. "You okay?" he whispered. She nodded but was quiet.

Adam rattled on with a constant stream of information about the caverns, how they were discovered, how deep the water was, and a bunch of other details Jayce wasn't retaining. He was sure Evelyn wasn't processing the information, either, as her eyes jetted back and forth, especially near low ceilings. Adam kept his focus on maneuvering the boat while he talked.

"I got you," Jayce said as he pulled Evelyn even closer. "Nothing's going to happen on my watch."

Adam pointed out various water creatures, then paused. "Evelyn, you okay? Jayce?"

Jayce looked up to see they were at a dead end. He'd been so worried about Evelyn and the way she was trembling, he hadn't had time to panic. Until now.

Evelyn knew what happened at this juncture. They were at the halfway point. The guides always turned off the lights so visitors could see how truly dark it was in the cave. She was pretty sure, under the circumstances, Adam wouldn't suggest that. And he didn't.

As they started back, Evelyn realized she'd

held her breath half the time, snuggled into the safety of Jayce's arms, and hadn't asked him once how he was doing.

"Is this as awful as you thought it would be?" She stayed close to him, the feel of his arm around her a memory she'd carry home with her and cherish later.

He flinched. "It's not something I'd want to do all the time, but I'll do it tomorrow and show my dad I can. But . . ." He got close to her ear and whispered, "I know you were nervous. I could feel it. Somehow, that kept me distracted. I wanted to be sure you were okay." His lips brushed her earlobe on the way to her cheek where he kissed her softly, sending a rush of emotion flooding over her.

As he stared into her eyes, she realized she'd never wanted a man to kiss her more than at this very moment. She eased out of his embrace and faced him. "I'm glad we did this."

"I'm glad it's half over." Jayce smiled as he cupped her cheek.

It was coming — the kiss — and she didn't want it to be in front of Adam. Her eyes drifted in his direction. Adam cleared his throat.

"We omitted one part of the tour," Adam said as he winked at Evelyn. "But I think you two did so well, you might want to experience the lights-out part."

Jayce stiffened as he lowered his hand. "Uh, lights out? For how long?"

"However long we want," Evelyn said softly as she brought his hand back to her cheek, holding it there while her eyes found his and held his gaze.

"I think I'm ready," Jayce said as a slow smile swept across his face.

Then everything went black, and even though Evelyn couldn't see the look in Jayce's eyes, she knew what he looked like right now. She felt it through his touch and the overwhelming emotion that came through in his kiss. He was slow and thoughtful at first, gradually becoming more exploratory, almost as if he was speaking to her with his mouth. And she was answering with all her heart. His closeness seemed comfortable and familiar, yet new and exciting at the same time, sending her stomach into a wild swirl. The kiss seemed to go on forever, and Evelyn had no desire for it to end.

When the lights finally came back on, she wiggled free, but Jayce and Adam laughed. "Caught!" Adam said.

Evelyn covered her face with her hands at first but eventually laughed along with them.

When they got back to the boat ramp, Adam began to tie up the boat. "Evelyn, you did really *gut,*" he said before he straightened and turned to Jayce. "And you seemed to do okay too." He paused, grinning. "Better than okay."

Evelyn took a deep breath. "I counted eight," she said as she squeezed her eyes closed.

"I wondered if you saw them." Adam took his hat off, then wiped a sleeve across his moist forehead. "I wasn't about to point them out."

"Eight what?" Jayce glanced back and forth between them.

"*Ach,* you must not have seen them." Adam counted on his fingers. "There were eight bats. Two of them were low hanging when we were all the way in the back. I was waiting for Evelyn to come unhinged, but you had her." He paused. "And I guess she had you too."

Evelyn latched onto Jayce's hand when he offered to help her out of the boat. "You thought I was trembling like that because I was afraid I *might* see a bat?"

"Um, yeah."

She laughed. "I just assumed you saw them too."

Adam waved. "I've got to go check on

things inside. Just make the hike up whenever you're ready."

"*Danki,* Adam. *Danki* so much." Evelyn might have hugged him if he wasn't on the other side of Jayce.

"Yeah, thanks a lot." Jayce extended his hand to Adam.

After Adam was out of earshot, Jayce smiled. "I need to take back something I said."

"Uh-oh. What's that? Were you not truthful? Was it worse than you said?" She felt horrible that she hadn't done more to help him with the experience, but he hadn't seemed to need it.

"Earlier, when I said I wouldn't want to do this every day . . ." He cupped her cheeks in his hands. "I think I would enjoy doing this every day."

He kissed her, and the ground shifted beneath her. Not a bat or any other winged creature could have pulled her out of the moment as she kissed him back with all the passion and emotion she could feel coming from him.

"Just like in the dark, that was a much better kiss than the first one I offered you," she said, grinning.

"I don't know. Let's see." He leaned in again, but when she heard footsteps, Evelyn knew a guide with a group was coming, so they separated and started the trek back up to daylight.

"Wow," Jayce said when they emerged from the cave. "I'm proud of us, but I'm even more proud of you. I had no idea you saw bats. Maybe butterflies won't seem so scary now."

She smiled as he opened her car door. "It all goes back to the fluttering," she said as she wagged a finger at him.

Before they left the parking lot, Jayce looked at her for a long time, then refocused on the road. "I enjoyed today, and that's not something I thought I'd be saying."

Evelyn had enjoyed certain aspects of their day, too, but she just nodded. Her thoughts were flying all over the place.

He glanced her way. "You know, we don't dress alike, and our lifestyles aren't anywhere close to the same, but are we really so different?"

Evelyn knew people who had gotten involved with outsiders, and it usually didn't go well. She was tempted to tell him, *"Oh, Jayce, you have no idea how truly different we are."* She calculated a list in her mind — the electricity issue, driving a car, detachment from outsiders as much as possible, an eighth-grade education on her end, the clothing . . . She could have gone on, but those were not the important things. Jayce had a good relationship with God. He was still finding his way, but so was she. And the fact that they could have healthy discussions about it meant more to Evelyn than the tangible differences. For her, that understanding of each other was more important than all the passion in the world. She'd loved her heavenly Father her entire life. She'd only met Jayce recently, but she smiled as she reconsidered her earlier thought.

"*Nee*, I guess we're not really so different," she said.

He wouldn't be here much longer. She would feel a sense of loss when he was gone, but she planned to soak up every moment she could with Jayce before that time came. She'd worry about the aftermath later.

NINETEEN

That night as they readied for slumber, Esther broached the idea of Jayce and Evelyn as a couple to Lizzie, listing the ways she and Lizzie might be able to encourage them.

"Remember when we arranged a private dinner for Marianne and Paul? We both saw how smitten they were. They would stare at each other all through worship service and the meals afterward, but they were both so incredibly shy. They just needed a gentle push." She tapped a finger to her chin.

"But Jayce and Evelyn are already spending time together. This isn't the same. And he isn't Amish," Lizzie replied.

Esther looked over at Lizzie, who was quietly tucked under the covers, her eyes open but staring at the ceiling. Esther was sitting up combing her wet hair. It had gotten so thin over the years. She remembered being Evelyn's age and having thick tresses of hair. "But Jayce will be leaving soon."

Lizzie remained unusually quiet.

"Are you hearing me?" Esther asked as she fluffed her pillows.

"*Ya,* I'm hearing you. But I don't think those two need a push from us. They're well on their way to an unhappy ending."

The negative statement was so unlike Lizzie, the eternal optimist, especially when it came to matters of the heart. "I know it seems that way since Jayce will be leaving, but sometimes we've intervened, and things worked out well. Just like with Naomi and Amos. We offered him a job so he would stay long enough for him and Naomi to realize they belonged together." She paused, searching her sister's expression, but Lizzie just kept staring at the ceiling as shadows danced overhead from the dimly lit lanterns.

When Lizzie didn't respond, Esther nudged her. "What's wrong with you? You haven't been yourself all day. Are you feeling unwell?"

"*Ya,* I guess you could say that." Lizzie pinched her lips together. She'd already removed her dentures.

"What's wrong? Are your teeth bothering you again?"

"*Nee.*"

Esther sighed. "Then what is it?"

Lizzie slowly looked at Esther, pushing

her lip into a pout. "I did a bad thing."

"*Ach,* Lizzie, what did you do?" She let out another heavy sigh as Lizzie whispered something unintelligible. "What? I didn't hear you."

"I opened the box." Lizzie turned her eyes back to the ceiling.

Esther's pulse picked up. She should reprimand her sister, but curiosity took over. "What was in it?"

Lizzie's eyes jumped back to Esther. "Aren't you going to yell at me?"

"I probably should." She waited.

"I unwrapped it, looked inside, then wrapped it in packing tape again."

Esther clutched the sheet with both fists as she sat perfectly still. "I didn't even notice the tape wasn't aged anymore like I did when Naomi first gave it to us." She paused. "Shame on you for doing that. Now, what was in it? I asked Gus if it contained important papers, and he said no."

Lizzie closed her eyes and shook her head. "*Nee,* it wasn't papers."

"Don't make me keep guessing." Esther relaxed her grip on the sheet. "Just tell me."

Lizzie didn't sit up, but she turned to Esther. "An urn."

"A what?" Esther tried to read Lizzie's expression. Her sister looked tormented.

"You mean, like an urn that —"

"*Ya,* with a person's ashes in it." Her eyes widened. "Why would Gus have someone's ashes? And didn't he miss them the past decade or so?"

No one in Esther's community believed in cremation. She wasn't sure if that was true for Amish all over the country, but it didn't really matter. Gus wasn't Amish. "That explains the grave expression on his face when I handed him the box — like he knew what was inside."

"I think maybe I've been cursed for opening it." Lizzie refocused on the dancing shadows as her bottom lip trembled.

"*Ach,* you're not cursed." Their people were superstitious, but this situation didn't seem to warrant that type of concern.

"*Ya,* I am." Lizzie spoke with strong authority. "Gus hates me, and I opened his box with a dead person in it. Those two things are a potent combination." She held up a finger, moving it around until it was in the light so Esther could see. "I haven't broken a fingernail in years. This one is ripped back below the quick."

Esther huffed. "Lizzie, that's probably from peeling the tape off that box."

Her sister held up her other hand. "*Nee,* I used a knife. And I haven't cut myself in

349

years either. Look!"

Esther pulled Lizzie's hand closer to inspect the cut on her thumb. "It's not even a bad cut, and those two things certainly don't mean you're cursed, just careless."

Lizzie rolled onto her side, faced away from Esther, and lowered the flame of her lantern. "*Nee*. I'm cursed. I always knew Gus would kill me somehow. Now, he's inadvertently done so."

Esther extinguished the flame on her lantern, then lay down. "You are not cursed, and Gus would never kill you. The man is a lot of things, but he's not a murderer. And just looking at an urn filled with ashes is harmless. Your only regret should be opening a box meant for someone else." Esther wasn't so glad now that they knew what it was. "I wonder who it is."

"I'll never know. I'll probably be dead by morning, cursed by the ashes of someone related or attached to Gus somehow."

"You will feel differently in the morning when you wake up." Esther finally got settled into bed, but she was wide awake. For over ten years, there had been a box with someone's ashes in the small house their mother had lived in for a while. Why? Who?

■ ■ ■ ■

Jayce had a bounce in his step as he passed the motor homes and limos. Jayce had loaded the equipment, but no one had emerged from the house. Gus was in his truck already, so Jayce got in.

"Kid, I ain't in a good mood, so don't give me any lip on the way to the caverns." Gus had his hands gripped firmly around the steering wheel as he glared at Jayce.

"Wow. What's up with you so early in the morning?" Jayce wasn't thrilled to be getting back on the boat today, but at least he knew he could do it. It wouldn't be the same without Evelyn by his side, but Veronica would be there, and other members of the crew. And his father would see that he'd pushed through this fear. He still wasn't sure about elevators, but he figured taking baby steps was best. His stomach churned just the same, but he'd suffer through it.

Gus grumbled. He was looking a little scraggly this morning, more so than normal. He hadn't shaved, his red-checkered shirt wasn't tucked in, and he had dark circles under his eyes, almost as if he'd been crying, which seemed unlikely. How many red-checkered shirts did the man own, or did he just wear the same one over and over again?

"That cat of mine is a floozy." His face turned red.

Jayce grinned. "That black cat I've seen coming and going out of your place?"

"It's supposed to be Naomi's cat, but the critter took up residence at my place." He looked at Jayce, his face glowing an even darker shade of red. "And now she's gone and gotten herself knocked up. What am I going to do with a litter of kittens?"

Jayce looked out the window when everyone started to come out of the inn and the motor homes. Then he turned his attention back to Gus. "Just give them away."

"And rip a mother's children away from her? That's a bit coldhearted, wouldn't you say?"

It would have been the last thing Jayce expected Gus to say. "Then keep them. Cats only have like four or five kittens, don't they?"

"How would I know? And that's four or five too many."

Jayce pulled his phone from his pocket and Googled it. "The average is four, but they can have as many as twelve."

"Wonderful." Gus lifted his hands from the steering wheel, returning them with a thud. "I'm sure that cat will reward me with a dozen." Amusement flickered in his eyes. "If there's a silver lining, I could take a few of 'em and throw them in Lizzie's bedroom. She's terrified of cats." He belly laughed, and his jowls got to bouncing.

Jayce decided to change the subject. "I'm planning to go in the boat with everyone today." He pushed his black sunglasses up on his head and glanced at Gus.

"That's great. You'll freak out, probably fall in the water, and I'll feel compelled to jump in and save yet another person." He shook his head. "Let me just tell you, that water is freezing."

"I'm not going to fall in the water." *At least I hope not.*

Gus started the old truck, then managed to shift into first gear to follow the cars, which were packed to capacity, as always. "Clearly, you're doing this to prove something to your father."

"And to myself," Jayce was quick to say. "But yeah . . . I'm anxious to see the look on his face when I say I'm going."

Gus didn't say anything, and the rest of the trip was quiet until they pulled into the parking lot at Bluespring.

"That phone of yours, can it look up just

about anything?" Gus's face was drawn and serious.

"Pretty much. Google is pretty smart. What do you need to know?"

"Where is Jug Rock?"

Jayce typed Jug Rock into his phone. "Here's what Wikipedia says about it." He read from his phone screen.

Jug Rock is a natural geological formation located outside of Shoals, Indiana, in the valley of the East Fork of the White River. It is composed of sandstone and is the largest freestanding table rock formation in the United States east of the Mississippi River.

"Then it lists an address in Shoals, Indiana," Jayce said. "It's about twenty miles from Montgomery."

Gus glared at him. "You can get all that information from a phone?"

"Yep." Jayce stepped out of the truck and took a deep breath, eyeing the entrance to the cave. After everyone poured out of the limos, Jayce pulled out the first load of equipment. He was happy to see that Veronica wasn't in a wetsuit. She'd be filming out of the water today. He started walking toward the entrance, his heart like a bass drum in his chest. Veronica came up beside him.

"How's it going with the Amish girl?" She nudged him.

Jayce smiled as thoughts of the day before soothed his pulse. "I like her. A lot."

"Think you'll stay friends after we go home?"

He repositioned a box under his arm. "Maybe I won't go home."

Veronica stopped walking. "You're kidding, right?"

Jayce shrugged. "I like it here."

She tucked her blonde hair behind her ears. "If you're saying this because of that girl, I'd be careful about overhauling your life to live the way they do." She shifted her stance and put a hand on her hip. "Listen, Jayce. I know you don't get along with your father, but you've got a good life in LA. And you said after this project, you'll have enough money to get your own place and get out from under your dad's thumb."

"Have you taken the time to really look around? It's peaceful here. The people are nice." He nodded at Gus after he walked by them. "Well, most of them."

Veronica grinned as she poked him on the shoulder with her finger. "Hey, no making fun of my hero."

Jayce laughed as his father walked by glaring at him. "We don't have all day, so hurry up!"

"I don't know how I ever dated him." Veronica shook her head.

"Neither does anyone else." Jayce started walking again, then made the usual number of trips back to haul the rest of the equipment. Finally, it was time for everyone to get in the boats.

"I'm going with you today, Dad." He stuffed his hands in his pockets since they were shaking.

His father snickered. "Um, really?"

"Yeah. I'll be going on the boat to help out."

His father stared at him, tipping his head to one side. "We don't need you to go today."

"Well, I'm going." Jayce felt good about proving to himself that he could do something he feared, but he needed to show his father too.

"No, you're not. We aren't going to be more than a couple hours anyway." His father walked to the far end of the dock and stepped into one of the boats. Jayce followed him, knowing he should just stay behind and let it go, but years of bullying pushed him forward.

"Why are you doing this? I finally tell you I'm ready to go, and now you're saying I'm not going." Jayce clenched his hands at his sides.

"Because we don't need you in the boat today. You'd only be in the way."

Jayce had never wanted to hit anyone so much in his entire life. As his hands balled into fists, he felt the fire in his chest, the pounding of his temples, and the urge to lash out at a man he loved but didn't respect. But then who would he be? What kind of person? Worse than his father? What would Evelyn think? More importantly . . . what would God think?

He relaxed his hands even though he was trembling. Surely his father would love for him to lose his cool in front of everyone. But the man's expression wasn't the usual mocking glare. There was something sad in his eyes, a look Jayce remembered seeing when his mother left. Jayce felt sick. About everything.

Gus cleared his throat. "I can stay back so the boy can go."

His father held the expression for a few long moments before he turned to answer. "Appreciate the offer, Gus, but you've kinda become our lifeguard." He smiled at Gus, then stepped into the boat. And just like that, his father was back to the man Jayce knew. Maybe he couldn't change. But Jayce could.

Jayce glanced at Gus, who opened his mouth possibly to argue, but he didn't say anything.

He glanced at Veronica, and she had the same sympathetic look he'd seen plenty of times. He avoided looking at anyone else as he turned and walked away. And he didn't stop walking when he got to the parking lot. Nor did he tour the property as he'd done in the past.

He walked to the road and just kept going.

Evelyn and her mother were hanging clothes on the line Monday afternoon when they both looked up as the sky became cloudy.

"It's not supposed to rain," her mother said while clipping a towel to the line.

"Hopefully those clouds will just pass over." Nothing was going to dim the sunshine in Evelyn's heart. She was too caught up in reliving her kisses with Jayce.

Her mother reached into her pocket for another clip. "I've noticed that dreamy look in your eyes all morning. And your *daed* is starting to ask more questions about the time you're spending with that boy."

"*Mamm,* can you please call him Jayce?"

Evelyn didn't want her mother to darken her spirits, especially when the sun broke through overhead and cleared the clouds, returning the atmosphere to mirroring her heart.

Her mother shook her head as she pinned up another towel.

"I'm a grown woman. Don't worry, *Mamm.*"

"*Ya,* you are. You are nineteen, and in most parts of the world, that's considered a grown woman. But I've lived longer, seen plenty, and I feel like you are going to get hurt. I'm merely imparting some of my wisdom to *mei dochder,* whom I *lieb* very much."

"And I appreciate that." Evelyn picked up the last towel in the basket and hooked it to the clothesline, irritated that her mother had dampened her mood. "I've got to get to work. I'm filling in for Katie this afternoon." As she started toward the house, she glanced over her shoulder. "And I'll be going out tonight."

Her mother didn't say anything.

About two and a half hours after Jayce had started walking, Gus pulled up next to him.

"Get in, Jayce."

It was the first time he could remember

the man calling him by his name. He wanted to keep walking off his anger at his father, but he was dripping in sweat and his calves ached from all the uphill roads.

"I don't want to talk about what happened." Jayce got in and slammed the truck door.

"Good. Neither do I. I have my own problems, and you're going to need to help me."

Jayce grunted. "Do you see how you phrased that? I think what you meant to say was 'I need you to help me.' Because I don't think I'm 'going to need to help' you."

Gus looked at him and frowned. "Quit talking in riddles. Your father said they are going to have a short screening of the movie Friday night down at the little community center. It ain't gonna be long, just the scenes filmed in the cavern, and two outside bigwigs are flying in for the viewing — investors, I think. Then you're all probably packing up and leaving earlier than expected."

Jayce's stomach dropped. He wasn't ready to go. He'd get more information from Veronica or one of the others. "What does that have to do with you needing my help?"

"I need nice clothes to wear, and I haven't bought clothes in decades."

This day just kept getting worse. "Are you asking me to help you pick out clothes?"

"And not kid clothes like you wear. Something classy."

Jayce looked down at his jeans and blue T-shirt before he turned to Gus. "Uh, I don't think a brief viewing in a small-town community center requires a tux or anything. Sure, people will probably spruce up a little, but —"

"It's not about that." Gus kept his eyes forward as he ground from second gear to third. Jayce had started hearing the sound in his sleep at night. "My daughter will be there."

"The one who hates you?"

Gus rattled off a few curse words, expletives that sounded weird coming from a guy his age.

Jayce shrugged. "What are you yelling at me for? You're the one that told me she hates you."

"After all these rides I've given you, are you going to help me or not? I'd ask Esther, but the chances of her knowing what's fashionable are fairly low."

"Yeah, I'll help you clean up your look." Jayce rubbed his chin. "Did my dad tell you for sure that you'll be in the background in this movie?" Gus wasn't the most likeable person, but he'd grown on Jayce, and Jayce didn't want to see him get hurt. It sounded like he was going to a lot of effort to be unknowingly humiliated.

"He assured me I will be in the movie."

Jayce slouched into the seat, still heated about the exchange with his father. "In case you haven't noticed, my father's a jerk. And he doesn't always tell the truth."

"Maybe you could have a little respect for the man." Gus glowered at him. "At least you didn't hit him today. I saw your hands fisted at your sides. He's provided you with a lifestyle most people will never have, and probably loads of money. Have a little gratitude."

"You don't know what you're talking about." With his head leaning against the seat, he turned to the older man. "As cliché as it sounds, money doesn't buy happiness. And I'd give it all up to live here."

Gus laughed. "You'd never make it, kid. You'd miss your fancy ways in Los Angeles. How many cars you got?"

"Two." Jayce thought about his Jaguar and his more practical Land Rover. He sat taller and stared out at the open fields. "But I wouldn't mind the occasional buggy ride."

"Kid, you've got messed-up thoughts. The Amish folks don't take 'the occasional

362

buggy ride.' It's their only mode of transportation unless they need to hire a driver to go farther than the horses can go. And if you're thinking about trying to convert to their godly lifestyle because of that girl, you're crazy."

Veronica had said almost the same thing. But another thought sailed into his mind, as if put there intentionally. "Do you believe in God?"

Gus visibly bristled, then softened a little. "There was a time I did." The regret in his voice was quickly followed up with, "Why are you asking me that? It ain't none of your business."

"When did you stop believing?" Jayce wasn't worried about making Gus mad. The guy was terminal when it came to grumpiness.

"The day something happened to make me stop believing." He glared at Jayce. "Which isn't any of your business."

"Yeah, you said that. So what happened?" Jayce kept his eyes on Gus, but the old man stayed focused on the road in front of him.

"Fine. You don't have to tell me. But I believe."

"Good for you." Gus sighed, opened his mouth to say something, but then snapped it closed again.

"I guess I had the opposite experience. Something happened to me one day, and I started to believe." He recalled the first time he went to church with Susan and the relationship with God that evolved thereafter. It became a sort of friendship that saw him through his roughest times when Jayce didn't think anyone understood him, only this Fatherly figure who seemed to stay close to him, then and now. God was the Father he'd never had.

"Good for you," Gus repeated. "Now, where do we need to go to get me some clothes?"

It was confusing why Gus's daughter, who hated him, was coming to the movie preview. Maybe she thought her father was coming into some money, and she wanted to worm her way into his life to snatch some of it. If the woman only knew . . . It was highly unlikely Gus would have even the tiniest cameo in the movie, and Brandon Clarkson wasn't about to pay him for it.

"How much do you want to spend on clothes?" Jayce glanced at him.

Gus gave him the usual look — an expression that made him look meaner than he really was. "I don't know. How much is a shirt and slacks?"

Jayce leaned his head to the left. "You

might think about replacing those worn-out running shoes too."

"Whatever. How much?"

Jayce rubbed his chin. "Hmm . . . for a decent shirt, some pants, and shoes, maybe three hundred bucks."

Gus downshifted so abruptly, Jayce had to grab the dashboard.

"Are you out of your ever-loving, God-fearing mind? I'm not spending three hundred dollars on clothes and shoes."

Jayce shrugged as he eyed his jeans. "I paid almost two hundred dollars for these jeans."

"Then you're an idiot. They have holes in them!" Gus shook his head after the outburst.

"That's the style." Jayce paused. "But maybe just go to Walmart. We can probably find you something decent there."

"And you think you could live here and wear Amish clothes? You're messed up in the mind."

"Gus, there are ways to get your point across without calling people idiots and telling them they have messed-up minds." He shook his head. Living like the Amish would be a challenge. He would enjoy living on a farm, riding around in a buggy, and ditching the demands in his life for something more peaceful. But he wasn't worthy — or ready — to commit to the type of lifestyle the Amish lived. He felt ready to commit to Evelyn, at least to see where things were headed. "You could be a little nicer is all I'm saying."

Gus was quiet, then finally said, "You sound like Esther, always schooling me on how to act."

"Maybe you should listen to her. Esther seems like a very nice person."

"Esther is the nicest person I know."

Jayce turned to him and smiled after noticing the endearing way he said her name. "Wow. You've got a thing for Esther."

Gus rattled off more curse words. "Shut up, kid."

Jayce frowned. "I doubt Esther likes you using those words."

He shook his head. "You just don't know when to be quiet."

But Jayce caught the hint of a smile on the old man's face, and he was pretty sure he'd hit the nail on the head.

TWENTY

Evelyn glanced around the small community center that usually hosted quilting parties, baby showers, or English book club gatherings. The room had been transformed into a mini movie theater with a huge screen in the front of the room and dozens of chairs with fancy white covers and dark-green bows tied around them — like she'd seen before at a wedding.

Off to the side two men in tuxedos were serving drinks from behind a table, and in the back of the room four more uniformed servers stood behind what smelled like a lavish buffet. Even more surreal was the fact that she, Lizzie, and Esther were in attendance. Rose must have opted out, and she was probably smart in doing so. The bishop would never approve. Evelyn had ignored the rule, justifying her presence because she was still in her *rumschpringe* and hadn't been baptized. She was a little

367

surprised the sisters had come because Esther wasn't the rule-breaker Lizzie was, and it was no secret that Lizzie didn't care for Gus.

Evelyn was taking any opportunity she could to be around Jayce, especially since she hadn't seen him all week. In addition to her work schedule, her mother had taken ill, which left Evelyn to handle all the household chores on her own.

"There you are." Jayce breezed up to her, so close she was glad there weren't any other Amish folks around besides Esther and Lizzie.

"Gus certainly cleaned up well. He must be excited to be included in the movie." She tried to keep from blushing as she thought about the last time she saw Jayce — and the kissing.

"I'm glad you're here," he whispered. "I've missed you. And yeah, I helped ol' Gus get spruced up. I think his desire to look presentable is because his daughter is supposed to be here." He looked at the wood floors, then raised his eyes to hers. "My dad isn't always the most honest person, and I have serious doubts Gus will even have a two-second spot in the film. I don't want to see him get hurt. He's an old grump, but he doesn't deserve that."

Evelyn wanted to tell Jayce she'd missed him, too, but he'd jumped to a different subject without a pause. "Gus would be embarrassed, and I don't want to see that happen either."

Jayce stared at her. "Can you spend the day with me tomorrow?" He lowered his gaze again, then locked eyes with her. "We're leaving Tuesday."

Evelyn's heart contracted like something was squeezing the life out of her. "I-I thought you were staying a month. That's not even three weeks." She heard the desperation in her voice, and while she'd known there would be a void when Jayce left, she hadn't realized how large it would be until now, when his departure was only four days away. She tried to focus on the times he'd said, "Maybe I'll stay." They were just words, but she'd held on to them tightly and let her heart get involved. She'd known better.

He ran a hand through his hair. "Yeah, I know. But the project is done, and Dad said it's time to go. It's a long drive." He seemed to be picking up on her response as he kept his eyes on her. "Can you hang around after this thing is over? Or maybe we can sneak out early, after they show the clip. It's pretty short, and then all the back patting will start and everyone will praise my dad for the great job he's done on these last few scenes." He nodded toward the back of the room. "Those two guys flew in last night. They're the biggest investors in the movie."

Evelyn nodded as she looked at two older men standing next to Jayce's father. They were all dressed nicely, and as she glanced around, she noticed everyone was wearing fancy clothes. Even Jayce had on crisp black slacks with a belt, a starched long-sleeve button-down shirt, and shiny black shoes. It was a far cry from his usual jeans and T-shirt.

"You look nice," she said barely above a whisper as she glanced down at her dark-blue dress covered by her black apron, then at her black ankle socks and black loafers. She'd never felt so out of place in her life. Would spending more time with Jayce tonight and tomorrow just make things worse?

He smiled. "You always look nice." His expression fell. "I take that back. You always look beautiful."

Her heart began to sing again, but it felt temporary. Eventually she'd regret ever meeting him.

Esther couldn't get over how handsome Gus

looked, even with his enlarged middle. He'd disguised it well with clothes that actually fit. He wore black pants with a black belt, a long-sleeve button-down shirt, a black-and-white tie, and black dress shoes, resembling half of the men in attendance. His gray hair was pulled back in a ponytail and he'd trimmed his beard.

She recalled the time she had helped Gus get cleaned up for his meeting with his daughter. He must have paid attention and taken it upon himself to better his appearance for this event, although Esther was sure it was mostly because his daughter would be coming. She hadn't seen the woman yet and wasn't sure what to hope for — that she showed up or that she didn't. There was a strong possibility Gus wouldn't be in the film, and he would be humiliated. If she didn't show up, he would be equally as hurt.

"Good grief, Esther. Quit gawking." Lizzie slapped her hands to her hips, and Esther felt her cheeks warming.

"I'm not gawking, just surprised. Gus looks . . . very nice." She grinned at her sister. "And you're still alive, not cursed."

"Well, clothes don't change a fella," Lizzie muttered with a sour expression. "He's still mean as a rabid hound dog, and I'm probably still cursed. He's just going to drag out my demise."

"You'd best behave." Esther nudged her sister's shoulder. "This is an important evening for Gus and all of the people here." She thought Lizzie had softened a little toward Gus since opening the box and finding an urn, but maybe she'd been wrong.

"*Ya, ya.* I know." Lizzie gasped and her eyes widened. "Look. That must be her, Gus's daughter, Heather."

Esther's stomach swirled in a nervous tornado of emotions as she nodded. The reunion between Gus and his fifty-something-year-old daughter last year hadn't gone well at all. She twisted and wrung her hands as the woman searched the room.

"Should we go help her find Gus?" Esther eyed the woman's black pantsuit. Her dark hair was styled in a short bob.

"She found him," Lizzie said when Heather began walking toward her father.

Esther said a quick prayer that all would go well.

"She's hugging him." Lizzie's eyebrows knitted into a frown. "Don't you think that's kind of fake since you said they were at each other's throats when she was here last time?"

Esther was surprised at Lizzie's attitude

toward Gus. She was acting protective. But she tended to bounce back and forth — she'd just said clothes don't change the man. Either way, Esther was glad that this reunion was starting off on a better note. And so far Lizzie had behaved.

"Look over there." Lizzie nodded toward Jayce and Evelyn. "They don't appear to belong in the same room together, but see how they're looking at each other."

"I know. I noticed it earlier." Sighing, she said, "Hearts will be broken after Jayce leaves on Tuesday."

Lizzie shrugged. "We'll see."

Esther clamped her jaw tight as she peered at her sister. "Do you know something I don't?"

"Of course not." Lizzie lifted her chin. "Only *Gott* knows how things will turn out with those two."

"Were Naomi and Amos invited to this event?" Esther asked.

"I don't know. We probably should have opted out, too, the way Rose did." Lizzie shook her head. "Esther, that girl is driving me *ab im kopp.*"

"Well, you're right. The bishop wouldn't approve of us being here, so Rose probably made the right decision." Esther sighed. "As for Rose, *ya,* the *maedel* talks a lot, but she's a hard worker and very kind."

Lizzie pouted. "Thankfully she hasn't broken out in any more of her midnight dance sessions."

Mr. Clarkson spoke above the crowd, saying it was time to begin. Esther and Lizzie found chairs in the back row, as did Jayce and Evelyn. Gus's daughter sat next to him in the fourth row. Everyone else was clustered together up front.

Gus looked over his shoulder and caught Esther's eye, as he'd been doing all evening, like he was making sure she hadn't snuck out. He turned back around quickly.

After Mr. Clarkson welcomed their two special guests, he introduced Veronica and the rest of the cast and crew.

"Obviously, we have a larger group of players," he said. "But it wasn't necessary for them to join us on this trip." He motioned to his team. "And we certainly couldn't have finished these challenging cavern scenes without this talented and creative group."

Everyone applauded, and Esther's stomach churned like it was making butter. As she twisted her hands together, she prayed Gus wouldn't be humiliated in front of his daughter.

"We had some unexpected turns of event

while filming, and . . ." Mr. Clarkson smiled. "Instead of giving you details, I think it will be more powerful to show you the clip." He nodded toward the back, then took a seat.

Gus glanced over his shoulder again, but this time he smiled.

Esther's chest grew tight as someone turned off the lights, and within seconds the big screen lit up. She tried to remember the last time she'd seen anything on a big screen, but all she could recall was walking through Walmart near the television section.

"Why isn't there any music?" Lizzie whispered when the inside of the cave became visible.

"I don't know. Maybe because it's an unedited clip." Esther had picked up on some of the movie lingo. It was hard not to when it was all they'd heard over the last two weeks.

"Do you think there will be any bad language?" Lizzie cringed.

"I don't know."

"What if there are naked people?" Lizzie put her hands over her eyes but peeked between her fingers.

"Lizzie, just be quiet and stop asking questions."

Esther held her breath. *Please let there be*

at least one shot of Gus's face in the movie.

Then there he was. Gus. Larger than life and filling up the entire screen as he pushed people out of the way and dove into the water. A woman dressed in a wetsuit standing on a boat near a low-hanging stalactite screamed, "She's drowning!" Another lady next to her got down on her hands and knees and peered into the water, crying, "Help her! Help her!"

After a moment Gus's head popped up from below the water, and he lifted Veronica up to others in the boat. They helped her on, and she began coughing up water and shivering. When she came to her senses, she turned to Gus, who was still in the water. With tears streaming down her face, she said, "You saved my life." Then the screen went black, and the lights came on. Everyone clapped.

Esther glanced at Lizzie, whose mouth hung open. She saw Gus looking over his shoulder at her, smiling, just as his daughter put her arms around him.

"Obviously we have more to show you, about thirty minutes more, but I wanted to pause and celebrate the man in this clip." Mr. Clarkson walked back up to the screen as someone switched on the lights. "Gus Owens, can you stand up, please?"

Gus hesitated but then rose to his feet. Esther's hand was covering her mouth, and Lizzie couldn't seem to lift her jaw.

Mostly speaking to the two gentlemen guests, Mr. Clarkson said, "Mr. Owens was originally slated to have a small part in the background." Esther still wasn't sure if that was true or not. "But in an unexpected moment, he turned out to be a hero and saved someone we all love very much. We found a way to work this shot into the movie since it appeared to be brilliant acting, even though no one was acting." His eyes found Veronica's, and the man's expression was tender. "Veronica would also like to address the crowd."

Gus started to lower himself back to his seat.

"Mr. Owens, can you please join Veronica at the front of the room?"

Esther's heart beat so fast she hoped she didn't pass out. Gus didn't like crowds, and he certainly didn't like being the center of attention. He slowly made his way up front, dragging his feet as if he were being led to a pirate's plank.

Veronica waited for him to stand beside her. The woman looked stunning in a knee-length red dress, her long blonde hair cascading past her shoulders. Tearfully, she turned to Gus before looking back at the audience.

"A few days ago, I asked Gus how he felt about having this scene included in the movie, because I had mixed feelings at first," Veronica said. "But in the end, we both agreed to let Brandon include it. I've never seen such bravery up close and personal." She hugged Gus, who barely put his arm on her back. His face was redder than Veronica's dress. When she withdrew from the hug, she reached for something on the table beside her and handed it to him. It was a plaque, and even though Esther was too far away to see what it said, she saw the tears in Veronica's eyes, and she knew in her heart the woman wasn't acting.

Gus couldn't even face the audience or her. He just nodded, eyes downcast, and said, "Thank you."

Mr. Clarkson shook Gus's hand. "Happy to have worked with you on this project." Then he handed Gus an envelope.

Esther glanced at Gus's daughter. Heather had a broad smile across her face. Was it because she was proud of her father? Or because of what might be in that envelope?

Seeing his father do the right thing by giving Gus the praise he deserved — Jayce hoped there was money in that envelope — and the way his dad looked at Veronica . . . There was love inside the man. And now Jayce was confused.

"Wow," he whispered to Evelyn. "I'm not sure who I'm more surprised by — my dad for being a decent human being or Gus for behaving so modestly and being so respectful." He shook his head. "The stars must all be in perfect alignment."

Evelyn nodded, but the look in her eyes told him something was wrong.

"Are you hungry?" He nodded over his shoulder toward the buffet. "Or do you want to sneak out of here?"

"I-I, um . . . whatever you want to do." She smiled, but it wasn't her real smile. She was definitely bothered about something. If her feelings were anything comparable to his, it was because he was leaving Tuesday.

"Let's grab something to eat real quick, then we'll sneak out and go somewhere to talk." He started walking but slowed when she didn't follow. He went back to her.

"I-I'm not feeling so well. Maybe I caught what *mei mamm* has. I think I'm just going to go home. *Danki* for inviting me to the screening, but I don't think I can stay for the rest." She stared into his eyes. "Bye, Jayce."

Then she rushed toward the door just as the lights went off again for the remaining scenes.

Jayce wanted to run after her. But his feet were rooted to the floor. What was the point? He'd be leaving in a few days. Maybe she'd realized that, too, and it was having the same effect on her.

Jayce had toyed with the idea of staying in Montgomery and paying to stay at the inn until he found a farm he could buy, but geography wasn't the only thing on his mind. He sat back down even though a chunk of his heart had just run out the door.

Evelyn cried all the way home, mad at herself for allowing her feelings to sneak up on her. After she got Millie settled in the barn, she did her best to dry her eyes. Light was coming from her parents' bedroom, her brothers' bedrooms upstairs, and the living room.

When she walked inside, her mother was in her robe on the couch. Normally she would have been in bed by now. Maybe not asleep but reading and tucked in for the night. She stood up and held out her arms. Evelyn raced into them. How was it that mothers just knew certain things?

"You'll be all right, *mei maedel*," she said

380

as she stroked Evelyn's hair. "Your *bruder* was in town earlier today, and he overheard one of the film people say they were leaving soon. I just had a feeling . . ."

"How did I let this happen, *Mamm*?" Evelyn stayed in the comfort of her mother's arms as her tears spilled. "I knew better."

"Our hearts don't always listen to logic, and I feared this for you." She eased Evelyn away. "You're in *lieb* with him, aren't you?"

Evelyn swiped the tears from her eyes. "Is that even possible — to fall in *lieb* with someone so quickly?"

Her mother walked her to the couch, and they both sat. She clutched Evelyn's hand and squeezed. "*Gott* puts people in our lives for a reason. He always has a plan, but the outcome isn't always what we hope for. You have to ask yourself what your purpose was in Jayce's life, and what his purpose was in yours."

Evelyn thought about how they'd conquered their fears together, at least some of them anyway. Maybe that was the sole purpose of their meeting. Instead of confiding her thoughts to her mother, she said, "All I know is that when he leaves, I feel like he will be taking a part of me with him."

Her mother twisted to face her, then gently dabbed at Evelyn's tears with her thumbs. "Do you want to go with him?"

Evelyn's eyes widened in shock at her mother's question. "*Nee,* of course not!" It was true. Nothing could tear her from the only place she'd ever known or from her family.

"Then the part of you he takes with him is a part of you he needs for reasons we don't understand. But you will heal, *mei lieb.* You will heal."

Evelyn tried to think of something she'd done for Jayce, something not tangible that he would take with him. Her heart was too tender to come up with anything. Instead, she buried her head in her mother's arms and wept.

"I knew better," she said through her tears.

TWENTY-ONE

Jayce suffered through the rest of the night, and by the time he got to his room he was miserable. He wouldn't see Evelyn again before he left on Tuesday, and it was obviously best that way. She was heavy on his heart, though, and it didn't help that just breathing the air in his room caused him to think about her. It was as if someone had planted an invisible field of lavender in his room. The aroma was pleasant, like Evelyn's soap, or shampoo, or whatever she used that made her smell so good.

Everyone had been right. Buying a farm and living in a place like Montgomery would be too much of a stretch, too different from everything he knew. He decided to go outside for some fresh air. As he sat on the inn's porch, some of the crew filed inside and others went to the motor homes.

He could talk to Veronica, but she would be celebrating with her friends, and a boozed-up conversation didn't sound appealing. When the screen door slammed, Rose stood on the porch.

"I heard everyone talking when they came inside. They said the evening was a big success. I hate that I missed it. I'm sure the food was *gut*. But I just didn't feel right about attending such a lavish event. And we aren't really supposed to watch movies or television. Did Evelyn go? I was surprised Esther and Lizzie went, but I guess it's because they've known Gus for so long. And . . ."

She kept going, but Jayce didn't hear any more. He couldn't take Rose's ramblings right now.

"I gotta go," he said as he forced a smile and hurried down the steps.

He paused at Veronica's motor home. There was enough booze inside to numb his pain for a while, but he'd walked away from all that. The music got louder inside, and between that and the generators and his spinning mind, his head felt like it would explode. He sprang forward and ran toward the cottage.

"You gotta let me sleep on your couch." Jayce pushed past Gus after the old man opened his door. He'd already changed into jeans and a ragged red T-shirt. "I need to be away from everyone. My father will be celebrating at the inn, and the others will be partying it up in the motor homes, and that Rose is a sweet woman, but I can't deal with her right now." He fell on Gus's couch and crossed his arms over his forehead. He didn't move until Gus poked his arm. The guy stood over him looking like he wanted to squash him.

"Kid, you ain't staying here. Get up" — Gus pointed to the door — "and get out."

Jayce rolled off the couch and stood, his fists clenched at his sides. Unlike Gus, Jayce was still in his dress clothes, his white shirt untucked atop black slacks. "You know, tonight you showed a side of yourself I hadn't seen before. You were humble and dignified. Why can't you act that way all the time?" He threw his arms in the air. "I don't have anyone. Don't you understand? My father wasn't himself tonight either. I want to believe he's noble and all that, but it's like the world fell off its axis, and everything feels strange."

Jayce wasn't sure when he'd started yelling, but anger and hurt had billowed up inside him as if they'd been stashed there for years. "I came to you for a place to lay my head for one night!" He threw his arms in the air. "But it's your house. I barged in." He dropped his arms, shook his head, and started toward the door. "Forget it. You wouldn't understand anyway."

"Oh, quit being so dramatic," Gus said as Jayce reached the door. "Fine, sleep on the couch if you want."

"No." Jayce grabbed the doorknob. He was trembling mad, so he just held his position and lowered his head. Then he felt a hand on his arm.

"Esther brought a chocolate pie over earlier today. I don't share my pies with anyone. But since you're being such a baby, you might as well stay and have some."

Jayce blinked back his tears and turned around. He wanted to punch the guy. Or hug him. Neither seemed appropriate, so he just nodded before walking back to the couch and sitting down again.

Gus came over and stood in front of him, nostrils flaring. "Geez, kid. You need to get a grip." He went around a counter into the kitchen area that wasn't even in a separate room. He brought a pie, three plates, and two forks to the coffee table, then went back around the counter and returned with a can of cat food, which he dumped on one of the plates.

"My floozy of a cat can't seem to get enough to eat." He set the plate on the floor near the definitely pregnant cat. "Here. Eat," he said as the animal gobbled up the food.

Gus sat on his corner of the couch and looked at Jayce. "Go ahead. Eat up." He waved toward the pie. "Esther makes the best chocolate pie ever. I'll reprimand myself later for sharing it with you, but you're a mess right now."

Jayce wasn't hungry, but he slid a slice of pie onto his place, then took a small bite.

"It's like medicine. Trust me." Gus crossed an ankle over his knee. "There ain't nothing Esther's chocolate pie can't fix."

After two or three bites, Jayce thought Gus might be right. "Congratulations, by the way," he finally said. "I hope my dad paid you."

Gus cleared his throat. "He did."

Jayce wondered how much, but Gus wouldn't know if it was a fair wage or not. He didn't seem all that interested in money anyway, based on the way he lived.

"If I had to guess, I'd say this is about the Amish girl and the fact that you're leaving Tuesday. I told you so." Gus reached for the pie and got himself a huge slice.

"You know, Gus, right now I don't need anyone telling me I told you so."

"And I don't need to be up past my

bedtime with someone sleeping on my couch. But since I'm already inconvenienced, you might as well get whatever's ailing you off your chest." He yawned, which tempted Jayce to leave, but he reached for another slice of pie instead. Gus might not have been right about the pie being an actual cure-all, but it was at least a temporary fix.

"I messed up," he said through a mouthful. "I want to stay, but I can't."

"No, you can't." Gus yawned again, which was starting to agitate Jayce.

"Why can't I? I know I said it, but why are you saying it?"

"You can't stay here cuz you ain't got the guts to do what it would take to live here. You'd have to sell your fancy stuff, and let's face it, kid. You're not cut out for this kind of lifestyle."

"How do you know? I like it here. I've always wanted to live on a farm or somewhere in the country. Just because my father hated it doesn't mean it's, like, in my DNA or something. I could make a life here. I could sell everything I own, take the money from this job, and buy a farm."

"You just said you can't." Gus raised an eyebrow. "Now you say you can. In less than two minutes you've flip-flopped. You don't know what you want. Go home on Tuesday with the rest of them."

"I think I'll stay." Jayce was shaking again, and the pie wasn't feeling like medication anymore.

"Then stay." Gus picked at a scab on his lower leg, which caused Jayce to want to hurl.

"Do you have to do that?" Jayce set his plate on the coffee table, forcing aside the empty glasses, cups, and newspapers.

"It's my house." He picked even more. "I know there's a tick burrowed in there." Glancing at Jayce, he grinned. "Hazards of country life. You up for that, kid?"

Jayce leaned his head back against the couch and closed his eyes.

Gus finally lowered his leg and stopped messing with the sore. "Here's the way I see it. You think you're in love with the Amish girl. You think you'd like to live on a farm. You think you'd like to get away from your father. You think all your problems will be solved if you make these radical changes to your life."

Jayce looked at him and waited.

"But you'd just be running away and toward something unfamiliar that might not work out." He shrugged. "Or it might be the best thing you've ever done." He laughed. "Although, I don't see you becoming Amish."

Jayce wasn't sure about that part, but he could imagine the rest. "Out of everything you said, you're right about one thing. I care a lot about Evelyn, and I don't know how that happened or how I let it happen."

"Yep. Women. They're at the core of all our problems." Gus shook his head.

Jayce decided to turn the tables. "How did it go with your daughter tonight?"

Gus shrugged. "She was pleasant enough. I'm sure she was just there to see if there was any money in it for her. I thought only you millennials felt that sense of entitlement, that life owes you something, but apparently my fiftysomething daughter falls into that category too."

"Did you give her the money my dad gave you?"

"Of course."

Jayce huffed. "Why, if you know she was only there for that?"

Gus stood and slowly started to the bedroom. "Because, trust me, kid. I did owe it to her. I wasn't a good father."

Jayce wished he could see Gus's face. There was such regret in the statement.

"Well, I wish you'd been my father." Jayce loved his dad, but he couldn't recall ever

390

having a decent conversation with him, and especially not one like he was having now with this grumpy old guy.

Gus stopped, and Jayce waited for him to turn around. He didn't. All he said was, "You'll be okay, kid." Then he closed the door to his bedroom.

Jayce ate more pie.

Evelyn was brushing Millie in the barn when she heard a buggy pulling into the driveway Saturday morning. Her brothers were off with their girlfriends somewhere, and her parents were in town at the lumber-yard. She wasn't in a hurry to see who it was. Any visitors would surely notice her swollen eyes from crying all night, and she wasn't feeling up to explanations.

"Well, we've kinda made a mess of things, haven't we?"

Evelyn gasped, spun around, and locked eyes with Jayce. "What are you doing here?"

"I asked if you wanted to spend the day with me." He stuffed his hands in the pockets of his jeans. "But you didn't really answer." Nodding over his shoulder, he said, "Lizzie said I could take their topless spring buggy since it's such a nice day. And her other one still smells like vanilla. I thought you might want to go for a ride." He stared into her eyes. "If you're feeling better."

He took a few steps toward her, rubbed Millie's snout, then found her eyes again. "I know why you left. And I don't think it was because you were sick. At least, not physically."

Evelyn hung her head before she looked back at him. "I thought it might be best to say goodbye instead of spending more time together." She put a hand to her chest. "Despite my best efforts not to care *too* much for you, I do. And it's a hopeless situation."

He took his hands out of his pockets, folded them across his chest, and kicked at the dirt before he looked at her. "Yeah, I know. And I let my heart get involved too. I care about you way more than I should." He paused. "So, hmm . . . What to do?"

"We haven't known each other very long. I guess that's to our advantage." Evelyn brushed hair from her face but didn't bother to tuck it beneath her prayer covering. She'd been out in the barn for a while and was sure she looked a mess.

He stepped closer to her and cupped her cheeks in his hands. "Evelyn Schrock, one thing I know for sure is that I want to kiss you." His lips descended onto hers, and she quivered at the sweet tenderness. She melted into him as her emotions skidded and swirled. Her knees trembled as he eased away. "But we do have some issues."

She tried to smile. "*Ya*, we do."

"So, do you want to go for a ride with me on this beautiful day and figure out what we're going to do?" His eyes pleaded with her, so she nodded. "I'm not sure there is a suitable answer, but we can try to find one."

"I'm not sure there is either. But I think if we go somewhere to talk and pray about it, *Gott* will help us figure things out."

Jayce kissed her forehead. "The power of prayer."

She smiled, genuinely this time. "*Ya.* I just need to leave my parents a note."

Jayce had already talked to God, and the Lord had responded. He knew what he needed to do. In some ways it sounded like a plan that was too far out to consider. But that was how Jayce knew he hadn't come up with the idea on his own. God was challenging him.

He'd tossed and turned on Gus's couch most of the night, trying to work out the best way to follow God's lead. The Lord hadn't given him all the answers, but He'd placed the thoughts in his mind, leaving room for free will.

"You look like a natural," Evelyn said as Jayce guided the horse onto a side street around the corner from Evelyn's house. He tried to pick up on any dual meaning. Did she want him to convert to the Amish faith?

As the sun rose above the midmorning clouds, Jayce tried to clear the fog from his brain. He wanted to explain his plan so she would understand his intentions without feeling any pressure. He waited until they were at the park where they'd eaten a picnic lunch. After tethering the horse, they walked to the picnic table and both sat on top of it.

"I've got to go home." He rubbed his temples before he looked at her. Evelyn's expression didn't reveal a thing. Surely this news didn't surprise her, but there was more to say. "I want to come back here, Evelyn, but I have to make sure I come back for the right reasons. I can't just run away from the only lifestyle I've ever known without more thought. There's a big world of alternate lifestyles that are different from mine. Just because I'm not happy where I am doesn't mean that buying a farm in Montgomery, Indiana, is the right thing to do. I'm smart enough to know that." He paused when she turned away from him. Gently, he touched her face, coaxing her eyes back to his.

"And I don't know if a person can fall in love in less than three weeks. But I know that I care about you more than anyone I've ever known, and I want to explore what's going on between us. I know there are risks with that. We could both end up hurting even more." He paused again. "Do you understand what I'm saying?"

She nodded, her eyes glazed with emotion. "I can probably summarize it." She stared at him long and hard. "Even if you choose to come back here, to make a different life for yourself, you could never transform yourself to be accustomed to our ways, to the Amish way of life, to our faith."

He propped his elbows on his knees and held his head in his hands. She rested her hand on his back.

"Jayce . . ." Her voice was shaky. "It's okay. I know in *mei* heart that I couldn't go to California and live in your world, so I understand that you can't be a part of the life I was meant to live. If you choose Montgomery as your future home, I can't see you in a romantic way because it leads nowhere, only to heartache for both of us. The most we could hope to be is friends. So I think you have to be very careful when you decide where you make your home, that your decision isn't based on anything to do with me."

He lifted his head and locked eyes with her. "That was all very well said and absolutely correct." He held her gaze. "And we can go round and round about this and bounce around the logistics, but it has everything to do with you, like it or not. That's why I'm going to leave Tuesday. I don't know if or when I'll be back. But to carry on, even long distance, isn't going to help me think straight." He smiled. "You're already in my head and heart way more than I ever thought possible."

A tear trailed down her cheek, and Jayce thought his heart might crumble to pieces as he leaned into her and kissed the tear away.

"But, Evelyn Schrock, if I come back, I want the whole package. The farm. You. The Amish lifestyle. All of it. I'm just not sure now that I can do it."

"An honest answer," she said with a slight nod as she swiped at her eyes.

"And if you've hooked up with a handsome Amish guy while I'm away, I can't fault you for that. It would be my fault for leaving you in the first place."

Evelyn wanted to tell him that she'd wait for him forever, but forever had different meanings for different people. She had no words.

"Last night when I was tossing and turning on Gus's couch . . ." She raised an eyebrow. "I know it seems like an unlikely place to go, but I just didn't want to be around my dad and the others, so I camped out there." He grinned. "Much to Gus's horror."

He took a deep breath. "But I kept dreaming about butterflies. It was the weirdest thing, and it took me back to our picnic and your fear of that butterfly. The dreams were so vivid that I looked online for a meaning I could relate to. I've heard that butterflies can be angels, spirit guides, and all kinds of messengers, but that didn't feel right." He took his phone from his back pants pocket, punched a few buttons, then said, "I found this, and it seems to fit where I'm at in my life, so I'll read it to you.

" 'When you see an abundance of butterflies, you're encouraged to pay attention to your cycles of growth. What parts of your personality and life could use a fresh start? A butterfly urges you to go after a life filled with grace and not run from a metamorphosis if your soul craves change.' " He paused, his eyes pleading with her. "So while I'm off finding myself" — he grinned — "it's so cliché, but you know what I'm trying to say . . . Maybe if you see a butterfly, you won't jump or be afraid, but instead try to embrace it for the message it might be offering. Or at the very least, think of me and know that I'm trying to get my head straight and in line with my heart."

As if on cue, a butterfly landed on Jayce's knee, and Evelyn gasped. She didn't jump up and run. She remained still beside the man she already knew she loved. Jayce's jaw dropped as they both stared at one of the winged creatures Evelyn had been so afraid of. Its fluttering took on a new meaning and feeling, almost sucking the honesty out of her like a syringe drawing blood from her heart.

"I'm going to take that as a *gut* sign and hope you'll be back."

As the butterfly lifted from his leg and flew away, Jayce leaned over and kissed her, passionately, and she knew his feelings for her were strong. But she also feared this would be the last time she kissed him, so she lingered in his arms as long as she could.

TWENTY-TWO

On Monday morning Esther stood next to Gus at the base of Jug Rock. She was unsure whether or not to ask him whose ashes were in the urn. When he'd asked her to go with him to the rock formation, she'd started to ask why, but then noticed the box under his arm. She'd been waiting ever since for him to tell her about the contents and why they were going to Jug Rock, which was supposed to be the largest freestanding table rock east of the Mississippi River. It looked like a giant mushroom in the middle of the woods to her. The local oddity had always drawn in tourists. Today it was just her and Gus.

He had pulled his truck off the highway, and they walked the path through the trees to the rock. Now they were just standing there, and even though Esther wanted to be respectful, she couldn't stand the suspense anymore.

"Gus, what are we doing here?" She watched as he opened the box. He'd already cut the tape, so he easily pulled out a plain silver urn and held it with both hands.

"This is where my parents had their first kiss, and they came here every year on their anniversary." He paused. "At least, that's what your mother told me."

Esther's pulse sped up. Was she finally going to find out Gus's connection to her family?

"What else did *mei mudder* tell you?" She tried to keep her voice even and not appear too anxious. "Are you going to tell me who we are paying respects to?"

Gus held the container tight against his belly as he stared at the rock. "Your mother and my mother were best friends, even closer after my father died. I don't remember him. He died when I was three. Then my mother was killed in a buggy accident when I was nine."

Esther stepped closer to him, not sure she'd heard him correctly. "A buggy accident? As in, she was in a buggy that was hit by a car, or . . ."

"Yeah, she was driving the buggy." He turned to Esther. "I was actually at your house when the accident happened. I think I was pushing you on the tire swing when

400

your mother came outside to get me and tell me the news. You'd have been about seven, I guess."

Esther lowered her head as she searched her memory. "*Ach,* Gus. I'm so sorry. I don't remember that." How could she forget something like that? But many memories she'd tried to hold on to had faded without her permission. Maybe she'd pushed the bad recollections from her mind.

"Well, it was a few decades ago." He shrugged.

"More than a few." She glanced up at him as her head swirled with this new information. "You and your mother were Amish."

"Yeah. But after my mother was killed, I got sent away to live with my aunt, who wasn't Amish. She made arrangements to have my mother cremated, even though your mother knew she wouldn't have wanted that. Your mother was able to convince my aunt to leave the ashes with her until I was ready to come back to spread them properly."

Esther was speechless.

"I didn't lead a very good life, Esther, and I was too ashamed to come back, too ashamed for everyone to see how my mother's son had turned out. But when I found myself with nowhere else to go, I came home. Your mother let me rent the cottage. Actually, I didn't rent it at first. She let me stay for free. I got a job at the local meat market, and then my social security checks started coming, and I've been paying rent ever since. I asked her not to tell anyone who I was out of respect for my mother, and she agreed. She told me she'd held on to the ashes for years and to let her know when I was ready for them. I wasn't at the time, and then I forgot about them. A terrible thing, for a son to forget about his mother's ashes."

Esther instinctively rested her hand on Gus's arm. She could feel his torment radiating like heat.

"Then your mom died, and I had no idea where they were." He looked down at the urn. "Now I do, and after thinking about it, I decided to spread some of her ashes here, some in the river that she loved so much, and the rest on my father's grave."

Esther's bottom lip quivered. Over the years she and Lizzie had speculated why their mother let Gus live in the cottage and why she'd made them promise he could live there the rest of his life. They'd concocted everything from affairs resulting in Gus being an illegitimate family member to all sorts of other nonsense. In truth their mother had been protecting her best friend's honor at the request of her son.

"I didn't know who else to bring with me . . . I didn't want to come alone." His eyes were moist, and Esther's heart was cracking.

She wasn't sure what to do. It wasn't any more customary to eulogize an Amish person's death than it was to be cremated. Amish funerals were more of a celebration of a person's life. But Gus hadn't grown up Amish past the age of nine.

"You don't gotta say anything." Gus opened the top, then with both hands he held the urn out and spread a portion of the ashes along the base of Jug Rock.

Sometimes there were songs during Amish funerals. Esther remembered the words to part of one that had been sung often, "Jesus My Shepherd." She began singing it softly in Pennsylvania Dutch, since she didn't know it in English.

Gus put the lid on the urn and stood straight and somber as Esther sang. She stood beside him, unmoving on the outside, but hurting for him on the inside. Birds chirped and chipmunks scurried around the fresh spring growth surrounding them.

Esther followed Gus when he started to walk back to the truck. From there they went to the widest fork of the East White River, then to the cemetery. When they returned to Gus's driveway outside the cottage, he killed the engine, and they just sat quietly for a while.

"*Danki* for asking me to go with you," she said softly.

"I'm sure you'll tell that sister of yours, but could you maybe not share the information with everyone else?" His head was low as he made the request. "And maybe convince Lizzie not to say anything."

"I will respect our *mudders'* wishes, Gus, and not say anything to others. I'll make sure Lizzie doesn't either." She glanced at the tire swing that still hung in the yard. The tire and rope had been replaced many times over the years, even though Esther and Lizzie never gave their parents grandchildren to swing on it. Visitors had enjoyed it. Esther wished she could remember the day Gus referred to, but maybe it was best that she didn't. A child finding out that his mother had been killed must have been horrific.

Esther respectfully waited for him to get out of the truck, but he just sighed, his hands resting on the steering wheel. She sat quietly until he turned to her. "Your mother was always kind to me. I can still remember

404

how tormented she was when she had to tell me that my mother had been killed. When I returned twelve years ago, it was as if not a single day had passed. I was like a prodigal son to her. But I was damaged. A mean old man who hadn't lived a good life my mother would have approved of. There's no redemption for some of the things I've done. I've carved a place in hell, and I'm sure my spot by the hottest part of the furnace awaits."

Esther couldn't imagine what Gus might have done over the course of his life, nor did she need to know. "There is always redemption, Gus. You may have given up on the Lord, but He has never given up on you."

One side of his mouth rose as he looked at her. "You're just like her, your mother. You make me want to be a better person." He lowered his gaze but then nodded toward the inn. "It's hard to believe you share the same DNA as that nutcase in there."

Esther had been trying to get him to be more compassionate, kinder to others, and to think before he spoke. It was a process that required time, but he'd shown progress.

"If you want to be a better person, you've got to treat people with respect, Gus." She narrowed her eyes at him. "And that includes Lizzie."

Frowning, he opened the truck door. Esther followed suit and opened hers, then went around the front of the truck. She could count on one hand the times she'd hugged Gus over the years, but this situation warranted it. She even kissed him on the cheek, which caused his entire face to glow a bright red.

"I believe in you, Gus, and so does *Gott.*"

"Yeah, well, I doubt that." He turned and shuffled to the cottage.

As she walked to the inn she let the tears roll down her cheeks. By the time she reached the porch, Lizzie had come outside. Thankfully, none of the movie people were around. Even the generators were turned off. The group seemed to do that sometimes during the day. Maybe they napped — she wasn't sure.

"What's wrong?" Lizzie's face was shriveled in a look of despair. "Why are you crying?"

Esther sat in one of the rocking chairs on the porch. Lizzie joined her, and Esther told her about the past few hours.

"So that old grump of a man has Amish blood." Lizzie blew out a puff of irritation and shook her head.

It was the straw that broke Esther. She

pounded her fists on the arms of her rocker. "Lizzie, I tell Gus repeatedly that he must treat you and others better, but you make no effort to get along with him!" Esther was surprised at her own rage, but the emotional day had caught up to her. She waited for Lizzie to fire back, but her younger sister just slouched into her chair.

"I remember that day," Lizzie said in a shaky voice. "I was the one Gus was pushing in the swing."

Esther's head snapped in her direction. "You would have been just five. How can you remember that?"

Lizzie shrugged. "Maybe because you just don't forget something like that. *Mamm* coming out, pulling Gus to the side, him screaming, then *Mamm* rushing him into the *haus* as she looked over her shoulder at me." She blinked a few times. "It's hazy, and I probably never would have remembered it if you hadn't brought it up. I don't think I understood exactly what was happening, but I knew it was bad. You weren't home, I don't think. Maybe you went somewhere with *Daed.* I don't know."

Esther strained her mind, but she couldn't recall such a tragedy. She suspected her parents had shielded her and Lizzie as best they could.

The sisters sat in silence for a while before Lizzie said, "You want some cough syrup?"

Esther faked a little cough. "My throat is a bit sore."

Their cough syrup was made from honey, rum, and lemon juice and strictly reserved for colds and sore throats. And moments like this one.

By the time Tuesday came around, Jayce was second-guessing everything he thought he'd worked through about Evelyn and a plan. The thought of not seeing her or even saying goodbye was tearing at his insides. They'd both agreed that Saturday's kiss would be goodbye, at least for now.

He stayed busy loading suitcases from the inn into storage compartments in the motor homes, while everyone else said their good-byes to Esther and Lizzie. Even his father was being particularly gracious, and that just muddled Jayce's state of mind even more.

He loaded most of the luggage, more than they came with, since the women had bought a lot of souvenirs. He glanced at the cottage, doubtful anyone would bother saying bye to Grumpy Gus Owens, except maybe Veronica. Jayce headed that way.

"What do you want?" Gus said as he

swung the door open.

Jayce smiled. He was used to this sort of greeting from the old man. "We're leaving. I came to tell you bye." He raised a shoulder, then dropped it slowly. "So . . . stay cool."

Gus frowned. "Stay cool? It will be summer soon, and it will be anything but cool."

"I might be back. I gotta go home and figure some things out." Jayce took a deep breath.

"No, you won't be back." Gus shook his head. "You ain't got it in you, kid."

Jayce grinned as he extended his hand. Surprisingly, Gus shook it and even smiled a little. "You never know, old man. You might see me again."

Gus looked at him long and hard. "I'll be hoping so."

Jayce lost his balance as his arm dropped to his side, but he regained his composure.

"Good luck with Esther. Don't wait too long. You're not getting any younger."

He laughed and hurried to leave before Gus could lash out. When he looked back over his shoulder, Gus was actually smiling a little and gave a quick wave before he closed the door.

Wow. This has been a whirlwind of a trip.

Evelyn stood at the living room window and

watched the caravan go by. One of the two limousines or two motor homes was carrying a piece of her heart. She sniffled when her mother came up behind her and wrapped her arms around her waist.

"If it's *Gott*'s will, he will be back, *mei maedel*. If not, he wasn't the one."

"I know." Evelyn had cried all morning. She didn't have any tears left, and she was sure her eyes showed the evidence. Her mother spun her around and kissed her on the cheek.

"Lucas said you fed the chickens and collected the eggs this morning." Her mother tipped her head to one side, her eyes questioning.

"*Ya.*" Evelyn took a deep breath. "I'm trying to work through some things."

Her mother smiled. "He also said he saw you running from the chicken coop when you were done."

"I didn't say I'd worked through them *yet.*" She forced a smile for her mother's sake. "And that red-and-white rooster is mean."

"I'm going to go make a batch of brownies." Evelyn's mother kissed her on the cheek again. "I'm here if you want to talk."

Evelyn nodded, but she turned around right away. All the vehicles were gone. *He*

410

was gone. Despite her best efforts, more tears found their way down her cheeks.

Sometime over the past two and a half weeks, one of Veronica's party buddies had taken a liking to Giovanni, and Jayce had snagged a ride in Veronica's motor home so the two could ride together in the limo. He wasn't sure why Giovanni didn't choose the motor home, but he didn't care. Jayce had his own bed to sleep in during the trip. His emotions, along with hauling all the luggage and packing everything up, had him feeling overly tired. The downside was that his father had managed to finagle his way onboard too.

Jayce was lying on the bed in the smaller of the bedrooms, his arms tucked behind his head. He was almost asleep when his father walked into the room, which caused him to lift up on his elbows. His father tossed an envelope at him.

Jayce opened it and noticed right away it was filled with hundred-dollar bills, more than they'd agreed on, it appeared. "You could have just written me a check," he said before yawning. "And this looks like more than we agreed on." Which was shocking, since the agreed-upon amount had been ridiculous.

"It is more. But you earned it." His father held his position and stared at Jayce. It was hard to read his subdued expression. "Why don't you just stay here? It's enough money for a down payment on a place and to get you through for a while."

Jayce shook his head, mouth hanging open. "Wow. You really want me gone from your place. Dad, I promise, I'll have my stuff out of your house as soon as we get back. I want out as bad as you want me out."

His father flinched. Then he turned to face the living room where Veronica was curled up sipping something red and reading a magazine. "Sometimes it doesn't pay to wait, and time can be the enemy. Time and a foul temper." He turned back to Jayce. "I didn't give her the time she deserved, and my temper has ruined most of my relationships. But I know what I want, and I'm going to make the necessary changes to prove to her that I can be the man she wants and deserves."

Jayce wanted to say, *"Who are you, and what have you done with my father?"*

"That's great, Dad." He wasn't sure how sincere the words were, or if Veronica would ever take him back, but at least his dad had a plan and had thought things through. On Saturday when he'd said bye to Evelyn, he thought he had it all worked out, a logical plan that made sense. He began to detail his plan to his father, surprisingly.

When he'd repeated almost everything he'd said to Evelyn, his father smiled sympathetically.

"Every time I look at you, I am reminded of the man your mother left me for — someone not much older than you are now. I've taken a lot of my anger out on you." He paused, sighing. "And others. But, believe it or not, I want you to be happy. If you want to go back to LA and see this very logical plan through, then of course you should do that. Or you could embrace what you feel today and go for it. There is no guarantee of a tomorrow." His father looked over his shoulder at Veronica again before he locked eyes with Jayce. "She's probably too young for me, and I shouldn't fault your mother for her younger man, but . . ."

Something in the pit of Jayce's stomach cramped, and he didn't hear anything else his father said.

"There is no guarantee of a tomorrow." What if he never saw Evelyn again? What if she found someone else while Jayce was off finding himself — which sounded really stupid all of a sudden.

An unusual quietness settled in. "You

always plan things out, Jayce," his father said. "I trained you in that regard. And it's not always a bad thing." He shrugged. "But sometimes it doesn't hurt to shake things up."

His father took a folded piece of paper from the pocket of his trousers. "This was obviously meant for you. I found it in the limo. I guess it was written before the writer knew you'd be traveling in the motor home." He handed the note to Jayce. "I confess. I read it." Shrugging, he said, "Maybe I was meant to read it." His eyes traveled to Veronica again. "You'll make the right decision."

His father smiled and walked to Veronica. She made room for him to sit beside her. Jayce couldn't hear what was being said, but the expression on Veronica's face told him his father was making progress.

He unfolded the note written on lined white paper and read.

Life is a journey to be enjoyed as much as the destination. But there is no guarantee of a tomorrow.

Jayce paused, recalling his father saying the same thing, obviously after he'd read this note.

414

Each day is a gift from *Gott* to be cherished. Fill your heart with the people you love. Cling tightly to your convictions, but allow room for change and growth. Be the person you want to be, and never forget that anything is possible. Above all else, stay wrapped in *Gott*'s presence and follow His lead. Think of today as tomorrow, in case tomorrow doesn't arrive with the expectations you've set forth. Sometimes it's okay to set logic aside and let the heart rule.

The note wasn't signed, but he could only think of one person who could have written it.

Jayce lay back, more confused than ever. *God, what do You want me to do? Am I defining Your thoughts and words in my head the way I want to?*

"What should I do?" he whispered aloud.

Then there was a loud boom. A blowout.

After they'd slid to a safe stop, Jayce just smiled.

Evelyn forced herself to go back out to the chicken coop. If Jayce ever did come back, she wanted him to see that she'd gotten over her phobia of birds. It wasn't going to happen overnight, but as she stood with her hands on her hips and faced off with the most aggressive rooster in the bunch, she said, "I'm going to win this battle."

She needed a distraction, and when she was around the chickens and roosters, she was on high alert.

Movement far down the road caught her attention. A man walking.

She dropped the feed pail she was holding, which sent the hostile rooster shuffling and squawking in her direction, followed by several hens. The blue T-shirt had her full attention. As Jayce's long dark hair blew in the wind, Evelyn's feet began to move toward him.

Had something happened? Was something wrong? Did she dare hope he might stay?

They walked toward each other down the middle of the gravel road, and with each step Evelyn increased her pace until she was standing right in front of him.

"What's wrong?" she asked as her heart pounded.

He shrugged. "The motor home had a blowout."

Her heart sank. "I'm sorry to hear that."

Jayce grinned. "Really? Because I kind of took it as a sign from God that I should stay."

Evelyn didn't say anything. Was he joking?

He took her face in his hands and kissed her, over and over again. When he eased her away, he held on to her arms. "I know what I want. And I know the logistics of all of this are complicated. So we can analyze it to death or just roll with it. I want to live on a farm. I know there are farms in most states, and I could go anywhere. But *anywhere* doesn't have you."

Evelyn's jaw dropped.

"We don't know each other well yet, and I'm not Amish. I realize that, but I know how I feel." He grinned. "I've never had this sick feeling in my stomach, or this pain in my chest. I guess I didn't know love could be so painful. And of all people, my father was the one who said something that made the most sense. He said there is no guarantee of tomorrow. I wonder where he got that from." He playfully rolled his eyes before his expression turned serious. "Will you date me if I stay? I can't give you any guarantee that I have what it takes to convert to the Amish ways any more than I can guarantee tomorrow, but I'd like to try."

Evelyn's heart swelled as a smile spread across her face. "Then let's accept the guarantee of this moment and take it one day at a time."

Jayce kissed her again. "I know I've made the right decision," he whispered.

Esther and Lizzie sat in the rocking chairs in the living room. It was eerily quiet. Rose had gone to town for groceries. All the movie people were gone, and Esther found herself surprised that she missed having other folks around. Maybe not as many as they'd had for the past two and a half weeks, but a few. When Rose returned it would be like having three or four people in the house. The girl could carry on enough conversations at one time to wear a person out. Esther decided to take advantage of the quiet.

Then there was a knock at the door, and Esther saw Gus on the other side of the screen. She cut her eyes at Lizzie, warning her sister to be nice. For once, Lizzie didn't respond by rolling her eyes or scowling. She just sat with a somber expression.

"What is it, Gus? Do you need something to eat or a slice of pie?" Yesterday had been a hard day for him. Esther opened the door to let him inside.

Gus's nostrils flared as he paced the room. "That cat had a dozen kittens!"

Lizzie covered her face and shook her head. "I knew it. I'm cursed."

"Oh, quit fussing," Gus said to Lizzie before he turned to Esther. "They all seem to be fighting for room to nurse." He scratched his head. "Am I supposed to do something?"

Esther pinched her lips together in her effort not to smile. "Everything should be all right, Gus. Whiskers will know what to do."

"What am I gonna do with thirteen cats?" Gus raised his palms. "Tell me, Esther. I can't have all those cats running in and out of the house."

Lizzie stiffened, her eyes suddenly wide. "Are they all black?"

At first Gus wouldn't look at her, but Esther gave him the same warning look she'd given her sister earlier. "Lizzie asked you a question, Gus."

He took a deep breath, kept his eyes on Esther, and said, "Four of the little things are black like the mama. The rest are black and white."

Lizzie shook her head. "We might as well be a coven of witches with all those black cats nearby."

They all turned at the sound of another knock at the door. Gus was closest so he pushed the screen open. "What are you doing here, kid?"

Jayce stepped over the threshold, and Esther smiled when she noticed two suitcases on the porch.

"Can I stay here awhile until I find a place of my own? I've decided to make Montgomery home."

Gus belly laughed. "Well, I'll be. You decided to stay around for the girl after all."

Lizzie jumped up and bounced on her toes, clapping her hands together like an excited child. "You and Evelyn?"

Jayce nodded. "Yep."

"Of course you can stay." Esther pressed her hands together, smiling.

"We know it hasn't been long, but we'd like to date and see how it goes." Jayce paused, looking down before he lifted his head and looked back and forth between Esther and Lizzie. "It was the weirdest thing. I had a conversation with my father that seems a little surreal right now, but in a good way. He said some things that shifted my way of thinking. And there was this note . . ." He paused, seemingly lost in thought. "Anyway, I asked God what I should do and" — he snapped his fingers — "boom! We had a blowout. It had to be a sign, and I already knew I didn't really want to leave."

Lizzie pressed her palms together and smiled. "Wonderful news. Um, not about the blowout, but we're glad you're staying."

Rose stumbled to the door carrying two bags of groceries, and Jayce was quick to open it for her.

"Oh no." Gus grumbled as he stepped aside for her.

"Jayce! What's happening?" Rose stopped barely inside the house. Jayce took the bags from her and placed them on the coffee table as she went on. "Is something wrong? Why is everyone here? Jayce, I thought you left, and —"

"Stop." Gus held a palm out toward her. "Stop talking."

Esther braced herself and said a quick prayer that everyone could just get along.

Gus peered at Rose, tilting his head slightly as he wrinkled his nose. "Rose Petal . . ." He glanced at Esther. "I mean, Rose . . . How do you feel about cats?"

"*Ach,* I *lieb* cats, especially kittens. They're so cute and playful. And they catch mice, and —"

"Stop." Gus raised his hand again. "Follow me. I've got a dozen cute and playful creatures you can help me with."

"*Ya,* of course." She looked at Jayce. "But what are you doing here?"

"I decided to stay. I'll rent a room until I can find a place of my own." He shrugged.

"When you realize you're in love, waiting to get started on a new life no longer makes sense."

Rose jumped up on her toes. "That's wonderful! I'm so happy for you and Evelyn."

If Rose ever had any intentions toward Jayce, she'd thankfully moved past them.

Gus grumbled something, then told her to go see the cats and he'd catch up with her. "I'm not sure if it's going to be worth it to let her help me with those kittens. Maybe if I tape her mouth shut."

"Gus, you behave around that *maedel.*"

Gus grinned at Jayce. "So, you've got it in ya after all." He shook his head. "Aren't we all just one big dysfunctional family?" He threw his arms in the air, shook his head, and shuffled toward the door.

Esther could have gone without hearing the word *dysfunctional,* but the fact that Gus referred to them as family was endearing.

Lizzie slowly stood. "Gus?"

Oh dear. Esther twisted the string of her prayer covering, willing Lizzie to be nice.

Gus folded his arms across his belly. "What?" He narrowed his bushy gray eyebrows at Lizzie.

"I'm sorry for your loss. It was me in the swing that day, not Esther. I remember now." Lizzie's voice cracked as she spoke, and Gus stared at her for a long time.

"Yeah, uh . . . Thanks."

Then he quickly turned to leave. "I'll be over at my house with jabber-box, my promiscuous cat, and a herd of kittens."

Esther blinked back tears. "That was very nice of you, Lizzie," she said after Gus was gone.

"*Ya,* well, don't get all emotional about it. He's still a grumpy old man."

The sisters and Jayce gathered by the window just as Rose was entering the cottage and Gus was slowly crossing the field.

"If we hurry, maybe we can whip up some lunch before Rose gets back." Lizzie twisted her hands together as if she'd come up with a diabolical plan. "We've got to find that girl a man. I don't have the heart to fire her, but she's going to give me a stroke with all that talking and a heart attack if I have to eat her cooking for much longer."

Jayce rubbed his stomach. "I bet I can put something together. I'm starving all of a sudden, and it's the least I can do for you agreeing to let me stay here."

"You're always hungry." Lizzie rolled her eyes, grinning.

Jayce picked up the two bags of groceries on the coffee table, smiled, and headed to the kitchen. Esther and Lizzie sat on the couch and propped their tired feet up on the coffee table.

"Do you think he knows we wrote the note?" Lizzie pressed her lips together as she turned to Esther. "I just couldn't stand to see that boy get away. We've been so *gut* by not interfering much, but I knew in *mei* heart that Evelyn and Jayce belonged together. They just need a little more time. Putting so much distance between them seemed too risky."

Esther stiffened. "You almost made those *kinner* sick with all that vanilla in your buggy." She paused, recalling the strong aroma in Jayce's room. Even though she tried to avoid the stairs, she made the trek up to check on things occasionally. "But the lavender was a nice touch. However, I believe I get credit for that note."

"I helped." Lizzie pouted and grumbled something under her breath.

"*Ya,* I suppose you did." She nudged her sister's shoulder. "But I'm not sure he knows we wrote it, and that's okay. Perhaps the note served two purposes. Maybe Jayce will be able to mend his relationship with his father. Some distance might help with that. It sounds like the timing was right for all concerned." She folded her hands in her lap. "And for that we can't take credit. *Gott* gets the glory for His perfect timing."

Lizzie nodded. "*Ya,* I agree. But we need to get busy on our next project. We must find someone for Rose." Lizzie tapped a finger to her chin.

"I agree. But for today, let's be happy with all the Lord has gifted us."

"Uh . . . *ya* . . . of course."

Esther smiled. Lizzie's wheels were churning. What could be coming next?

EPILOGUE

Esther, Lizzie, and Rose cleared the table after supper as they'd been doing on Wednesday evenings for a few months now, unless they had overnight guests, which was less likely during the week.

Gus always sat at one end and Lizzie at the other. They were more tolerant of each other, but that was mostly because they avoided each other except for the Wednesday evening suppers. Both had been given strict instructions not to say or do anything to disrupt the weekly gatherings or they would be excluded from the next meal. They must have taken Esther seriously because, so far, they'd only taken a few jabs at each other, which landed them with firm warnings.

Jayce bought a farm only two weeks after the film crew left The Peony Inn. It was where he and Evelyn would make their home and raise a family after they were married. They were wrapped up in wedding plans, and Jayce was taking the necessary classes to be baptized into the faith. The decision hadn't come easily for the boy. He'd spent a lot of time with the bishop and elders, asking questions and learning as much as he could about the Amish faith. In the end and after much prayer and consideration, he'd said it was the only organized religion — as he called it — that was a good fit for him.

Amos and Naomi attended the weekly meals unless they were visiting Amos's family in Ohio, which they tried to do every few months. It was a joyous time when the twins arrived right on schedule. Esther and Lizzie served as grandparents on Naomi's side of the family even though they weren't biologically related. They spent as much time with the girls as possible. Naomi and Amos named them Regina, after Lizzie and Esther's mother, and Eve, after Amos's great-grandmother.

Life was good for everyone, except Rose. Esther, Lizzie, and Jayce had finally taught her to cook. She still made the occasional mistake, but overall her culinary skills were much improved. They hadn't, however, been enough to snag a man since none lasted long enough for Rose to cook for.

Her moods shifted faster than Esther could keep up with sometimes. Understandably. She'd be so excited to meet a new man, then devastated when he stopped asking her out.

Esther joined Lizzie in the living room after everyone had left. Rose was upstairs in her room.

"What are we going to do about that girl?" Lizzie asked. "We've set her up with three nice Amish fellows, and they all ran faster than a cat with its tail on fire." She groaned. "Speaking of cats, I'm surprised I'm still alive with all those black creatures running around. They're even more dangerous now that they're full-grown."

Gus had found homes for all of them but two, and he had those spayed when he took Whiskers to the vet. "You know the mother mostly stays inside, and the other two keep the mice away and don't bother you."

"They cross *mei* path at least once a week."

"Let's get back to Rose," Esther said. "We both know she talks too much, and we've gently tried to talk to her about that. She is such a beautiful woman, inside and out."

"Yep. She just can't keep her mouth closed." Lizzie kicked her socked feet up on the coffee table next to Esther's.

"Sometimes I think she talks so much because she's nervous." Esther frowned. "She's almost twenty-four."

"Practically an old maid." Lizzie crossed her ankles. "Maybe we should talk to the herbal doctor in Orleans. Maybe there is a natural medicine to make her be quiet."

"Lizzie, we don't want to change Rose's personality." Although, the thought of less chatter was an appealing idea.

"I have one more person for her to meet." Lizzie gave a taut nod of her head. "And I have high hopes for this one."

Esther slumped her shoulders. "I don't know, Lizzie. After the last fellow quit calling so abruptly, Rose was upset for weeks. I think she is growing depressed. I know she cries sometimes, especially after the Wednesday suppers. She sees how happy Amos and Naomi are, and we're all watching Jayce and Evelyn plan their wedding. I think she's happy for the other couples, but also sad."

"*Ach,* well, we can't give up. That's not our way."

"Who is the fellow you want to introduce her to?" Esther asked.

"You don't know him." Lizzie twirled the string of her prayer covering. "He's . . . um . . . perfect."

Esther frowned. "What do you mean? Is

429

he Amish? I feel like Jayce was an exception, an *Englischer* who was willing to put in the work to convert to our ways. It's always so unlikely that an outsider will choose to do that."

"He's Amish." Lizzie slouched into the couch.

"Lizzie, what do you have up your sleeve?" Esther was intrigued and worried at the same time.

"Don't you worry about a thing." Lizzie didn't look at her. She just patted her on the knee.

Esther was already worrying.

ACKNOWLEDGMENTS

Thank you to my readers for following me on this amazing journey. Your loyalty and support keeps me motivated to continue writing stories that I hope inspire and entertain.

I have a wonderful publishing team at HarperCollins Christian Publishing. Thank you to everyone involved in the process, especially my brilliant editors, Kimberly Carlton and Jodi Hughes.

To my agent, Natasha Kern, another big thank you for all you do!

I'd be lost without my friends and family, so a huge thanks to all of you.

My fabulous friend, marketing guru, and advisor on most topics — Janet Murphy — I couldn't do it without you.

To my street team, Wiseman's Warriors, you gals are awesome! Thanks for all you do to promote my books.

God has blessed me more than I could

have ever imagined. It's so cool how He does that. Thank you, my heavenly Father.

DISCUSSION QUESTIONS

1. Evelyn and Jayce are drawn to each other right away. Besides physical attraction, what are some of the other qualities they find endearing about each other?

2. Despite being matchmakers by nature, Esther and Lizzie agree that encouraging a romantic relationship between Evelyn and Jayce wouldn't be good for the young couple. But there are several things that Lizzie and/or Esther end up doing to nudge Jayce and Evelyn together. What do the sisters do in that regard?

3. Gus continues to be a work in progress, and Esther is determined to help him be a better person. What are some instances when Esther succeeds?

4. Why do you think that Gus and Jayce ultimately end up forming a friendship? Is it because Gus and his daughter don't get along, and also because Jayce and his father don't see eye to eye? Or is there

more to their relationship?

5. Evelyn and Jayce both tend to share their vulnerabilities openly with each other. What are some examples of this?

6. What do you think would have happened if Jayce's father hadn't found the note and read it to him? Would Jayce have eventually come back to Montgomery? And what about his father? After Brandon reads the note, we see a softer side of him. Do you think his conversation with Veronica leads to reconciliation?

7. Rose is a sweet woman who talks a lot. While there is more to be revealed about Rose in the next book, can you speculate as to why she is so chatty? Is she nervous? Perhaps she just can't corral her thoughts and verbalize them without rambling? Or is there another reason for Rose's chattiness?

8. Evelyn is afraid of any creature with wings. Jayce has a hard time being in enclosed spaces. Together, they work to conquer their fears. Without each other, do you think that either of them would have worked through their phobias alone?

9. It is obvious that Esther and Gus have a soft spot for each other. Do you think their feelings for each other run deeper than friendship? If so, why?

10. Imagine you are a young woman or man in your twenties. You fall in love with an Amish person. Could you do what it takes to convert to the Amish way of life? If not, what are the things that would hold you back?

11. What do you hope will happen in the next and final book in the Amish Inn series?

ABOUT THE AUTHOR

Bestselling and award-winning author **Beth Wiseman** has sold over two million books. She is the recipient of the coveted Holt Medallion, is a two-time Carol Award winner, and has won the Inspirational Reader's Choice Award three times. Her books have been on various bestseller lists, including CBD, CBA, ECPA, and *Publishers Weekly.* Beth and her husband are empty nesters enjoying country life in south-central Texas.

Visit her online at BethWiseman.com
Facebook: @AuthorBethWiseman
Twitter: @BethWiseman
Instagram: @bethwisemanauthor

The employees of Thorndike Press hope you have enjoyed this Large Print book. All our Thorndike, Wheeler, and Kennebec Large Print titles are designed for easy reading, and all our books are made to last. Other Thorndike Press Large Print books are available at your library, through selected bookstores, or directly from us.

For information about titles, please call:
  (800) 223-1244

or visit our website at:
  gale.com/thorndike

To share your comments, please write:
  Publisher
  Thorndike Press
  10 Water St., Suite 310
  Waterville, ME 04901